Sheila Bugler grew up in a small town in the west of Ireland. After studying Psychology at University College Galway (now called NUI Galway) she left Ireland and worked as an EFL teacher, travelling to Italy, Spain, Germany, Holland and Argentina.

She is the author of a series of crime novels featuring DI Ellen Kelly. The novels are set in South East London, an area she knows and loves.

She now lives in Eastbourne, on the beautiful East Sussex coast. Eastbourne is the location for her series of crime novels featuring investigative journalist Dee Doran.

When she's not writing, Sheila does corporate writing and storytelling, she runs creative writing courses, is a tutor for the Writers Bureau and is a mentor on the WoMentoring programme. She reviews crime fiction for crimesquad.com and she is a regular guest on BBC Radio Sussex.

She is married with two children.

Also by Sheila Bugler

YOU WERE ALWAYS MINE

SHEILA BUGLER

First published in the United Kingdom in 2022 by

Canelo
Unit 9, 5th Floor
Cargo Works, 1–2 Hatfields
London SE1 9PG
United Kingdom

A CIP catalogue record for this book is available from the British Library.

Print ISBN 978 1 80032 732 0
Ebook ISBN 978 1 80032 731 3

Cover design by Black Sheep

Cover images © Depositphotos, Shutterstock

Look for more great books at www.canelo.co

Printed and bound in Great Britain by Clays Ltd, Elcograf S.p.A.

MIX
Paper from
responsible sources
FSC® C018072
FSC
www.fsc.org

For my brilliant agent, Laura Longrigg. This one's for you!

One

It was a Friday afternoon in August when Cassie MacNamara walked out of her job in the middle of her shift without telling anyone why she was leaving or where she was going. Cassie's sudden disappearance was a worry for her boss, Jennifer, but not a surprise. Because in the days leading up to that Friday, Cassie's behaviour had become increasingly erratic. Jennifer had tried speaking to her about what was going on, but Cassie had brushed off her concern. Shutting down the conversation and withdrawing further into herself as the week progressed.

On the Friday in question, Jennifer had been putting a colour on Marge Hall's stringy grey hair, trying to pretend she was interested in Marge's incessant chatter while also keeping an eye on Cassie.

'Did I tell you Ruby's going to be an actress? She's got her heart set on it and, according to her drama teacher, she's got the talent to go all the way. She could even win an Oscar one day if she puts her mind to it. We're so proud of her, I can't tell you.'

Marge's eyes in the mirror bored into Jennifer, daring her to contradict this bold statement.

'I can imagine,' Jennifer replied, choosing not to say what she was really thinking. Namely, that becoming an award-winning actress seemed a slightly ambitious aspiration for Marge's four-year-old granddaughter.

On the other side of the salon, Cassie was cutting Selma Wetherwick's hair in total silence. More than once, Jennifer had watched Selma try to make small talk but she'd clearly given up and was now flicking through the pages of a magazine while Cassie sliced off chunks of her thick black hair.

Fridays at the salon were always a busy time. Along with Cassie, two of the other girls were working and there was a steady stream of clients coming in to get their hair sorted in time for the weekend. With the radio playing through the wall-mounted speakers and the hum of different conversations taking place between hairdressers and clients, it would be easy not to notice there was something wrong with Cassie. But this was Jennifer's salon and she noticed everything.

If it was Sonia or Charlee or Maya acting like that, they'd be on a warning by now. But Jennifer had always treated Cassie differently, giving her the easiest clients and letting her take time off at short notice even if it meant moving appointments around. The other girls didn't like it, of course. Jennifer was sure they bitched about it behind her back. Not that Jennifer cared. If Sonia or Charlee or Maya didn't like the way Jennifer ran her salon, there was nothing to stop them getting a job elsewhere.

'Of course, not having children of your own means you can't understand what it's like to be a grandparent. The thing is, Jennifer, grandchildren are an exceptional gift. Take my little Ruby, for example...'

Marge was right. Jennifer couldn't understand what it was like to be a grandparent. But she doubted it was very different to the all-consuming love Jennifer felt for her own child, taken away from her when he was only a few hours old.

'All done,' she said, interrupting Marge mid-flow as she wrapped the final piece of foil around a clump of coloured hair and peeled off the latex gloves she'd been wearing. 'Can I get you something to drink?'

'A cup of tea would be lovely thanks, Jennifer. Milk and two sugars. Two bags and leave them to stew for a bit before you add the milk and sugar.'

Jennifer walked away as Marge continued giving instructions. She'd been taking tea orders from Marge Hall every second Friday for the last five years. If she didn't know by now how the woman liked her tea, chances were she never would. Normally, Jennifer would ask one of the girls to make the tea. But they were all busy and it was a relief to get away from Marge into the peace and quiet of the little kitchen at the back of the salon.

The sounds from the salon muted as Jennifer closed the door and put the kettle on. A new song came on the radio. Dusty Springfield, 'Son of a Preacher Man'. As the opening guitar chords started up, Jennifer was transported back to 1977. A Brighton nightclub. Slow-dancing with a man Jennifer had briefly believed was the love of her life. Forty-something years ago but Jennifer could still remember, as if it was yesterday, every detail of that night they'd shared in Brighton.

Alone in the kitchen, Jennifer gave herself a few precious moments to remain in the memory of that night. As the final chords of the song faded away, she reluctantly dragged herself back to the present and set about making Marge's cup of tea. On the radio, the news had come on. A round-up of local stories, including the discovery of a young woman's body washed up on the beach near Beachy Head.

'Police have confirmed that the woman is seventeen-year-old Grace Parker from Eastbourne. Grace, niece of businessman turned TV celebrity Joey Cavellini, has been missing since last Friday. Her family have issued a statement, thanking everyone for their support and asking for privacy as they come to terms with their loss.'

Jennifer poured water from the kettle over the two teabags she'd placed in the cup, noting the slight tremor in her hand. Over the last week, Grace Parker's face had seemed to smile out at Jennifer every time she opened a newspaper or switched on her TV. Until this moment, the dead girl's friends and family would have been holding out hope that she would be found alive. A hope that was now well and truly crushed.

3

Grace Parker's disappearance had been dissected in endless conversations between the salon staff and their clients over the last week. All that would start up again now, everyone greedily going over the details of the girl's fate, speculating about how she'd died, whether it was from natural causes or something more sinister. It was the sort of salacious gossip that Jennifer found distasteful, although she would never say that. Women didn't come to her salon just to get their hair done. They came to share secrets about their husbands, to whisper stories about their neighbours and their friends. They came for the chat – that special form of gossipy, giggly conversation that only happens when groups of women are together without the censorious presence of men.

Leaving the cup on the counter, Jennifer walked back to the salon. Cassie's face in the mirror above Selma Wetherwick's head was greyer than Marge's hair before Jennifer had put the colour in. And her eyes, when she turned to look at Jennifer, were wide and haunted.

'You should take a break, Cass,' Jennifer said.

But Cassie didn't answer. The scissors in her hand dropped to the floor. As the metal blades clattered onto the tiles, Cassie turned and walked past Jennifer into the kitchen.

'Cassie!'

Jennifer hurried after her, moving as fast as her formidable bulk would allow. Cassie wasn't in the kitchen when Jennifer got there, but the back door – the one that led to the alley running along the back of the salon – was open. Jennifer ran into the alley, scanning left and right, trying to work out which way Cassie had gone. She ran the length of the alley and onto the street. But there was no sign of Cassie anywhere.

Back in the salon, a sea of faces turned to look at her. Selma was still in her chair. Her half-chopped hair hung in damp strands down her shoulders; her mouth was opening and closing like she had things she wanted to say but she didn't know how to get the words out. And Sonia, breathless and pink-cheeked, was gesturing to the two women standing at the main entrance to the salon.

'The police are here,' Sonia whispered. 'They're looking for Cassie.'

Two

Dee Doran was driving her new, cherry-red Mazda MX-5 convertible along the steep, winding road that rose up from the western edge of Eastbourne town towards the chalk white cliffs at Beachy Head. She was meeting her cousin, Louise, for lunch at the Tiger Inn in East Dean. And she was late. As she crested the hill and the rolling green fields of the South Downs stretched out in front of her, she pictured her cousin sitting at a table outside the pub, her manicured fingernails tap-tapping restlessly while she waited.

It was a perfect summer's day. A warm breeze brushed against Dee's skin as she followed the road up towards Beachy Head and the Belle Tout lighthouse, perched on the top of the cliffs. A clear blue sky spread out over a matching blue ocean. To the west, Dee could see the jagged outline of the Seven Sisters, a series of white cliffs that ran from Beachy Head to the Cuckmere Valley.

A helicopter appeared, flying along the edge of the cliffs. Despite the warm sunshine, Dee shivered. Anyone living around here was familiar with this sight. Beachy Head, world-famous for its beauty, also happened to be the country's number one suicide spot.

Two police cars were parked on the grass at the top of the cliffs behind a line of yellow and black police tape. No ambulance, which meant whatever poor soul had been found, they'd already been taken to the hospital. Or, more likely, straight to the morgue. Without realising she was doing it, Dee slowed as she drove past, thinking of the ripple effects of a tragedy like this. Because death was never just about the person who'd died, it was also about all those left behind.

The sound of her phone ringing distracted her. She knew it would be Louise, calling to see why Dee wasn't already at the Tiger Inn. Unlike Dee, Louise was never late for anything. This was because she planned her days in minute detail. She would have set aside one hour, exactly, for her lunch with Dee and would be in full rant mode when Dee showed up fifteen minutes later than scheduled.

With Beachy Head behind her now, Dee sped past Belle Tout and on to Birling Gap, where the road curved inland towards East Dean, the picturesque village which Sherlock Holmes had supposedly moved to in the latter years of his life. As she pulled into the village car park, her phone started ringing again. Ignoring it a second time, she concentrated instead on finding a parking space. The car park was almost full; tourists and locals using it as a starting point for a walk over the Downs to the white shingle beach at Birling Gap.

Grabbing her bag, Dee got out of the car and hurried towards the pub. Situated on the village green with tables outside, the Tiger Inn was something of an East Sussex institution. Established in the sixteenth century and once popular with smugglers, the pub's idyllic location in the heart of the rolling South Downs meant it was always busy. To Dee's dismay, all the outside tables were occupied. The pub's oak-beamed interior was lovely, but she'd been looking forward to eating in the sunshine.

At the entrance, she pushed open the heavy wooden door and walked inside. It took a moment for her eyes to adjust after the bright sunshine. When they eventually did, it was clear that Louise wasn't in here.

Back outside, Dee checked the tables and the surrounding area once more. Still no sign of her cousin. Remembering the phone calls she'd received earlier, she took her phone out of her bag and scrolled through her call log. Two missed calls and a voicemail. She was about to listen to the voicemail when her phone started to ring again, and Louise's name flashed up on the screen.

'Lou, where are you?'

'I could ask you the same question,' Louise said. 'I was waiting for you for almost fifteen minutes. I don't understand why you're incapable of being on time for anything.'

'Did you get my message?'

'I haven't had a chance to listen to it yet.'

'I can't make lunch,' Louise said. 'Something's come up at work and I had to rush off. I'm sorry.'

'It's okay. These things happen.'

As editor of the local newspaper, Louise often had to drop things at short notice when a story broke.

'It's Grace Parker,' Louise said. 'They've found a body.'

A man and a woman in late middle age were eating lunch at one of the tables on the grass, sharing a bottle of white wine that glowed pale green in the sunlight. A fat chip dropped from the woman's fork and a white seagull swooped down from the sky and caught it as it hit the ground.

'Dee?'

'I'm still here,' she said, remembering the helicopter and the police cars she'd passed earlier.

'She was washed up off the coast near Beachy Head,' Louise said. 'You know what that means, right?'

'I've got to go,' Dee said.

'Dee, there's nothing you could have done.'

Dee hung up, without replying. The heat of the sun suddenly felt intolerable. As she looked around for some shade, Dee noticed people were watching her. It was only when she lifted her hand to brush a strand of hair out of her eyes that she noticed her face was wet. Tears for a young woman she'd only spoken to a handful of times.

'Are you okay?'

A middle-aged woman, wearing her hair tied back with a colourful scarf, was standing in front of Dee.

'Fine,' Dee said, wiping her face with the sleeve of her shirt. 'Just got a bit of bad news, that's all.'

'Oh I'm sorry, dear. Is there anything I can do?'

Dee shook her head. There was nothing anyone could do. It was too late for that.

Three

Dee lived in a modern, glass-fronted house situated on a quiet stretch of beach between Eastbourne and Pevensey Bay. The house, designed by her architect father, had been her childhood home. She'd moved back when she left London seven years ago, following the break-up of her marriage. At first, coming home had felt like an admission of defeat. Gradually, however, she'd fallen back in love with her childhood home and now she couldn't imagine ever wanting to live anywhere else. There was something magical about waking up in the morning and watching the sun rise over the horizon and pour its red light across the flat, black sea. Or sitting on her deck in the evenings, letting the stress and worry of a difficult day slip away as night crept in across the wide open sky.

As she pulled up outside the house, she saw another car was here already. The car was empty but, when Dee walked around to the back of the house that faced onto the beach, she saw two women standing on the deck. One of them was peering through the bifold door that separated the inside of the house from the outside. The other was standing with her back to the house and seemed to be taking in the view.

'Can I help you?' Dee said.

She recognised the woman who was trying to see inside her house. She was Detective Inspector Rachel Lewis of East Sussex CID. Until recently, the partner of Dee's on-off boyfriend, Ed Mitchell.

'Hello, Dee,' Rachel turned away from the house to look at Dee. 'You got a few minutes?'

'What were you doing back here?' Dee asked.

'We rang the doorbell,' Rachel said. 'But there was no answer, so we came around the back to see if you were out here.'

'You were looking through my windows,' Dee said, 'like you thought I was in there and was ignoring you.'

'We didn't think anything of the sort.' The other detective smiled warmly at her. Taller and younger than Rachel, she was a vision. Ebony skin, eyes the size of plates that shone like polished stone and a smile that made you want to step right into the warmth it promised. 'DC Ade Benjamin,' the vision said. 'Beautiful place you've got here.'

'Thanks.' Dee recognised she was being charmed but didn't mind, because how could she when someone this gorgeous was doing the charming? She imagined Ade Benjamin was the sort of detective who was adept at getting suspects to tell them exactly what she wanted to hear. 'I assume you're here because of Grace Parker,' Dee said.

'Any chance we could do this inside?' Rachel asked. 'I'm melting out here.'

'Sure.' Dee stepped onto the deck, lifted the plant pot beside the back door and took up the key she kept there.

'You're practically asking to be burgled keeping your key there,' Rachel commented as Dee unlocked the door and stepped into the welcome coolness of the house.

'Can I get you anything to drink?' Dee asked, choosing not to point out that her family had kept a key in the same spot ever since the house had been built when she was just ten years old and the house had never been burgled.

'I'd love a coffee,' Rachel said. 'If it's not too much trouble.'

'Have you got any Diet Coke?' Ade asked.

'I'm afraid not,' Dee said, feeling ridiculously regretful for not having stocks of Diet Coke she could offer.

'Never mind,' Ade replied. 'Rachel's always telling me I drink too much of the stuff.'

'Because you do.' Rachel gestured to the sofas and chairs scattered around the open-plan living space. 'Mind if we sit down?'

'Be my guest,' Dee said. Pointlessly, because Rachel had already settled herself into the armchair Dee normally sat in.

As the kettle boiled, she switched it off and put some of the hot water into the cafetière to warm it before adding the fancy coffee that Ed had insisted on buying recently.

'Do you know yet how Grace died?' Dee asked. 'I know the location of the body most likely means she took her own life. But she didn't strike me as the sort of person to do something like that.'

'We can't discuss any of that with you,' Rachel said.

'Not officially,' Dee said, resisting the urge to say something snarky. 'But you could give me some idea, surely.'

'It's too early to say what happened,' Ade said.

Dee focused on pouring coffee and asking Rachel if she wanted milk or sugar, while she tried to get her thoughts in order.

'So why are you here?' she asked eventually.

'After Grace disappeared,' Rachel said, 'you came into the station and gave a statement in which you said that you knew Grace Parker. She'd contacted you a while back asking for help.'

'That's right.'

'We've read your statement,' Ade said, 'but now Grace's body has been found, we'd like to go over what you told us again, if that's okay?'

'Of course.' Dee couldn't see how it would help their invest-igation, but she didn't have anything to hide and couldn't see the harm in answering whatever questions they had. She put Rachel's drink on the low table beside the chair she was sitting in and sat down on one of the other chairs, further from the window with no table beside it for her own drink.

'About six months ago,' she began, 'I got an email from Grace asking me to help investigate an alleged miscarriage of justice.'

'You didn't know her before she got in touch?' Ade asked.

'No.' Dee shook her head. 'But it's not unusual to get emails like that. I'm a journalist who specialises in looking into historical crimes. Grace's email intrigued me, so we arranged to meet.'

Dee paused, remembering the vibrant young woman she'd met that day. It was impossible to think of that bright light extinguished forever.

'That's when she told you what had happened to her parents,' Rachel prompted.

'Yes.'

Again, Dee stopped speaking as she remembered that strange conversation. When they'd met, Grace told Dee that, sixteen years ago, her father, Paul Cavellini, had been killed. Grace's mother, Cassie, was subsequently charged with his murder, found guilty of manslaughter and served ten years of a fifteen-year prison sentence.

After the trial, Grace was adopted by Paul's sister, Trish Parker, and her husband. Grace Cavellini became Grace Parker. Her adopted parents took out a child arrangement order forbidding Cassie from having any contact with Grace. The arrangement order was in place until Grace turned eighteen. A birthday that was due to take place in two months, but now would never happen.

'Grace told me she didn't believe her mother had killed her father,' Dee told Ade and Rachel. 'She wanted my help proving it.'

'But you told her you couldn't help,' Ade said.

'Not immediately,' Dee said. 'I could see how much it meant to her so I said I'd look into it. I started by trying to find Cassie Cavellini, Grace's biological mother. It took a while for me to track her down because these days she uses her maiden name. I wasted a lot of time looking for Cassie Cavellini instead of Cassie MacNamara.'

'It must have been a surprise to discover Cassie was also living here in Eastbourne,' Rachel said.

'It certainly was.' Dee took a sip of her coffee before continuing. 'Especially as Grace didn't seem to have any clue her mother was living so nearby. When I asked Cassie about it, she told me she knew the child arrangement order meant she couldn't have any contact with her daughter, but it didn't stop her from living in the same town if she wanted to.'

'What was your impression of Cassie when you met her?' Ade asked.

'I liked her well enough,' Dee said. 'But I got the impression she was hiding something from me. I wasn't interesting in working with someone who wasn't being straight with me. So I called Grace and told her I wasn't going to pursue the story. She was very gracious about it, considering how desperate she'd seemed when we met.'

'You never spoke to Grace after that?' Ade asked.

'No.' Dee sighed. 'I got in touch with Cassie when I heard Grace had disappeared. I felt I had to. She was sick with worry over it. I can't imagine how she's coping now.'

The two detectives shared a glance with each other.

'What's wrong?' Dee asked.

'We haven't been able to find Cassie to tell her about Grace,' Ade said. 'That's why we're here. We thought you might know where she was.'

'Hang on,' Dee said. 'You mean her daughter's death is all over the news before anyone's bothered to tell her what's happened? She's the girl's mother, for Christ's sake.'

'Biological mother,' Rachel said. 'Trish Parker is her mother by law.'

Dee opened her mouth to reply, but Ade jumped in first.

'We're doing everything we can to find Cassie. We really don't want her to hear about Grace's death before we've had a chance to speak to her first.'

'Isn't it too late for that?' Dee's bitterness turned to anger. 'Grace's death is already public knowledge.'

'That wasn't intentional.' Rachel had the decency to look embarrassed. 'The news leaked out before we had a chance to speak to Cassie.'

'How?'

'You know her uncle is Joey Cavellini?'

'Yes.' The relationship between the dead girl and the celebrity businessman had been extensively covered by the press.

'He had to ID the body,' Rachel said, 'Trish wasn't up to doing it, so Joey offered. He got ambushed by the press afterwards. As you can imagine, the Parker family home has been under siege from journalists ever since Grace went missing. We'd asked Joey not to speak to any journalists, but that's a difficult thing to do when there are hordes of them surrounding your sister's home. They caught him at an extremely vulnerable moment and took full advantage of that.'

Dee felt a rush of compassion for the man who had looked so smooth and in control during the public appeals he'd been making since his niece first disappeared.

'Of course that's terrible,' she said, 'but it doesn't change anything. I have no idea where Cassie is. I imagine she's probably heard the news by now and has gone somewhere to be alone with her grief. Because, let's face it, speaking to the police is not going to be high on her list of priorities right now.'

'We should get going.' Rachel drained her mug and stood up. 'Do us a favour, Dee. If Cassie contacts you, tell her to get in touch. We really do need to speak to her.'

Later, long after the two detectives had left, Dee sat on her deck watching an orange sun sink down beneath a sea that looked as if there was a fire burning beneath its surface. She could hear her phone ringing, inside the house, but she didn't go to answer it. The only person she wanted to speak to right now was Grace Parker.

Dee wanted to tell her she was sorry. The day she'd told Grace she couldn't help her, she had been busy. Distracted, she had ended the call as quickly as possible because Grace was just another thing on her to-do list that needed to be crossed off. What Dee should have said, but didn't, was that Grace was a beautiful young woman with her whole life ahead of her, and she owed it to herself to focus on her future and let the past stay in the past where it belonged. Now Grace was dead, and Dee would never get the opportunity to tell her how glorious her life could have been.

Four

For a brief but perfect moment, in the half-filled space between sleeping and waking, Grace was still alive. Freya's brain hadn't yet caught up with the new reality of a world in which her sister no longer existed. She'd been dreaming. The details already fading, seeping into the grey light that trickled through the gaps between the curtains and the window. A single memory from the dream remained. Grace, dancing barefoot on white sand; sunlight reflecting off a turquoise sea and her sister's blonde hair swirling around her as she moved. An explosion of colour that faded along with the rest of the dream until there were only fragments left, like tiny pieces of ash floating in the air after a fire.

Freya opened her eyes. The wall opposite glowed green, reflecting the light from the radio beside her bed. As the digits changed from 04:59 to 05:00, everything came rushing back. The shock and the horror and the gut-churning, stomach-emptying grief. It was too huge for one person to contain. She could feel the pressure of it building up inside her body, forcing its way up her throat and out her mouth. Wailing, she pressed her fist against her lips, trying to block out the sound, but it kept coming with a force she couldn't contain.

By the time the wave of grief had passed, the digits on the clock were at 05:23. Outside, a squabble of seagulls screeched their angry greeting to the start of a new day; the world carrying on as if nothing had changed. She had no memory of feeling like this after her father left. Instead, she had lived most of her life with an emptiness and confusion she never knew how to resolve.

She'd only been three when he walked out on his family to live with the woman who was now his wife. Too young to understand her loss, or process it properly. Over the years, she had learned to deal with the complex feelings that sometimes made life so difficult. But now, in the aftermath of her sister's death, all the strategies Freya had learned seemed woefully inadequate.

She didn't want to have to do what was required to get through another day. Drag herself out of bed, put her clothes on and find the strength to keep going today and tomorrow and all the endless ones after that. But getting through was what she did, what she would have to do. Because Freya Parker was an exceptionally positive person who excelled at making the best of whatever challenges life threw her way.

Every day, she had a set of goals that helped her navigate this strange and confusing world. The goals kept her anchored, and feeling in control. She would need them now, more than ever. If she focused on being the best student, the fastest runner, the leanest and fittest of all her friends, she could push to the back of her mind the other, more complex thoughts and feelings she didn't know how to deal with.

She closed her eyes, breathed slowly and counted to ten, then threw back the duvet, got out of bed and put on her running gear. She ran five days a week, fifty-two weeks of the year. Today was Day Five for this week. The only time she'd missed a Day Five was when she'd been in hospital having her appendix out three years ago.

She crept downstairs, not wanting to wake her mother, who would try to stop her from going out. Who, if she had her way, would stop Freya doing anything in her life ever again.

Peeking out the sitting room window, she could see it was too early for the journalists who had plagued the family for most of last week. Relieved she didn't have to deal with them for another few hours, she took advantage of their absence to leave by the front door instead of sneaking out the back.

Outside, the sky was pink-stained with promise. Colour seeped into the pale streets, driving the night further west over the rolling hills of the South Downs. As she ran down the road towards the sea, Freya could see the outline of two container ships on the horizon, fuzzy and grey in the morning mist.

She ran along the seafront to the start of the Downs, then onto the path that led up, up, up towards the top of the first hill. Never once did she slow down or pause for breath. At the top, she kept running, faster now as the ground levelled out, along the side of the white cliffs that stretched along the coast to Seaford, ten miles away.

The world sped past in flashes of colour: pink and blue, green and white. All of it blurring as she started to cry. Tears running down her face, sobs shaking through her body. Memory after memory slamming into her, all ending with the doorbell ringing and a softly-spoken woman with dark hair and badly fitting trousers saying she was sorry, so very sorry for their loss.

Freya ran through the tears and the memories and the burning grief, only stopping when her stomach heaved. She doubled over, spitting out the thin trickle of vomit, waiting for the nausea to pass. When she lifted her head and looked around, she realised where she was and why her feet had taken her here this morning.

This was it. The spot they said Grace had jumped from. Although Freya didn't believe that was what had happened, because she knew Grace better than anyone and knew she'd never have done something like that.

The area was cordoned off by a line of black and yellow police tape. Freya wanted to move forward, duck under the tape and stand at the edge. To look down at the crashing waves and imagine what it would be like, to throw yourself off into the empty space beneath. But there was a police car up here too, with a policeman sitting inside, watching her. She knew if she moved towards the tape he'd get out of the car and want to know what she was doing.

She jogged past the car, stopping further along the cliffs and looking down, all the way to the calm blue sea lapping gently against the white rocks. Except there was nothing calm about that sea. It had taken her sister's body and thrown it against the rocks, again and again, until she was battered and broken and unrecognisable.

'It's for tonight. What do you think?'

The memory was so sudden and so real, almost as if she was back there that afternoon in Grace's bedroom. Watching her sister smile at her reflection in the mirror before she twirled around, the red dress fanning out from her waist.

'You're going on a date?'

Grace's smile had turned into a giggle.

'You won't believe it when I tell you who with.'

She'd been right about that. Freya felt it again now, the stab of angry jealousy when Grace had told her.

'Are you okay?'

The policeman had got out of the car and was walking towards her. He was tall, with short blond hair and blue eyes so pale they were almost white. He smiled and she hated him.

'My sister's body was found here yesterday,' Freya said. 'So no, I'm not okay actually.'

He reached out and touched her arm, the contact like an electric shock. The first person to touch her since her world had been ripped inside out.

She shook him off and stepped back, out of reach. 'Leave me alone.'

He said something, but she didn't hear him. She'd already turned away from him and was running, faster now that she'd got her breath back. Feet pounding against the hard soil, her mind replaying the same image: her sister's body, tipping head first over the edge, falling down and down and down.

Five

On Monday morning, the police released a statement confirming that Grace Parker had been murdered. Dee switched the TV on while she made breakfast. A local news channel replayed a clip of an appeal issued by Grace's adopted mother in the week the young woman was missing. Trish Parker was accompanied by her brother, the TV personality Joey Cavellini. Unlike his sister, Joey looked relaxed and well-groomed as he appealed for anyone with information on his missing niece to contact the police.

'If you're watching this, Grace,' he said, looking directly at the camera, 'please come home. We all miss you and love you so much.'

The screen faded, replaced by a photo of Grace with her boyfriend Lloyd Armstrong, who, according to the news reporter, was currently 'helping the police with their enquiries'. Grace and Lloyd looked happy in the photo. He had his arm around her shoulders and she was looking up at him, laughing.

Dee hit the pause button on the remote and looked at the photo, as if she might find some clue to what had happened to Grace. But there was no hint of anything bad. Grace and Lloyd were an attractive couple. He was tall, dark and very handsome. Grace was pale and petite, with a head of white blonde curls that hung loose and wild around her smiling face.

In the photo, she looked vibrant and happy and heart-breakingly alive. She also looked remarkably similar to Cassie MacNamara, her biological mother. Not for the first time, Dee thought how odd it was that the two women could have lived in the same town all these years without anyone ever noticing the resemblance.

There was no mention of Cassie on the news, but Dee knew it was only a matter of time before a journalist discovered the link between the murdered teenager and her troubled past. Because sixteen years ago, Cassie MacNamara had been convicted of killing her husband, Grace's father.

Dee had called Cassie over the weekend and left a message, but Cassie hadn't got back to her. She picked up her phone to call Cassie again, then changed her mind. She knew where Cassie lived because she'd driven her home after she'd been with the police. Dee decided to drive out there now and try to speak to Cassie in person.

On the drive to Cassie's house, Dee once again went back over the two times she'd spoken with Grace Parker. She had liked the young woman enormously. There'd been an energy to her, combined with a cheeky charm. Dee guessed there were a lot of people who found Grace Parker quite irresistible. Dee herself had been instantly charmed when they met. And later, when she'd called Grace to say she wasn't going to investigate Paul's murder, Grace had been so polite, telling Dee she under-stood entirely and thanking her for taking the time to consider her request.

Dee remembered, during their first conversation, Grace had told Dee how she wanted to become a human rights lawyer. She had spoken with such passion and energy that Dee had left the conversation convinced Grace would make a success of whatever she decided to do with the rest of her life. Later that evening, Dee had told Ed that Grace Parker was a young woman with a bright future ahead of her. Dee couldn't have known, at the time, how wrong she'd been.

Pulling up outside Cassie's house, Dee was struck again by how bleak and isolated it was. A single-storey, grey stone building with a roof that sank in the middle and rotted wooden window frames. There were no other properties nearby, just flat yellow fields that stretched all the way to Hailsham in one direction and Pevensey Bay in the other. Cassie had told Dee she loved living here. Said that when she came out of prison, she'd needed peace and quiet. This little house in the middle of nowhere gave her exactly that.

It was only after she'd knocked on the front door and got no answer that Dee realised she should have phoned first to check Cassie would be here. She was about to knock again, when she heard the shuffle of footsteps inside the house and, a moment later, the front door creaked open.

A woman, about five foot tall and almost as wide, stood in the doorway staring at Dee. From the expression on her face, it was clear she wasn't happy with what she saw.

'Who the hell are you?'

Resisting the urge to ask the same question, Dee smiled and introduced herself.

'I'm a friend of Cassie's,' she said. 'Is she here?'

'Why do you want to know?'

'Listen,' Dee said, losing her patience. 'I've no idea who you are, and I'm not particularly interested in finding out. Is Cassie here or not?'

The woman took a step closer and it took all Dee's willpower not to shove her back. 'In case you didn't realise, Cassie has suffered a terrible loss. She's grieving and she doesn't want to see anyone. So why don't you sod off back to wherever you came from and leave us alone?'

'I've got a better idea,' Dee said. 'How about you go back in there and tell Cassie I'm here. If she doesn't want to see me, I'll go. But you don't get to make that decision for her. And if you shut the door in my face, I'll keep knocking on it until you'll have no choice but to open it again. Because I am very happy to spend my entire day sitting out here in the sunshine until you tell Cassie that I'm here.'

She thought the woman would say no, but after a long, drawn-out moment, she gave an almost imperceptible nod.

'Wait here.'

She shut the door, but Dee was at least fifty per cent confident she'd be back.

Less than a minute passed before the door opened again. This time, by a barely recognisable Cassie. Grief had distorted her face, twisted it into something terrible.

'I had to come,' Dee said. 'I've been thinking of you all weekend and I needed to tell you how dreadfully sorry I am. Grace was such a lovely young woman. You would have been so very proud of her, Cassie.'

Cassie's face crumpled and she started to cry.

'I'm so sorry.' Dee stepped forward and wrapped her arms around Cassie's body.

'I can't believe she's gone,' Cassie said, pulling away from Dee and using the sleeve of her faded sweatshirt to rub her face. 'Do you want to come inside?'

'You think that'll be okay with your friend?'

'Jennifer's just looking out for me,' Cassie said. 'She's one of the few people in my life that I trust.'

Dee followed Cassie down a narrow hallway, that stank of cigarette smoke and stale food, into a small kitchen. Jennifer was sitting at the table, but when she saw Dee, she stood up and told Cassie she was going to the shops.

'You've got no food in,' she said. 'I know you don't feel like eating at the moment, but at some point you'll need to eat.'

She gave Cassie a hug and swept past Dee.

'So,' Dee said, as the front door slammed shut so hard the whole house vibrated. 'How do you and Jennifer know each other?'

'She's my boss,' Cassie said. 'Owns the hair salon where I work.'

'What's her problem with me?'

'She's suspicious of everyone,' Cassie said. 'Trust me, it's not just you. Once you get to know her a bit she'll be fine.'

Dee had no desire to get to know Cassie's boss any better, although she refrained from saying this.

'She knows Grace is your daughter,' she said instead.

'Jennifer's one of the few people who know the truth,' Cassie said. 'She's been amazing to me.'

Dee knew it was only a matter of time before some journalist worked out the connection between the dead teenager and Paul Cavellini's murder. She also knew there was no point saying this to Cassie, who looked like she was barely keeping it together.

'She was murdered,' Cassie said, her voice barely more than a whisper. 'Who would do something like that, Dee?' Before Dee could respond, her mobile phone started to ring. Fishing it out of her bag, she saw Ed's name on the screen and diverted the call. She'd call him later, when she was finished here.

'None of this feels real,' Cassie said. 'The single thing that's kept me going all these years has been her. Without her in my life, I don't know who I am or how I'm meant to carry on living while she's dead. It's not right. No parent should outlive their child. What am I going to do, Dee?'

Dee was saved from having to find a response to that impossible question by the sound of someone knocking on the front door.

'I'll get it.' She pushed her chair back and stood up, part of her selfishly relieved to escape the claustrophobic atmosphere of Cassie's too-small kitchen.

She opened the front door and, for the second time this morning, found herself face to face with someone who clearly wasn't pleased to see her.

'Dee?' Rachel said. 'What are you doing here?'

'I came to see how Cassie was doing,' Dee said. 'What's your excuse?'

'I don't need any excuse. Cassie's expecting me. I called earlier and told her I was coming to see her. I'll be speaking to her in private, by the way. Just in case you were thinking of hanging around to listen in to our conversation.'

'I wouldn't dream of it.' Dee stood back to let Rachel into the house. 'I've left my bag in the kitchen. I'll grab that and leave you to your *private* conversation.' She used her fingers to make mock speech marks when she said 'private'. Surprisingly, Rachel didn't appear irritated by the gesture, which, even Dee had to admit, was more than a bit childish.

'How do you think she's doing?' she said instead.

'I haven't been here long enough to tell,' Dee said. 'From what I've seen, she's barely coping.'

'Grace would have been eighteen in a few months,' Rachel said. 'After that, there wouldn't have been anything stopping Cassie from making contact. The timing of this makes it seem even crueller than it already is.'

'Let me know if you think there's anything I can do?' Dee said.

'Make sure she knows you're there for her,' Rachel said. 'There's not much you can do apart from that.'

Ever since she'd met Ed, he'd maintained that Rachel Lewis was one of the very best people he'd ever met. As Dee drove away from Cassie's house, she thought that he might just be right about that. Which wasn't surprising, because in all the time she'd known him, he was rarely wrong about anything.

Six

Ed's car was parked outside Dee's house when she got back. She found him sitting on the deck with a pot of coffee and a pile of newspapers on the table in front of him.

'Where have you been?' he asked, standing to give her a perfectly placed peck on the cheek.

'I decided to go and see Cassie,' she said.

'Poor woman,' Ed said. 'It's hard to imagine what she must be going through. Is there anything I can do?'

'I don't think so.'

'I was starting to worry you wouldn't be back in time.'

In time for what, Dee was about to ask, before she remembered.

'Lunch!' she said. 'You know I wouldn't let us be late for that.'

'I know you most likely completely forgot about it.' Ed grinned. 'Come on, Doran, admit it.'

'Me, forget?' Dee said, doing her best to sound shocked. 'Never! I've got one quick phone call to make and then I'm ready to go.'

As she said this, she started rooting around in her bag, trying to locate the phone. But even after she'd emptied the contents onto the table beside Ed's stack of newspapers, she couldn't find it.

'I must have left it in Cassie's,' she said. 'It's your fault, you know. You called me while I was there and I took my phone out to see who was calling.'

'But my call went straight to voicemail,' Ed said.

'I was with a grieving mother,' Dee said. 'I planned to call you as soon as I left.'

'So why didn't you?'

'I didn't have my phone, did I?'

She was about to ask if they could drive to Cassie's house and pick up her phone before going to lunch, but she changed her mind. If they did that, they'd definitely be late and it wouldn't do her any harm to be without her phone for a few hours.

'Come on,' she said instead. 'Let's get going. I'll drive.'

'Won't you want a glass of wine with your lunch?'

'I've got to work this afternoon,' Dee said. 'So it's probably best I don't have a drink. But you're a man of leisure these days. You can have a pint of Harveys and then a nap in the afternoon.'

'Lucky me,' Ed replied, but he didn't sound as if he meant it.

Until three months ago, he'd been working alongside Rachel Lewis as a detective with Sussex Police. He had always planned to retire in his early fifties and when he finally decided it was time to leave, he'd seemed relieved. Since then, however, Dee suspected the adjustment to being a man of leisure was proving harder than he'd expected.

'Rachel was at Cassie's just now,' Dee said, as they walked to her car.

'How's she doing? We keep saying we'll meet for a drink and a catch-up, but she never seems to have any time.'

'She seemed fine.'

'She puts on a good front,' Ed said. 'She'll be taking this hard. Murder investigations are never easy, and when it's a young person who's been murdered, that can really get to you.'

'Especially when the victim is a young woman with her whole life in front of her,' Dee said.

'You know what?' Ed took Dee's hand in his and squeezed it. 'Let's not talk about Rachel or the investigation over lunch. Let's talk about us and all the exciting things we want to do over the next few years.'

'Sounds good to me.' Dee smiled, as some of the tension drained from her shoulders. She felt looser and lighter than she had a few minutes earlier. It was something she'd started calling 'the Ed effect', although she would rather die than let him know this. No matter how bad things were, Ed always seemed to know what to do to make her feel better.

It hadn't always been plain sailing between them. There was a time when Dee had thought their relationship was over for good. Yet, somehow, they seemed to always gravitate back to each other. This time round, they'd promised to take things slowly, enjoying each other's company while also giving themselves as much space as they both needed. It was an arrangement that, so far, seemed to be working pretty well.

–

They ate lunch at the Eight Bells in Jevington, a tiny village six miles outside Eastbourne. The food was every bit as good as they'd come to expect from their many visits to the pub. Ed had booked a table outside and they sat side by side, looking out over the rolling green fields and low hills of the South Downs National Park.

Dee was glad she'd decided to drive. It would only take one glass of wine for her to suggest that they spent the rest of the afternoon in bed together. Even without the wine, she'd found herself more than once on the verge of inviting him back to hers as soon as lunch was finished. Which was a terrible idea, because she had at least three hours of work waiting for her this afternoon.

'What was she like?' Ed asked, after they'd ordered their food.

'Grace, you mean? I thought we weren't talking about this over lunch.'

'Sorry.' He held his hands up apologetically. 'You don't have to answer if you don't want to.'

'It's okay,' Dee said. 'I'd like to talk about her. She was lovely, Ed. Bright and bubbly, full of personality. And she was interested, you know? As well as sharing details of her own life, she asked me lots of questions about myself too. Even when I told her I wasn't going to look into her father's murder, she took the news really well. Said she respected my decision and thanked me for my time.'

'Are you going to be okay?' Ed asked.

'Me? Of course I will. Why do you ask?'

'Because I know you. What's happened is terrible, but it's really not got anything to do with you. You've got such a big heart, which is one of the things that make you such a special person. But that big heart of yours also means you take on too much of other people's pain. Sometimes at the detriment of your own well-being.'

'I can't turn my back on someone when they need me,' she said. 'You're not telling me that's what I should do, are you?'

'I'm just looking out for you, that's all.'

'I know,' Dee said, 'and I appreciate it, Ed. But I'm fine. Really I am.'

'So you're not going to do anything stupid, like decide you owe it to Grace to take another look into her father's murder?'

'Would that be such a bad thing?'

In fact, over the weekend, she'd been thinking that's exactly what she was going to do. She felt guilty. She could have – should have – done more for Grace while she was alive.

'I think you had very good reasons for deciding not to investigate,' Ed said. 'Those reasons don't change just because Grace is dead.'

Their food arrived shortly afterwards and Dee did her best to pretend she was enjoying herself. But her thoughts kept returning to Cassie.

She had ordered fish and chips, something she regretted now. Stodgy, fried food on a hot summer's day was rarely a good idea. She managed about half the fish and a handful of chips before putting her knife and fork together and pushing the plate to one side.

'No good?' Ed asked, in between mouthfuls of steak and kidney pie and mashed potatoes. Clearly, he wasn't going to let a bit of sunshine get in the way of his own enjoyment of the food.

'I wasn't as hungry as I thought,' Dee said.

'Mind if I take a few chips?'

He didn't wait for her to answer, reaching out and piercing his fork into several of the chips congealing on Dee's plate.

'I'm buying a camper van,' he said.

'You're what?'

'Now I'm retired, I want to do a bit of travelling.' He put his fork down and took Dee's hand. 'A European road trip. What do you think?'

The proposal was so out of the blue, Dee had no idea what she thought about it.

'Um, I think that sounds like a great plan,' she managed eventually. 'When would you go?'

'Not me, *we*. I want us to go travelling together. I need a new adventure. If I have to live out the rest of my years playing golf and doing the *Times* crossword every day, I'll be dead before I'm sixty. There's a whole big world out there and I want to see lots of it before I pop my clogs.'

'Well,' Dee said, carefully, 'I'm all for adventures. Of course I am. It's just come a bit out of the blue, that's all. I'll need a bit of time to get my head around the idea. I mean, what about my work?'

'There's more to life than work,' Ed said. 'But I'm not asking you to make a decision right now. Just promise me you'll think about it?'

'Yes of course.' Dee gave him a smile that she was sure looked as forced as it felt.

Normally, after eating they would have stayed for another drink, then gone for a gentle stroll along one of the paths that led from the pub into the nearby forest. Today, Dee couldn't wait to get back home and be alone, away from Ed with his talk of adventures and his plans for a future she wasn't at all sure was what she wanted.

Seven

Ed wasn't happy about their afternoon being cut short, pointing out that Dee's world wouldn't fall apart if she had to be without her phone a little longer. Dee knew this was technically true. But she also knew she would feel a lot better once she was reunited with her rectangular friend. Promising to call Ed later, she dropped him home and drove across to Cassie's house.

This time, no one came to open the door after Dee knocked on it. Reluctantly, Dee decided her best option was to leave and come back later in the hope that Cassie would be back by then.

She was walking back to her car when it suddenly occurred to her that Cassie might be in there, just not answering the door. This thought was rapidly followed by a series of images, each one featuring Cassie inside the house unable to move because she'd had a fall or taken an overdose or... The images kept coming and Dee knew she couldn't leave without making sure Cassie was okay.

She banged on the front door several more times, calling Cassie's name. When she got no response, she peered through each of the windows on either side of the front door. Through the first window, she saw a sitting room, TV, a cheap-looking armchair and a faded rug that didn't quite cover the scratched laminate floor beneath it. The other window belonged to a bedroom. Single bed squashed between the wall and a chest of drawers, a carpet with an ugly swirling pattern in mustard yellow and brown, a framed photo on the chest of drawers. No Cassie in either room.

Dee walked around to the back of the house. A metal door with frosted glass. She rattled the handle, but, unsurprisingly, the door was locked. As she stepped away from the door to peer through the window, she saw a movement on the other side of the frosted glass.

'Cassie!' Dee banged on the glass and rattled the handle a few more times. When no one answered, she took a step back and looked along the back of the squat grey building as she considered what to do next. The window was too high for her to look through. When she tried to look through the frosted glass, all she could see was a kaleidoscope of blurred colours and her own, distorted reflection. Yet she had definitely seen something a moment ago.

After a futile fifteen minutes searching under various rocks for a spare key, Dee took another wander around the house. This time, she checked the windows to see if she could open any of them. They were sash, with rotting wooden frames that all needed replacing. The sitting-room window was locked, but, when Dee tried the bedroom window, it slid up easily. Not quite believing her luck, she pushed it up as far as it would go. Which wasn't far, but she figured there was just enough space for her to crawl through if she was careful.

Cursing herself for not losing the two stone in weight she'd been threatening to shed for the last three years, Dee pulled herself onto the windowsill. With a bit of grunting and a lot of effort, she was just able to wriggle through the gap beneath the open window.

Entering a room this way was far from ideal. As she fell forward, Dee put her hands out to protect her face as she landed heavily on the threadbare carpet. She had scratched her stomach on the rotting wood on her way in. Lifting her top, she saw she had a narrow cut beneath her belly button which felt worse than it looked.

Despite the tired furniture and the awful carpet, Cassie had clearly put a bit of effort into making the room as nice as possible. The bed was made up with a matching duvet set, white with a pattern of bright red flowers. A lime and mandarin diffuser stood on the top of the chest of drawers and, beside it, the photo Dee had seen when she looked through the window earlier.

The photo was of a much younger Cassie with a small baby in her arms. No prizes for guessing who the baby was. The look of pure joy on Cassie's face was all the proof Dee needed that this photo had been taken shortly after Cassie became a mum. The photo was a powerful, and poignant, reminder of the strength of maternal love and how much Cassie had lost.

Dee was about to pick up the photo to take a closer look, when she heard a floorboard creaking on the other side of the closed bedroom door. She held her breath, listening for more sounds. When she heard another creak, followed rapidly by the sound of someone breathing heavily, she crossed the bedroom quickly and pulled open the door.

The corridor outside was empty.

'Cassie?'

Dee looked left towards the front door, and right towards the kitchen. When she didn't see anyone, she wondered how real the sounds were that she'd heard. Was it possible that her over-active imagination had heard things that weren't really there?

The door to the kitchen was open and she could see her phone, sitting on the table where she'd left it. As she walked down the corridor to get it, the hairs on the back of her neck prickled. Yet each time she turned around and scanned the space behind her, it was empty.

She had one missed call and a voice message. When she saw the missed call was from Louise, Dee dialled the number for her voicemail and listened to her cousin's message.

'Dee? It's me. Can you call me as soon as you get this? It's urgent.'

Immediately, Dee's thoughts turned to Daisy and Ben – her niece and nephew.

She was in the middle of calling Louise back, when something heavy smashed into the back of her head. It happened so fast she barely had time to register it, before the scuffed black and white lino was racing towards her. She hit the ground hard, pain shooting up her right arm and hip. Her phone fell out of her hand, skidding out of reach across the lino.

She grabbed the leg of the table and tried to pull herself up, but a foot shot out, kicking her hand. Screaming, Dee reached out, trying to grab the foot, but the person attacking her was too fast. A kick to her side sent the air whooshing out of her body, another kick followed to the back of her head. Dee roared, a combination of fear and rage and frustration.

Holding onto the leg of the table a second time, she hauled herself up. Warm liquid was running down her face, getting into her eyes. When she wiped it away, her hand was smeared with blood.

She looked around for her attacker, her fists up ready to fight, but the kitchen was empty. Holding her breath, she moved into the hallway, eyes scanning left and right and straight ahead, ears listening out for any sound. But she didn't see or hear anything out of the ordinary.

The hallway, so dark earlier, seemed lighter now. As Dee approached the front door, she realised why this was. The door, locked shut moments earlier, was wide open. She went outside, but there was no one out here.

On the other side of the overgrown hedge that separated the garden from the road, a car engine revved into life. Dee caught a flash of colour as the car sped away. She raced out to the road, but the car had already disappeared around the sharp bend in the road.

Her attacker was gone, and Dee had no way of finding out who they were or what they'd been doing here.

Eight

Before

Cassie's phone pinged with a new text message. When she saw Mark's name on the screen, she deleted the message without reading it.

'Everything okay?' Paul was standing in the doorway, watching her. Always watching. As if he knew she was keeping secrets from him.

'Fine.' She smiled and lay back down on the sofa, her eyes fixed on the TV. The volume was down low, so she could listen through the baby monitor while he put Grace to bed.

'Who's sending you messages?' Paul asked.

'Lizzie. She wants to know if I fancy meeting for a drink.'

'That's not a bad idea.' He crossed the room, knelt on the floor beside her and kissed her cheek. He stank of garlic and beer and her stomach roiled as he wrapped his arms around her. Strange to think she'd once convinced herself she loved him. 'You haven't been out in a while,' he said. 'A drink with Lizzie will do you the world of good.'

'I don't have any money to go out,' she reminded him. 'The money you give me for housekeeping is barely enough to get the basics we need each week. There's never anything left over.'

'You'll have to get a bit better with budgeting.'

He stood up and moved away. He didn't like it when she complained about money, but sometimes she couldn't help it. He had no idea how tough it was, constantly struggling to make ends meet. This wasn't what he'd promised when he'd asked her to marry him.

'I do my best,' she said.

'Well, your best clearly isn't good enough.' He ran a hand through his hair, a sure sign that he was stressed. 'It's not my fault, Cassie. I've been working for Joey for over a year now and I'm still on the same salary as when I started. He keeps promising to review it, but whenever I try to speak to him about it, he changes the subject. I've a good mind to look for work somewhere else. Plenty of jobs out there for someone like me, I reckon.'

Cassie gritted her teeth to stop herself saying something she'd regret. They'd gone over this so many times before, always ending up in the same place with Paul moaning about having to work for his older brother. Never once acknowledging that Joey had given him a job when no one else would.

Not for the first time, Cassie reflected on the bad choice she'd made. There was a time she could have had either of the Cavellini brothers. Before Joey grew bored with her and moved onto his next conquest. On the rebound, Cassie had been flattered when Paul asked her out. It was only later, after she'd married him, that she realised he was no better than his brother. They were both selfish bastards who didn't care about anyone except themselves.

'Things will get easier,' Paul said.

As if to prove the lie, the doorbell rang. Paul and Cassie looked at each other, both knowing who it was.

'She's not going to leave us alone until she has her money,' Cassie said.

Paul scowled. 'She knows I'll pay her back as soon as I can. Maybe if you were a bit more careful, we'd have had something to give her by now.'

The accusation stung, but Cassie knew better than to argue back. She still had the bruises on her arm from the other day, when he'd grabbed her and held her until she apologised for making him feel bad for going to the pub with his mates to watch the football.

The doorbell rang again, but Paul made no move to go and answer it.

'What are you going to do?' she asked.

'Keep your voice down,' he hissed. 'She'll go away in a minute.'

But that didn't happen, because when the doorbell rang again, it woke Grace up and she started screaming. The sound was so loud anyone standing outside would be able to hear it and know the house wasn't empty.

'Jesus Christ,' Paul hissed. 'I told you she needs to be taken out every day. If you keep her indoors all the time, how do you expect her to be tired enough to sleep?'

Cassie would have told him she had, in fact, taken Grace to the park earlier. But he had already stormed out of the room, slamming the door so hard the walls vibrated. Through the closed door, she could hear Paul and Trish shouting at each other. Arguing about the money Trish had lent Paul to pay for his lavish marriage to Cassie and, so far, hadn't paid back.

Grace had settled again, her wails turning to snuffled sobs followed by peaceful silence. Cassie wanted to go and check on her, but she couldn't face having to pass the front door, where she would certainly be seen by her sister-in-law.

Instead, she went to the window and looked out. She could see Trish's shiny blue BMW parked on the road outside the house. It terrified Cassie to think of the money they owed Trish. Ten thousand pounds. How were they ever going to find that?

Paul had told her it was money left to him in his parents' will. A lie that Cassie had been too willing to believe. In fact, he had borrowed the money from his sister because Trish had told him there was no rush paying it back. But then, Trish had lost her job while she was on maternity leave and now she needed the money to continue living in the big house she shared with her husband, Conor, and their daughter, Freya.

If Cassie had known about the money, she would never have married him. But she'd been pregnant and scared and Paul had seemed like the answer to all her problems, offering her the security she desperately craved. It was only later, after Grace was born, that Cassie had realised her whole marriage had been built on a lie and Paul was no better than any of the other men she could have chosen instead.

Her phone pinged again with another message.

> I really need to see you. Call me.

Her fingers hovered over the phone, thinking of the different things she wanted to say to him. But what was the point? She'd made her choice when she first found out she was pregnant. It was too late, now, to change things.

She heard the sound of the front door slamming shut, then Paul's footsteps as he crossed the hall and went into the kitchen. When she heard the fridge door opening and the hiss of a can of beer being opened, rage bubbled up inside her. That was Paul's answer to everything: crack open a beer and forget about the responsibilities of being a parent with debts that needed to be paid.

If she'd known it was going to be this difficult, she'd never have agreed to keep the baby and get married. She loved Grace, of course. But being a parent was such hard work. Especially when you had no money and no friends, apart from Lizzie who didn't count because she'd made it crystal clear she didn't want anything to do with Cassie ever again.

In the kitchen, Paul had switched the radio on and was humming softly along with the Arctic Monkeys. Sounding, Cassie thought viciously, as if he didn't have a care in the world. In that moment, as she listened to his humming and pictured him drinking beer from the can, she hated him and she wished more than anything in the world he was dead.

Nine

Dee called Louise on the drive back home. This time, Louise answered.

'I got your message,' Dee said. 'What's wrong? Is it one of the kids?'

'The kids are fine,' Louise answered. 'But I thought you'd want to know that we're about to publish a story on our website confirming that Grace Parker was adopted, and Cassie MacNamara's her biological mother.'

'Shit.' Dee breathed in, the action causing her aching ribs to hurt more than they already did. 'Tell me it wasn't you who leaked the information?'

'You're really asking me that?'

'Sorry,' Dee said. 'So how did they find out?'

'An anonymous call came through earlier,' Louise said. 'Rita took the call, and when she looked into it, the information checked out. There's nothing I could have done, Dee.'

'I know,' Dee said. 'And I appreciate you calling to let me know, Lou. I really do. But I've got to call Cassie and warn her.'

'Before you go, there's something I've been meaning to ask you. When you first told me about Grace and Cassie, you said there was a child protection order forbidding Cassie from making any contact with Grace.'

'That's right,' Dee said, 'what about it?'

'I keep thinking, if it was me, if I was living in the same town as my child, no child protection order in the world would stop me from trying to see her.'

'Cassie knew if she broke the order she'd end up back in prison.'

'I don't think that would be enough to stop me,' Louise said. 'Are you sure that in all this time she's never once got in touch with Grace?'

'Grace told me she hadn't seen her mother since the adoption,' Dee said. 'Why would she lie about that?'

'To protect Cassie.'

'So let's say they did meet up,' Dee said. 'Does it make any difference?'

'It doesn't make Cassie look good,' Louise replied. 'And believe me, Dee, if they were seeing each other and that gets out, the press will crucify her. Listen, I've got to go. You've got an hour before the story goes live.'

After she hung up, Dee thought about what Louise had said. Both Grace and Cassie had been adamant the child protection order had never been broken. But Louise was right, it was possible they'd lied about that.

As well as her sore ribs, Dee had a thumping headache and a cut on her forehead that was stinging like hell. She'd managed to clean off the blood with some tissues she'd had in her bag, and her fringe hid the cut. She felt far worse than she looked. Right now, she wanted nothing more than to sink into a hot bath and have a large glass of chilled wine before crawling into bed. But before she could do any of that, she had to find Cassie.

Using the car's display unit, she scrolled through her contacts, found Cassie's number and made the call. Cassie picked up almost immediately.

'Cassie, where are you?' Dee said.

'I'm at the seafront,' Cassie replied. 'I had to go give another statement to the police. I came down to the beach afterwards, but the truth is, I don't know what I'm doing. Has something happened?'

'I need to see you,' Dee said. 'Tell me which part of the beach you're on and I'll go straight there.'

Twenty minutes later, Dee was walking along the promenade east of the pier looking for Cassie. It was difficult to spot Cassie among the throng of tourists and locals out in force to enjoy the summer sunshine. After about ten minutes, Dee eventually saw her, sitting on the beach facing the sea. When Dee sat down beside her, Cassie looked surprised, as if she'd forgotten all about them meeting up.

'How are you doing?' Dee asked, wincing at the stupidity of the question.

It was obvious, just by looking at her, that Cassie was barely holding it together. Her arms were wrapped around her body, as if she might fall apart otherwise. She had dark rings under her eyes, the only patch of colour in her too-white face.

She was holding the end of a rolled-up cigarette between her thumb and forefinger. She took a final drag, blowing a stream of smoke into the air, and stubbed the tip out on a white rock. When she threw the cigarette onto the ground, Dee picked it up. Normally, she was more than ready to reprimand anyone she saw littering the beach, but in this instance she kept her mouth shut. Cassie had enough to be dealing with without having to endure a lecture from Dee as well.

'I can't do this,' Cassie said softly.

Dee stayed silent, knowing there were no words that could make this better.

'I keep thinking of all the other parents who have lost children. How did they keep going? Then I think of Trish, and even though I hate her for taking Grace from me, there's part of me that wants to see her. Because she's the only other person in the world who could possibly understand what this feels like. Do you think I should speak to her? I have no idea what I should do. It's like part of my brain has shut down and I'm walking through this fog where I can't see anything properly.'

She stopped speaking and the silence stretched out between them while Dee tried to think of something to say.

'I don't think you should be alone right now,' she said, eventually. 'Would you let me take you back to mine for a bit? You can stay as long as you want.'

Cassie shrugged. 'I don't care where I go.'

'Well, in that case, you're coming with me.' Dee stood up and held her hand out. After a moment, Cassie reached out and took it. Dee pulled her up and together they walked across the shingle back towards where Dee had parked her car.

They were on the promenade, about to cross the road, when Cassie abruptly stopped walking. Dee opened her mouth to ask what was wrong, but, when she saw Cassie's face, the words stuck in her throat. Cassie looked terrified.

'What is it?' Dee asked, but Cassie didn't reply.

Dee followed the direction Cassie was looking in and saw a young woman walking towards them. As she drew closer, Dee realised she was more a teenager than a woman. A tall, very thin girl with dark hair tied back in a too-tight ponytail and a pinched white face.

The girl drew up in front of Cassie and pointed at her.

'I know all about you,' she hissed. 'You think you were so clever keeping it a secret, but you're wrong. This is all your fault. I don't care what the police or anyone else says, I know she's dead because of you.'

Ten

Freya scrolled through the contacts on her phone, looking for Iris Allen's number. Iris was the family liaison officer who'd been assigned to them a few days after Grace first disappeared. She was a bland, uninteresting woman. The exact opposite, in fact, of Grace, who had attracted people to her like moths to a flame.

Until now, Freya had done everything she could to stay out of Iris's way. She found the woman insufferably irritating, with her gentle voice and endless offers to make cups of tea. As if tea could, somehow, fix all of this.

But after seeing Cassie MacNamara, Freya knew she couldn't keep quiet any longer. She needed to break her promise to Grace, the one she had sworn on her own life she would never tell to another living soul. But that promise had been made when Grace was still alive and neither of them had any inkling that she wouldn't live to see her eighteenth birthday.

Freya expected to get a recorded message, but when she called the number, Iris Allen answered almost immediately.

'Um, it's me,' Freya said. 'Freya Parker?'

'Hello, Freya.' Iris's voice was soft and sympathetic, which irritated Freya. She didn't want sympathy; she wanted the police to do their job properly and arrest Cassie MacNamara for causing her sister's death.

'I need to see you,' Freya said. 'There's something I haven't told you.'

'I can be at the house in ten minutes,' Iris said. 'Or, if you don't want to talk there, I can meet you somewhere else.'

'The house is fine,' Freya said, after a moment. 'Thank you.'

–

The journalists were still there, gathered in secretive groups outside the house, waiting to pounce the moment they saw Freya. She sneaked around the back to avoid them and entered the house through the kitchen.

Iris was already here, sitting at the table with another detective Freya recognised from last week. She searched her mind for the detective's name, but it wouldn't come to her. Mum was there too, frowning at Freya.

'Iris says you want to talk to her about Grace,' Mum said.

'That's right.'

'I wish you'd spoken to me first,' Mum said. 'I've called Joey and he's on his way over. I think he should be with you when you talk to Iris.'

'I don't need Joey with me,' Freya said, trying not to sound irritated at the suggestion.

The last thing she wanted was her uncle sitting beside her, monitoring everything she said. She could handle this perfectly well without him.

'I disagree,' Mum said.

'I'm eighteen, Mum. If I don't want anyone else with me, then I don't have to have them. I'll be fine, honestly. You don't need to worry.'

It was a pointless thing to say because her mother always worried. Even before this, she had been a worrier. Constantly anxious about every little thing her daughters did, nagging and worrying and over-parenting to an exhausting degree. It was no wonder Grace had railed against it. Unlike Freya, who always tried to placate her mother and do as little as possible to give her any further reasons to worry.

On the beach earlier, she'd believed for one crazy moment that Grace was still alive. Until she realised, with a deadening certainty, that the woman walking towards her couldn't be

Grace. Then, as the woman had got closer, Freya could see the differences. This woman was older, and her skin was dull in a way Grace's had never been. She had a pattern of tiny crows' feet at the corner of each eye, and there was a haunted look in her face that made it difficult to look at her for too long.

It was the first time Freya had seen her, but she knew immediately who she was. She looked too like Grace to be anyone else. Thinking back to that moment, Freya knew she should have walked past without saying anything. But the sight of her, alive and walking along the seafront, had triggered a surge of sudden rage that made Freya want to lash out.

'I thought you were meeting your friends today.'

Mum's voice dragged Freya back to the present moment.

'That's later.'

They were going to light a fire and have some drinks in memory of Grace. It had been Marissa's idea. She had taken on the role of grieving friend with fervour, acting as if this was her tragedy and hers alone. It was stupid. Grace hadn't even liked Marissa. She had tolerated her because she was Freya's friend, but she'd told Freya — more than once — she thought Marissa was a self-centred airhead.

'Where would you like to do this?' Iris asked.

'If you don't want Joey,' Mum said, 'maybe I should sit with you.'

'No.'

She smiled at Mum, wanting her to know there was no need for her to worry. Freya knew what to say to the police. More importantly, she knew what *not* to say.

'Let's go into the sitting room,' she said, taking a glass from the cupboard and filling it with tap water. 'We'll be more comfortable there.'

As Freya led the two detectives down the hallway, the noises inside her head grew quieter. She could see a way forward now. She knew what she needed to do. She was back in control.

'So,' Iris said, once they were sitting down, 'how are you doing, Freya?'

She shrugged, not bothering to answer such a stupid question.

'I appreciate how hard this must be for you,' Iris continued. 'And I want you to know that Ade and I are here to help you in whatever way we can. Ade is working with Detective Inspector Rachel Lewis on the investigation. You remember Rachel?'

'Of course,' Freya said.

She looked at the detective whose name was Ade, Freya remembered now. Pronounced 'Ah-day' but spelled 'Ade' because it was short for Adesanya, as she'd explained to Freya at some point over the last week. She didn't look like a detective, Freya thought. If you saw her in a bar, you'd think she was a model or an actress.

'Are you able to tell us why you wanted to see us?' Ade asked.

'The last time we spoke,' Freya said, 'I told you how Grace changed after she found out what happened to her father.'

'You said she was very upset about it,' Iris said. 'Hardly surprising, really. It must have been a difficult thing for her to process.'

'The thing is,' Freya said, 'it was Cassie's fault that Grace found out about her dad. That's what I wanted to speak to you about.'

'We're listening,' Ade said.

'Grace always knew she was adopted,' Freya continued. 'It was never a secret in our family. It could hardly be anything else. We're the same age but have different birthdays. It's obvious we're not related by birth.'

'But you were as close as sisters?' Ade said.

'We were.' It hurt, saying it. Close didn't seem an adequate word to describe the way you felt about someone who had been in your life for as long as you could remember. To imagine living her life without Grace was so inconceivable Freya didn't know how she was going to be able to do it. 'We were very different, but that didn't matter. Mum loved us equally. There was never any doubt about that.'

48

Not entirely true, but there was no need for the detectives to know every detail of their lives.

'In what ways were you different?' Ade asked.

In all the ways that mattered, Freya wanted to say. Grace was free-spirited, chaotic and didn't care what anyone thought of her. The exact opposite of her uptight sister, who craved control and order because without them she was unable to manage the anxiety and crippling self-consciousness that made everything so difficult.

'Lots of ways.' Freya looked from one detective to the other. 'But you don't care about that, do you? You want to know about Cassie. I should have told you before, but Grace made me promise never to tell anyone. I'm sorry.'

She felt a thrill as she watched their body language, the way they both leaned forward slightly, waiting to hear what she had to say.

'It's about Cassie and Grace,' she said. 'And the secret they had.'

Eleven

Cassie was sitting on the deck when Dee got up the following morning. Dee made a pot of coffee and carried it outside along with two mugs.

'It's beautiful here,' Cassie said, as Dee poured the coffee and sat down beside her. 'You're lucky.'

'I know.' Dee took a sip of coffee and looked around her. Strange, now, to think she'd spent so much of her early life desperate to leave. She couldn't ever imagine living anywhere else. She'd always assumed Ed felt the same way. Although they tended to avoid speaking about the future, in some vague way she'd imagined that if they stayed together he would one day move in here with her. Yet from their conversation yesterday, it seemed he had other plans entirely.

'Does anyone live down there?' Cassie pointed at the mobile home further along the beach.

'Not at the moment,' Dee said, swallowing down the familiar pang of loss. 'The family who lived there moved to Canada a while ago, and it's been empty since. I keep thinking I should rent it out again, but first I need to redecorate it and I never seem to find the time to get around to doing that.'

'You own that place too?' Cassie asked. 'Wow.'

Dee drank some more coffee, embarrassed at how privileged her life was compared to Cassie's.

It was another scorching hot summer's day. Not yet nine in the morning and waves of heat were already rising off the beach. The sea was calm and clear, its surface so still that it was impossible to see where the water ended and the sky began.

'Thanks for letting me stay last night,' Cassie said.

'You're welcome,' Dee said. 'Did you manage to get any sleep?'

When they'd come back here yesterday afternoon, Cassie had gone straight to bed in the spare room and Dee hadn't seen her again until this morning. It hadn't stopped Dee worrying, though. At one point during the night, she'd dreamed she'd found Cassie's body washed up on the edge of the shore. The dream had been so vivid, Dee had had to get up and check Cassie was okay.

'A little,' Cassie said. 'I kept thinking about Freya, wondering if I could have handled that situation a bit better.'

She was referring to their encounter with the angry young woman on the promenade yesterday. Afterwards, Cassie had told Dee the woman was Freya Parker, Grace's adopted sister.

'There's not much else you could have done,' Dee said, although that wasn't entirely true. If it had been her, she'd have tried to talk to Freya, find out why she was so angry and why she blamed Cassie for her sister's death. Instead, Cassie had turned and fled, seemingly terrified of what else Freya might have said.

'She was so angry,' Cassie said. 'It took me by surprise, you know? But I guess people don't always act sensibly when they're grieving. Tell me, Dee, why did you decide not to help Grace?'

'I thought she was better focusing on her future instead of dredging up the past,' Dee said.

She didn't add that she hadn't entirely trusted Cassie the first time she met her, deciding now probably wasn't the best time to say this.

'Maybe you were right.' Cassie sighed. 'I didn't mean to sound rude. It's just so hard, you know?'

'I know.'

They sat in silence for a while, drinking their coffee and watching the tide roll slowly out. After a few minutes, Dee decided it was time to tell Cassie what had happened yesterday. She lifted her fringe to show Cassie the cut on her forehead.

'This happened just before I met you yesterday. I'd driven over to your house because I'd left my phone there by accident.'

Her mind flashed back to that moment in Cassie's kitchen. The attack, that had seemed to come out of nowhere, the fear and helplessness as she lay on the ground while her unknown attacker laid into her.

'But you have your phone,' Cassie said, 'because you called me, remember?'

'I had to climb in through your bedroom window to get it,' Dee said. 'Sorry, I shouldn't have done that, but you weren't there and I needed my phone.'

Cassie frowned. 'I don't mind you climbing through my window to get your phone, but I'm not sure why you're telling me this now.'

'Because there was someone else in the house. And whoever it was, they clearly didn't want me being there.'

'I still don't understand,' Cassi said. 'How could someone have been inside my house?'

Dee told Cassie how she'd been attacked, starting with the blow to the back of her head and finishing with the sound of the car driving away from Cassie's house. When she'd finished, Cassie was visibly distressed and Dee wondered if telling her had been the wrong thing to do.

'This is about Grace, isn't it? Whoever attacked you, it wasn't a burglar. No burglar in their right mind would want to break into my house. You only have to look at it to know there's nothing worth stealing in there. Do you think it was Lloyd? I know he's a suspect. They'd split up, you know. On the news, they're saying he's her boyfriend, but they weren't together when she was killed.'

'How do you know all that?' Dee said.

'The police must have told me, I guess.'

It seemed strange to Dee that the police would reveal any information like that to Cassie. Then again, she wasn't a detective, so what did she know?

'How would Lloyd Armstrong know where you live?' Dee asked.

Cassie shrugged. 'You found me, didn't you?'

'But I'm an investigative journalist. I'm used to finding people who don't want to be found. Besides, that's not the point. Whoever it was, we need to tell the police what happened.'

Cassie shook her head. 'No. No way. I can't face speaking to them right now.'

'Why on earth not?'

'Because of the way they've treated me ever since Grace went missing.,' Cassie said. 'They think I killed her, you know. As far as they're concerned, once a killer always a killer.'

'If they really believed that,' Dee said, 'they wouldn't have let you go.'

'They let me go plenty of times after Paul was killed,' Cassie said. 'It didn't stop them arresting me, did it? I'm sorry, Dee. But I really don't want to tell them about what happened to you. I mean, it's not like you're badly hurt or anything.'

It crossed Dee's mind then that it could have been Cassie who had attacked her yesterday. She couldn't think why Cassie would do that, but it was the only reason Dee could think for her determination not to report the incident to the police.

'Listen to me,' she said, deciding to try one more time. 'I can understand you're scared, because of what happened before. But this is completely different. You were living with Paul when he was killed. The police know about the child protection order, which means they know you haven't seen Grace since she was given up for adoption. They have no reason to think you had anything to do with what happened to her.'

Abruptly, Cassie put her mug on the table and stood up. 'I need to use the loo.'

After Cassie went inside, Dee watched a woman and a young girl further along the beach. The girl was running in and out of the sea, squealing with laughter as the water splashed her legs.

Dee thought of Cassie and all the precious moments like this that she'd missed out on with her own child.

Deciding she needed more coffee, Dee stood up to go and put the kettle on. As she stepped into the living room, a draught of cool air hit her. She paused, trying to locate the source of the breeze. The front door was open.

The downstairs bathroom was empty and there was no sign of Cassie here or anywhere else in the house. Running outside, Dee looked up and down the quiet road. Nothing. Back on the beach, there were plenty of people out and about, but none of them were Cassie.

The mobile home, the only other property out here, was locked up and empty. Pushing away thoughts of happier times, Dee focused on looking for Cassie and not thinking about the hole in her life ever since her neighbours had moved away.

She walked for forty minutes, before giving up. Cassie was gone.

Twelve

Over the next few days, Dee tried several times to speak to Cassie, with no luck. Cassie wasn't picking up her phone and when Dee drove out to her house, it was empty.

Cassie's relationship to Grace Parker had been picked up by the national press. It felt to Dee that each time she opened a news website, there was another story about Cassie and the crime she'd been convicted of. She couldn't help worrying that being in the media spotlight once again had tipped Cassie over the edge. The more days passed with Cassie still missing, the more Dee's anxiety increased.

Despite her earlier reservations about Cassie's innocence, Dee had a burning need to find out as much as she could about the circumstances surrounding the death of Cassie's husband. Even if all she discovered was proof of Cassie's guilt, at least then she would know for sure she'd done all she could.

One of the first things she did was try to track down the detective who'd led the police investigation that had resulted in Cassie's conviction. His name was David Verney. At the time of the murder, he had been based in South Croydon. When Dee called Croydon police station to speak to him, she was told that David Verney had retired several years ago and the police were not at liberty to give out his contact details to members of the public.

Luckily, when she looked him up on the internet, she got a hit straight away. David Verney had his own website. He worked as a 'crime consultant' offering a range of services for crime-fiction writers. An interesting niche area, Dee thought as she looked through his website. She wondered whether this might be something Ed could turn his hand to, and made a note to suggest it to him when they met later in the week.

Dee sent David Verney an email, explaining who she was. Knowing he wouldn't want to speak to her if he realised she was trying to clear Cassie's name, she told him instead she was writing a 'where are they now?' piece, sixteen years after the murder. She also mentioned that she'd met Grace before she was killed, hoping that might pique his interest.

It was tempting to spend all her time digging deeper and deeper into the events surrounding Paul's murder, but that was a luxury Dee couldn't afford. When she'd first moved back home, Dee had struggled to find work. Gradually, however, her career had taken off again, and she had built up a solid reputation as a freelance journalist who could be trusted to write informed and balanced opinion pieces on a range of issues, from miscarriages of justice through to the plight of illegal immigrants. Following the recent success of the non-fiction book she'd written about two local murders, she had been commissioned to write another book that her publisher was expecting to see in two months' time. She was on track to finish in time, but only if she stayed focused on the book instead of allowing herself to be distracted by other things.

Alongside her writing, Dee's career had recently expanded into TV and radio. This included regular slots on a frothy early-evening TV programme called *The Big Chat*. Dee's role on the show was to give her perspective on a range of 'women's issues'. The programme was about as deep as a bag of crisps and none of the topics were covered in any real detail, but Dee thoroughly enjoyed the time she spent recording it with people half her age and twice as gorgeous.

Tomorrow, Dee was going to London to record this week's episode; the topic under discussion was going to be 'Botox: would you ever?' Although Dee knew her own view on this, she decided she should read up on the topic. After breakfast, instead of working on her book, she typed 'Botox' into her internet search engine and started reading.

Two hours later, she'd read enough to be able to talk about it without sounding either too preachy or too ignorant when she was taking part in the debate (although she realised calling it a debate was a stretch too far, and 'ten minutes barely touching the surface' was a better description of what would actually take place). To her surprise, she'd also discovered her opinion on Botox had changed from 'never' to 'why the hell not if it makes someone feel a bit better about themselves?'

Resisting the urge to immediately look up Botox treatments in Eastbourne, she went onto the deck to take a screen break and soak up some early-afternoon sunshine. This stretch of beach rarely got busy, but, today, there were more people out here than Dee was used to. Normally, she liked the peace and solitude, but watching the young children playing in the water and hearing their squeals of laughter travelling across the shingle made her happy.

She would have stayed out in the sunshine a bit longer, but her mobile phone started ringing. When she went inside to answer it, she saw Rachel Lewis's name on the screen. Anticipating bad news, Dee answered the call with shaking fingers.

'Rachel, have you found her?'

'I assume you're referring to Cassie,' Rachel said.

'Of course.' Dee rolled her eyes. 'Who else would I be talking about? I'm worried about her, Rachel. The last time I saw her, she was in a bad way.'

'You've already told me that,' Rachel said. 'The last two times you phoned. And as I've told you before too, we can't help Cassie if we don't know where she is. We've put an appeal out, asking for anyone with information about her whereabouts to get in touch.'

'So if you're not calling about Cassie, then why are you calling?'

'I've got some more questions about the attack you reported.'

Despite Cassie's misgivings about telling the police what had happened, Dee had felt obliged to tell Rachel about the attack at Cassie's house.

'Fire away,' Dee said. 'Although I'm pretty sure I've told you as much as I can about what happened.'

'You say you didn't see your attacker,' Rachel began. 'But you must have had some impression of them.'

'Not really,' Dee said. 'I never got to see their face, did I?'

'Think,' Rachel said. 'Is it more likely it was a man or a woman? A big person or a small person? Any little thing you can remember might help.'

'I think it was a woman,' Dee said slowly. 'But I've no idea why I think that.'

She closed her eyes and forced herself to remember.

'Sandals,' she said suddenly. 'When they kicked my hand, I saw their foot just for an instant. I'm pretty sure I saw a sandal.'

'Colour?'

'Blue. Pale blue, or maybe grey. But it looked like a woman's sandal, not a man's.'

'Anything else?'

'No,' Dee said, after a moment. 'Sorry, Rachel.'

'Is it possible the person who attacked you was Cassie?' Rachel asked.

'I don't think so,' Dee said. 'Whoever attacked me drove off in a car. Cassie doesn't drive. And I went to meet her on the beach immediately afterwards. How would she have got there so quickly without a car?'

'Maybe someone gave her a lift,' Rachel suggested.

'It's possible, I guess.' Dee frowned. 'Why are you suddenly asking about Cassie, Rachel?'

'I'm just exploring some ideas,' Rachel said. 'You see, I'm still trying to work out why Cassie suddenly disappeared. You said she left your house abruptly, without even telling you she was leaving. You must have a theory about why she'd do something like that.'

'We were talking about the child protection order,' she said. 'Cassie was worried you'd think she had something to do with Grace's death. I told her you knew about the child protection order, so you'd know she hadn't seen Grace since she'd been given up for adoption.'

'Ah,' Rachel said. 'Now it's starting to make sense.'

'It is?'

'Did she talk to you much about Grace?' Rachel asked, ignoring Dee's question.

'Grace was practically all Cassie talked about,' Dee said. 'She would have been eighteen soon. When that happened, there was nothing stopping Cassie from trying to contact her. She knew she'd have to go through the official channels, and there was no certainty Grace would want anything to do with her. But she was clinging onto the hope of seeing her child again. For Grace to die – and in such horrible circumstances – so close to her eighteenth birthday is just terrible.'

But even as Dee said this, she heard Louise's voice repeating what she'd said the last time they spoke. *'I keep thinking, if it was me, if I was living in the same town as my child, no child protection order in the world would stop me from trying to see her.'*

'You're right about the child protection order,' Rachel said. 'Grace's parents didn't want Cassie having any contact with her daughter, either while she was in prison or when she came out. Did Cassie ever talk about breaching the protection order?'

'No.'

'Then I'm afraid she's been lying to you,' Rachel said. 'You see, it turns out Cassie and Grace had been meeting in secret for the last six months.'

'Shit.'

'There's something else,' Rachel continued. 'The night she disappeared, Grace was on her way to meet Cassie. According to Cassie, Grace never turned up for their meeting. But we only have Cassie's word for that. What we do know is that Friday night is the last time Grace was seen alive.'

Thirteen

Two days later, Dee got a reply from David Verney, the detective who'd led the investigation into Paul Cavellini's murder.

> Dear Dee,
>
> Thanks for your email and apologies for not getting back to you before now. Having seen the news over the last few days, the timing of your email has intrigued me. Happy to chat. Feel free to drop me an email or give me a call.
>
> David

Beneath his name was a mobile phone number he could be contacted on. Dee made a pot of coffee, carried it out to the deck and called him back.

'David Verney.'

'Mr Verney? This is Dee Doran. I got your email this morning. Thanks so much for getting back to me.'

'I wasn't going to,' he said. 'You wouldn't believe the number of journalists who've contacted me over the years wanting to speak to me about that case. I've turned them all down.'

'Why make an exception for me?' Dee asked.

'I'm writing my memoir,' David said. 'I covered a lot of interesting cases in my time, but the Cavellini murder was the biggest one I ever worked on. It's a key part of the book. You told me in your email that you met Grace. I'd like to know more about that. If you knew her, you must have your own theory about who killed her and why.'

'I'd be happy to tell you what I think if we could meet up,' Dee said, knowing she had to tread carefully. If he was writing a book about the murder, it might be harder than she'd first realised to get him to open up to her. Anything he might know, he'd be saving for his book and would be unlikely to offer it up to Dee. Unless she could find something to offer him in return.

'I've seen the photos of her on the news,' David said. 'She's the spitting image of Cassie, you know. So, you think Cassie killed her own kid or did someone else do it?'

Dee scowled at her phone. She suspected meeting David Verney was going to be a chore, not a pleasure.

'When Grace first went missing, Joey gave a statement begging her to come home,' David continued, oblivious to Dee's displeasure. 'So I knew she was his niece, although I had no idea then that she was Paul's kid. I should have worked it out earlier. Feel a bit foolish for missing it, if I'm honest. It all came flooding back to me, of course. Poor Joey and Trish had already lost both their parents. It was very hard on them to lose their brother as well.

'Joey and I stayed in touch over the years. He's a great guy, as down to earth now as he was back then. Hasn't changed a bit, despite all his fame. Amazing to see how well he's done for himself. He built his business from scratch, you know. Now, everyone has heard of Cavellini Constructions, the UK's leading house builder.

'I've always thought his success was down to his commitment to family. Paul and Trish both worked with him in the early days. In fact, Paul was still working for Joey when he was killed.'

This was news to Dee, and she filed the information away to think about it later.

'I wasn't at all surprised when Channel 4 made their move,' David continued. 'Reality TV shows about business and making money are a big deal these days. I can't think of anyone better than Joey to host a show like that.'

Dee had actually met Joey Cavellini at a TV awards ceremony earlier this year. She had been invited as a guest of the two young people who hosted *The Big Chat*. She'd gone along for a laugh and, at one point in the evening, someone had introduced her to the entire cast of *Make Me a Millionaire*, the reality TV show that had made Joey Cavellini a household name. He hadn't made any sort of memorable impression on her, so she would have to take David's word that he was 'a great guy'.

'He never told you his sister had adopted Grace?' she asked.

'Not a word. But why would he? Joey's always put family before anything else. Him and Trish are very close. It's understandable they didn't want anyone knowing the kid Trish adopted had a killer for a mother.'

'Do you think we can meet up?' Dee said, keen to move the conversation along. 'I'd love to pick your brains about the initial investigation.'

'Okay. You're in Eastbourne, I think?'

'That's right.'

Interesting, she thought. He had obviously done his research before deciding to contact her.

'I'm in Bexhill, just down the road from you. How about Wednesday morning?'

Dee hesitated. Wednesday was four days away. She would prefer to meet him before then. On the other hand, it gave her time to do some research and come up with information she could share with him in exchange for something back.

'Wednesday's perfect,' she said.

He gave her the name of a coffee shop in Bexhill and they arranged to meet there at eleven o'clock on Wednesday.

After hanging up, Dee opened her laptop to work on her book. It had started out as a non-fiction account of the Irish diaspora in the UK, looking at how Irish immigrants' experiences had changed over the years. Somewhere along the way, however, it had become a much more personal account of her father's life. Last year, Dee had been reunited with one of her

Irish cousins. Ever since then, the tug of her Irish roots was becoming stronger. While her father had been alive, she had rarely spoken to him about how he'd felt having to leave Ireland at the age of just sixteen and start a new life in a new country. Now he was dead, her need to understand his life had become important.

In preparation for writing the book, she had travelled around the country speaking to Irish people living in England – asking them what they missed about 'home' and exploring the differences between Irish and English cultures. With Ed, she had also travelled to Ireland, where she'd spoken to as many people as she could find who had known her father.

Once she had gathered all of this information, she had set about turning it into a story that people would want to read. Normally, the act of writing about her father consumed her. This morning, she found it difficult to concentrate. She kept thinking of Cassie, wondering where she was and whether it was possible she could have had something to do with Grace's death.

Eventually, Dee shut her laptop and stood up. She needed someone she could speak to, get another person's opinions on the different thoughts swirling around inside her head. Usually, that person would be Ed. But he was playing golf today, followed by lunch with an ex-colleague. He wasn't due to see Dee until this evening, and she couldn't wait that long.

She got her phone and called Louise.

'I don't suppose you're free for a coffee and a chat?' Dee said. 'I know it's Saturday, and you're probably crazy busy with the kids, but I could really do with a chat if you've got any free time?'

'Martin's here today,' Louise said. 'So I've actually got a bit of time to myself, for a change. In fact, he's taking the kids to the beach in a bit. Why don't you come over around half two?'

'Perfect. Thanks, Lou. I'll see you then.'

Dee hung up and checked the time. It was approaching midday. Which meant she could squeeze in a swim in the sea before driving across to Louise's house. Avoiding the accusing sight of her closed laptop, Dee went to get changed into her swimsuit.

Fourteen

'Freya!'

Her heart sank, as she recognised the voice. Turning around, she saw Patrick Keenan walking towards her, with a goofy smile on his face.

'I can't stop,' Freya said. 'I'm on my way to meet someone and I'm running late.'

'No problem,' Patrick said. 'I just wanted to say hi. Did you get my message?'

She nodded.

He'd sent her a long message on Instagram, saying how sorry he was about Grace and to let him know if she ever needed someone to talk to. She hadn't replied to the message, because it had annoyed her. It made it seem like they were still friends, when actually they hadn't really been friends for ages. There was a time when they'd been close. Never boyfriend-girlfriend close, but they'd hung out together and enjoyed each other's company. He'd made her laugh and she'd thought he was sweet. That was before Freya met Lloyd Armstrong and realised boys like Patrick were immature and a bit pointless.

'Which way are you going?' he asked. 'I can walk with you, if you'd like?'

They were on the seafront. Saturday afternoon in summer, and the place was heaving. Families and dog walkers and the air thick with the voices of overexcited children. Heat making the air shimmer and her skin prickly with sweat.

'I remember what it was like after my dad died,' he said, when Freya didn't reply. 'The grief, how it hits you. It's like this big wave that's so strong you think you might drown under the weight of it.'

Freya's mouth opened, then closed again, without any words coming out. He had described so perfectly how she was feeling.

'Sorry.' He held up his hands. 'If you don't want to chat, that's fine. We can just walk for a bit and not say anything if you'd prefer.'

'I'd prefer it if you left me alone, actually.'

She turned around and walked away quickly, but not before she caught the expression on his face. Surprise mingled with something she wished she hadn't seen: pity.

She walked as fast as she could without running, hoping he had the sense not to follow her. The encounter had left her feeling shaken and uncertain. She hated the thought of anyone pitying her, especially a loser like Patrick Keenan.

As the pier came into sight, Freya's heart started beating faster and her stomach did that flip-floppy thing it did when she got nervous. She tried telling herself it would be all right, that she'd done the right thing getting in touch. Even if Lloyd hadn't seemed particularly pleased to hear from her when she finally found the courage to call him yesterday.

Meeting at the pier had been his idea. Freya had suggested they go for a drink somewhere, but he'd said no to that. She hadn't objected at the time, but now she wished they were meeting somewhere else. Because the pier reminded her of Grace.

There'd been a time, when they were much younger and before the fire destroyed much of the original pier, when they'd come here all the time. Grace, especially, used to love the slot machines that pinged and trilled and swallowed up all the coins the sisters saved up just for this moment.

As they'd got older, they'd stopped coming here so much. After the fire, the slot machines were gone and Grace and Freya found other things to entertain themselves during the hot summer months that seemed to stretch out endlessly all through their teenage years. Until this summer, when now all that stretched out in front of Freya was a vast, empty nothingness.

She had arranged to meet Lloyd at the end of the pier at two thirty. But when she arrived, five minutes late, there was no sign of him. Most visitors to the pier didn't come this far, and today Freya was the only person here. She leaned over the railing, looking down at the waves that lapped against the sides of the pier.

It would be so easy, she thought, to tip herself over and disappear into the sea. She imagined herself sinking down into the black emptiness of the ocean, and she thought how much she would welcome the oblivion that followed.

Freya leaned forward a little more, her ponytail swinging against her face. She had a sudden image of Grace, so vivid it was almost like she was here in front of her. She let herself believe, for a moment, that Grace was alive and dancing across the turquoise ocean, a bottle of Prosecco in one hand and a cigarette dangling from the other. Except it wasn't real, because Grace was dead and Freya would never see her dance again.

She closed her eyes and took a deep breath. And suddenly, she wasn't leaning over the railings. She was being yanked back. A hand on her shoulder, arms wrapping around her body and holding her too tight.

'Freya. Jesus Christ. What the hell were you thinking?'

Lloyd, she realised, her face flushing with embarrassment. Surely he hadn't really thought she was going to jump?

'I was just looking at the sea,' she said.

He let her go and took a step back, as if he was keen to put some distance between them.

'Sorry,' he said. 'Maybe I overreacted. I'm a mess at the moment. Jumping at the slightest sound, feeling like everyone's looking at me any time I leave the apartment.'

'Is there anything I can do?' Freya asked.

He looked exhausted, and she felt a pang of guilt, knowing this was partly her fault. Ever since Grace had disappeared, the police had acted as if Lloyd had had something to do with it.

'There's nothing anyone can do,' he replied. 'So, what did you want to talk to me about?'

'Have you spoken to the police recently?'

'Feels like all I do these days is speak to them. They've interrogated me, taken all my stuff – phone, laptop, computer, the lot. They searched my apartment too, looking for her necklace and cardigan.'

The night she disappeared, Grace had been wearing a white cardigan and the silver olive-leaf pendant that Lloyd had bought her. Neither the cardigan nor necklace had been with Grace when her body had been found. There was a photo in circulation, taken of Grace that night before she walked out of the Dew Drop Inn in town and was never seen again.

'I've had to buy a new phone,' Lloyd said, 'because they can't tell me when I'll get mine back.'

'Hey.' He reached out and touched her arm. 'I shouldn't be moaning to you about the police. I'm sorry.'

A shock of electricity tingled through her, and she pulled her arm away, angry at herself for reacting like this. Angry at him for the power he didn't even know he had over her.

'There's something you should know,' she said, deciding it was best to get it over and done with. 'In the months before she died, Grace had been meeting up with her birth mother.'

'She what?'

'They found each other by accident,' Freya said. 'Cassie's been living in Eastbourne ever since she got out of prison. They were in the same coffee shop one afternoon, and Grace recognised her from the news stories she'd read about her father's murder.'

'How long ago was that?'

'Six months, I think.'

Lloyd shook his head. 'She was meeting her mother for six months and she never told me about it? Well, that just says it all really. I knew she'd been up to something behind my back. I thought it was another bloke, but it wasn't that. Jesus, Freya. How do you think it makes me feel finding out that she couldn't talk to me about any of this?'

'I'm sorry.'

'Not your fault,' he said.

'I thought the police might have mentioned it to you.'

'No.' Lloyd frowned. 'They asked me about Cassie, but I told them I didn't know anything about her. Hang on a sec, you're telling me that all this time they've known Cassie was seeing her daughter in secret but they never once mentioned it to me?'

'Well, they didn't always know. She'd begged me not to tell anyone. You see, Cassie was breaking the conditions of the child protection order by meeting up with Grace. After Grace disappeared, I didn't see the point of telling the police. I thought Grace would turn up and, when she did, she'd be glad I hadn't told anyone. I didn't want to get Cassie into trouble.' She sighed. 'I realise now I was wrong. My mum and my uncle have told me that enough times. But, at the time, I thought I was doing what Grace wanted.'

'So what changed?'

'I saw Cassie. A few days after they found Grace's body. Something inside me flipped. It felt wrong that she was alive and well and walking along the seafront as if she didn't have a care in the world, while Grace would never have the chance to do that again. And it struck me that it could have been Cassie who killed her. I mean, she's already killed once before. Grace was obsessed about trying to prove Cassie didn't kill her father. But what if she was wrong about that? What if she found something that proved the opposite – that Cassie was guilty? Grace was on her way to see Cassie the night she disappeared. I think she confronted her about her father, they had a row and Cassie killed her.'

She stopped talking, painfully aware she'd said more than she should have.

'Fucking hell,' Lloyd hissed. 'All that time when you had important information that could have taken some of the heat off me, and you kept it to yourself? I thought we were friends, Freya. But you're as bad as she was, aren't you? First Grace lied to me, and now you too.'

'I'm sorry,' she said, but it was too late.

Lloyd had already turned and started walking away from her. When she ran after him and put her arm out to pull him back, he pushed her away from him so hard she stumbled and almost fell.

'Lloyd,' she called, but he didn't turn around or acknowledge he'd heard her.

As she watched him leave, she tried to remember why she'd felt it had been so important to keep Grace's secret, what part of her had chosen to protect Cassie over Lloyd. But all she could think was how badly she had messed up, and how she wouldn't blame Lloyd if he never wanted to see her again.

Fifteen

Louise lived in Meads, an affluent part of Eastbourne nestled between the sea and the start of the South Downs National Park. Her house was on a leafy street lined on either side with detached period properties.

'Ignore the mess,' Louise said, leading Dee through the pristinely tidy house to the back garden. 'Tell me, how was London? The kids are very excited about seeing you on TV.'

She was referring to Dee's appearance later this evening on *The Big Chat*. Dee had travelled up to London yesterday to record the show. The news that Dee was going to be a regular guest on the show had caused hysterical levels of excitement in Louise's household. With the exception of her husband. A fact that went entirely in his favour, as far as Dee was concerned. Over the years, her feelings towards Martin had migrated from a vague dislike to something approaching fondness. He might be a boring old git, but he was a boring old git with a heart of gold who adored his wife and kids and worked hard to make sure they wanted for nothing.

'I'm not sure the content is suitable for Ben and Daisy,' Dee said, referring to Louise's children. 'We're talking about Botox.'

'What's wrong with that?' Louise frowned and Dee noticed, for the first time, how remarkably unlined her forehead was when she did this.

'You've done it?'

'Duh.' Louise waved a hand in the air dismissively. 'And before you ask, I told Daisy what I'd done and why.'

'I'd like to know the answer to that one too,' Dee said.

'Because it makes me feel better.' Louise scowled. 'Is that a problem?'

'Of course not.'

In fact, during the recording, Dee had argued quite passionately in favour of women having Botox if it made them feel better. She'd said she really couldn't see the harm in it. So why, now, did she feel so unaccountably irritated by her cousin's smooth, unlined forehead? Because, Dee concluded silently, she was a hypocrite.

'We're having wine?' Dee asked, noticing the wine bottle in a cooler on the table outside beside a pair of Waterford Crystal wine glasses.

Dee recognised the glasses. They had been a wedding present when Louise and Martin got married, which must have been at least fifteen years earlier. Dee wondered how on earth Louise had managed to keep the glasses for this long without breaking them.

'It's the weekend and the sun is shining and we hardly see each other these days,' Louise said. 'I thought we should celebrate getting to spend some time together. Plus, we're getting a takeaway this evening, which means I don't have to worry about cooking dinner. I've got a few hours to myself for once, and I can't think of a better way to enjoy them than sitting in the sunshine with you.'

'Sounds good to me.' Dee smiled and sat down on one of Louise's exceptionally comfortable garden chairs.

'So,' Louise said, after she'd poured wine for them both. 'Any specific reason for this surprise visit?'

'Cassie MacNamara,' Dee said. 'I can't stop thinking about her. One minute, I'm worrying how she's doing and wishing I'd done more to help her. The next minute, I'm wondering if she killed her daughter.'

'Wind back for me,' Louise said. 'I know Cassie's gone into hiding, but is there anything specific that makes you think she could have done something like that?'

Louise listened carefully as Dee told her how Cassie had, apparently, broken the conditions of the child protection order by meeting Grace in secret.

'Well,' she said, when Dee had finished, 'you can hardly blame her. It must have been awful not being able to see her daughter. I can't say I'd have done anything different if I was her. Although, bad as Martin can be sometimes, I can't imagine ever wanting to kill him.'

Louise took a sip of her wine and frowned.

'Sorry, that sounded awful. You say Grace was on her way to see Cassie when she disappeared? How do the police know this?'

'I'm not sure,' Dee said. 'Grace had a boyfriend, didn't she? Lloyd Armstrong. Maybe he told them.'

'Maybe.' Louise didn't sound convinced. 'I know him, you know. And Grace. She worked at Albertine's, the wine bar in Meads that Lloyd owns. I go there sometimes with my yoga group. Although I doubt we'll continue going there now. You know a lot of people think Lloyd killed her?'

'And what do you think?' Dee asked.

'I don't know. I mean, I've always found him a bit of a fraud. He lays on the charm, but you can see it's all an act. There was something slightly off about him and Grace.'

'Off how?'

'Well, he's quite a bit older than her for starters. And he was always watching her. One time, I was there for lunch and Grace was serving a beer to some guy about the same age as Lloyd. He was by himself and she hung around his table for a bit, chatting to him. The moment Lloyd saw her, he called her away. He seemed really angry, although I couldn't work out why. It was only later, when I thought back on it, that I realised he was jealous because she'd been speaking to another bloke.'

'You can't know that for sure,' Dee said.

'Maybe not, but I know what I saw. You know she was only seventeen? Lloyd is twenty-eight. Eleven years older than her, and he was her boss as well. That's not a good situation for any young woman to find herself in.'

'He's certainly the most likely suspect,' Dee said. 'I read somewhere recently that two women a week are killed by their partners or ex-partners in England and Wales.'

'Surely if Lloyd killed her he'd have been arrested by now?'

'Not if the police haven't found any evidence yet,' Dee replied. 'What have you heard about that, Lou?'

Apart from the police, Louise was likely to know more details about Grace Parker's murder than anyone else. As editor of the local paper, she had connections everywhere and would have shamelessly used those connections to discover as much information as she could.

Dee drank some more wine, letting the alcohol and warm sunshine work their magic while Louise updated her on everything she'd learned about Grace Parker's murder.

'She was dead before she fell,' Louise said. 'The injuries to her body are consistent with her being run over by a car. The driver obviously thought they could make it look like suicide by throwing her off Beachy Head. Stupid really, given what we know about forensics these days. Alongside her injuries, flecks of paint have been found on her clothes.'

'Paint from the car?'

Louise nodded. 'A silver Nissan Juke.'

'How on earth do you know all this?' Dee asked, genuinely in awe of Louise's ability to extract this much information from a supposedly confidential murder investigation.

'A good journalist never reveals her sources,' Louise said primly. 'You know that.'

'How did the killer get her body to Beachy Head?' Dee wondered.

'I assume whoever hit her bundled her into their car and drove her there,' Louise said.

'So we're looking for someone strong,' Dee said.

'Or two people,' Louise suggested.

Dee frowned, not liking the idea there was more than one person out there who'd been involved in ending a young woman's life. Somehow, this made the horror of Grace's death seem even worse.

'At least the police know what car they're looking for,' Dee said.

Grace's killer clearly didn't realise that paint was powerful forensic evidence. A few years earlier, another young woman had been run over outside Dee's house. From the tiny pieces of paint found on the victim, the police were able to identify the make and model of the car that had killed her. Just as they'd done now, if Louise's information was correct.

'Cassie can't drive,' Dee said, 'and she doesn't have a car. Which must surely rule her out as a suspect?'

'How do you know she can't drive?'

'She told me.' Dee realised as she said this that she had no way of knowing if it was actually true or not.

'You know what I want to know,' Louise said. 'How has Grace's death suddenly become your problem?'

'What do you mean?'

'I mean, you called me because you needed someone to talk to. Because you're worrying about Cassie and you're trying to work out who killed Grace and why. But none of this is any of your business, Dee. You're already busy enough with your book and the TV show. Why this too?'

'I couldn't help Grace when she was alive. Now she's dead, I feel like I owe it to her to do what she wanted.'

'I think that's bullshit,' Louise said. 'This is about you, not Grace or Cassie.'

'What's that supposed to mean?' Dee asked.

'You've struggled since Ella and Jake left. I wonder if maybe you're unconsciously hoping Cassie could be some sort of replacement for Ella. Because I really can't see any other reason why you're so obsessed with all of this.'

Until last year, Ella and her young son Jake had rented the mobile home next to Dee's house. Jake had been born soon after Ella had moved in, which meant Dee had known him his entire life. Not having children of her own, she had doted on the little boy, loving him as much as she'd ever loved anyone. Then, last autumn, Ella's other half, Tom, got offered a job in Canada that was too good an opportunity to turn down. Their absence had left a hole in Dee's life that she hadn't yet managed to fill.

'That's not why I'm doing this,' she said, unsure which one of them she was trying harder to convince.

'Then why?' Louise asked.

Luckily for Dee, in that moment Louise's two children burst into the garden, followed by their dad. As the children ran to Dee to hug her and tell them all their news since she'd last seen them, Dee was able to put Cassie and Grace and Ella and Jake out of her mind for a few precious moments.

Sixteen

Sun-drenched drops of water sprayed up around her as Dee rose out of the clear blue sea. It was late on Sunday afternoon. She'd spent most of the day working, alternating between her book and Google, before coming out here to clear her mind.

When she was swimming, there was nothing else except this: water and sky and wide open space. Slices of sunlight cut through the surface of the water, flashes of white shot across the clear blue sky from the seagulls swooping down to scavenge whatever tasty titbits caught their ever-watchful beady eyes.

She swam until her legs ached and the tension across her shoulders and chest had melted away. Lying on her back, Dee followed the criss-cross streaks of chemtrails from the planes that flew in and out of Gatwick airport. She remembered Ed's camper van announcement, and tried to picture the two of them travelling across Europe together. She could see the appeal of the open road, but her mind kept snagging on the details – the lack of space and privacy, the basic cooking facilities, having to share a chemical toilet for large chunks of time. The more she thought about it, the more she convinced herself it was a stupid idea. They were both too old to go haring around Europe like a pair of lovestruck teenagers.

She came out of the water and located the towel she had left on the shingle. Wrapping this around herself, she walked back up the beach. As always, her attention was drawn to the empty mobile home. The familiar feelings of loss sitting like a heavy stone in the pit of her stomach as she thought about the family no longer living there.

Dee was almost at the house when she noticed the silhouette of a tall man walking towards her. For a split second, she thought he was her old friend Trevor Dubber. Except Trevor was dead, killed in a fire while rescuing a young boy. And when she saw him properly, she realised this man didn't resemble Trevor as much as she'd first thought. He was taller, his face narrower and not quite as symmetrically perfect. She knew who he was, though. Joey Cavellini, Grace's uncle and the brother of Cassie's dead husband. Instinctively, Dee drew the towel tighter around her body, feeling exposed and vulnerable in the knowledge that they were alone out here.

'Dee?' He gave her the benefit of a full-wattage smile that revealed a set of teeth so white she felt she should shield her eyes from their brightness. 'I'm not sure if you remember me. We met earlier this year at the Broadcast Awards.'

'I remember,' she said, although their encounter had been so brief she was surprised he did. She must have been one of many not very famous people he'd met that night.

'Nice place you've got,' he said. 'I have a seafront apartment on the other side of town. I thought my views were good, but this is spectacular. I own a place in London too, but I spend quite a bit of my free time in Eastbourne because it's where my sister lives. She moved here after her husband walked out on her, when the girls were still young. She thought it would be a good place to bring up kids. Ironic, isn't it?'

A breeze was blowing in across the beach, causing goose-bumps to rise along Dee's overexposed skin. She knew if she didn't have a hot shower she would start shivering.

'I need to go inside,' she said. 'You're welcome to wait on the deck while I get changed. After that, you can tell me why you're here.'

As she walked past him towards the house, she thought he could also tell her how the hell he'd found out where she lived. In her line of work, Dee sometimes made enemies. Not everyone liked an investigative journalist digging up past secrets.

Because of this, she'd always made sure only a handful of people knew where she lived.

When she went inside to shower, she locked the back door so he couldn't come inside. She didn't think Joey Cavellini was here to hurt her, but he'd turned up at her house out of the blue and she wasn't taking any chances.

Twenty minutes later, she came back outside to find him slumped in a chair, his face in his hands.

'I've made some coffee,' Dee said, touching his shoulder.

He glanced up and she saw how exhausted he looked.

'Thank you.' He took the mug she held out for him, wrapping his hands around it.

'I'm so sorry about Grace,' she said, sitting down opposite him.

'I can't believe she's gone,' he said. 'None of us can. I don't know how much you know about my family, Dee, but we've already been through so much. Our parents died in a car crash when we were still in our teens. I'm the oldest, so I was responsible for looking after Trish and Paul after we lost Mum and Dad. Then, just as it felt like we were getting back on track, Paul was killed. That changed everything, of course, but we did our best to move on. Trish and Conor adopted little Grace. But then their marriage broke up and Trish was left to bring the kids up by herself. The girls were only three when their dad left. Trish has done her best, but it hasn't been easy. And now this. Trish will never get past losing Grace. None of us will.'

'I really am sorry,' Dee said. 'But I'm not sure why you're here. Is there something you think I can do to help?'

'We need to find Cassie,' he said.

Dee had met this man only once before. They'd spoken for less than five minutes. He had no way of knowing she had ever met Cassie or had promised to look into Paul's murder. 'Why on earth do you think I'd know where she is?'

'I got a phone call earlier,' Joey said. 'A friend of mine, an ex-detective. He called to see how I was doing and if there was anything he could do to help. When I told him we were desperate to find Cassie, he suggested I speak to you.'

'David Verney,' Dee said, remembering the detective had told her he was still in touch with Joey Cavellini. 'What exactly did he tell you about me?'

'He said you'd reached out to him recently, because you were writing a story about Paul's murder. And that you'd met Cassie and Grace.'

'What else did he tell you?' she asked.

'Not much,' Joey said. 'He told me where you lived, of course. I wouldn't be here otherwise. You don't mind, do you?'

Dee did mind. A lot. When she'd spoken to David, he hadn't tried to hide the fact he already knew she lived in Eastbourne. Clearly, however, his research had been more thorough than she'd realised.

'I don't like people giving out my address without checking with me first,' she said.

'Sorry.' Joey held his hands up. 'I wouldn't have come if I'd known it would upset you.'

'It's okay.' Dee waved away his apology. He wasn't the one who'd done something wrong. 'Listen, Joey. If I knew where Cassie was, I'd tell the police. I'm afraid I have no idea where she's gone.'

'I shouldn't have come,' he said. 'I can see that now. I'm not behaving rationally at the moment, that's the problem. Cassie almost ruined my family once before, and now it feels as if she's doing the same thing again.'

'Grace was her daughter,' Dee said. 'You don't really think she could have killed her own child?'

'I think she's capable of anything,' Joey said. 'You may not know this, Dee, but there was a protection order that prevented Cassie from trying to contact Grace. We've only just found out she breached that order. They were meeting in secret for the last few months. Trish suspected something was wrong. Grace had become moody and withdrawn. Now we know why. That woman had turned her against us.'

'How do you know that's what she was doing?' Dee asked.

'Trish and Conor got that child protection order because we knew Cassie couldn't be trusted to keep away when she came out of prison. They needed to keep Grace safe. We all did. She was our last link to Paul – or so we thought. Turns out Cassie fooled us there, too.'

'What do you mean?' Dee's stomach tightened.

'Paul was a great father,' Joey said. 'He doted on Grace and would have done anything for his little girl. When he first got together with Cassie, we were happy for Paul. He'd always held a torch for Cassie, so it was good to see he'd finally got what he wanted. We naturally assumed Cassie felt the same way. It was only years later we discovered how much Cassie had deceived all of us.' He paused. 'When she was ten, Grace had appendicitis. Before the operation, the doctors needed to check her blood type. Her parents assumed it would be A-positive because that's what Trish and Paul both were. Turned out Grace's blood type was O-negative. I don't know how much you know about blood types, but an A-positive parent can't have a child with O-negative blood.'

'I didn't think the science was as exact as that,' Dee said, scrabbling through the bits of genetics she'd picked up during her career.

'It's not,' Joey replied, 'which is why, a few months later, I persuaded Trish to get a DNA test done. The results showed, beyond any doubt, that Trish and Grace were not related by blood. Paul wasn't Grace's biological father.'

Seventeen

The following evening, Dee had arranged to meet Ed for a drink at Levels wine bar, situated at the back of the Grand Hotel. She had considered going to Albertine's, the wine bar where Grace had worked, but a quick internet check told her it was currently closed.

The sun was setting as Dee walked into town. The sea and beach were bathed in the pink glow of the sun setting beneath the ridge of the South Downs. The seafront grew busier the closer Dee got to the town centre, tourists and locals taking advantage of the four-mile-long stretch of beach.

Year on year, Eastbourne's reputation was changing. Previously, the town had been best known as a place where people moved to after they retired. God's waiting room. These days, it was better known as a beautiful seaside resort perfect for families who didn't want to jump on a plane but still wanted a slice of seaside living for their holidays. In the aftermath of a global pandemic, it seemed to be more crowded this summer than ever before.

Passing a couple with a toddler, Dee's thoughts inevitably turned to Jake and Ella. When they'd first moved to Canada, they had kept in touch regularly. There had been Zoom calls with the family, and email updates from Ella. Recently, however, the Zoom calls had become less frequent and Dee couldn't shake off the fear that soon they would stop altogether. Jake was getting older. Over time, he would forget that he'd ever lived in a little house on the beach in Eastbourne next door to a woman who had loved him fiercely and completely.

Ella had invited Dee to come and visit them, but they'd never got as far as turning the suggestion into an actual plan and Dee doubted they ever would. Ella and Jake had moved on, were building a new life for themselves in Canada. The last thing they wanted was Dee guilt-tripping them with her neediness.

Surprisingly, when she arrived at the wine bar, there was no sign of Ed. Surprising because she was fifteen minutes late and Ed was a stickler for punctuality. Pleased with herself, Dee ordered a glass of Sussex Blend and carried it to one of the tables outside on the street.

While she waited, she took her phone out and scrolled through the latest news stories on Grace's murder. Nothing new since the last time she'd looked, but there was plenty of speculation about whether Cassie might have killed her own child. It was one week since the police had issued their statement confirming Grace had been murdered. It seemed to Dee that the investigation had hardly moved forward since then.

Frustrated, Dee put her phone down and took a sip of wine as she scanned the street for Ed. She felt a twinge of unease, wondering where he could be. She thought about phoning him, then decided against it. If it was the other way around and she was running late, nothing would annoy her more than Ed phoning to check up on her. Far better to chill out and let him get here when he was ready. Besides, the longer he took, the more time she had to think about Cassie.

Dee had called her after Joey's visit yesterday. Cassie's phone had rung out, but she didn't answer, so Dee had left a message asking her to please call. So far, Cassie hadn't done that. It had occurred to Dee, after Joey left, that he might have been lying about Grace's father. But without asking Cassie directly, Dee had no way of knowing for sure.

She needed to speak to someone, other than Joey Cavellini, who knew Cassie. But apart from knowing where Cassie lived, and that she worked as a hairdresser, Dee knew very little about her. Then she remembered there was someone she could talk to. If she could find her. Cassie's boss.

The last time they'd met, the woman had made it clear she didn't approve of Dee. But now Cassie was missing, she might be a bit more forthcoming. Especially if Dee could convince her she really did have Cassie's own best interests at heart.

The problem was, in a town like Eastbourne with more hair salons than any woman could ever need, finding the right one wasn't going to be an easy task. Especially when Dee couldn't, for the life of her, remember the name of Cassie's boss.

Think, she told herself, going back over her encounter with the woman. Cassie had mentioned her name at one point, Dee was sure of that. Jane, Gillian, something with a 'J' sound at the beginning. The name was there, at the edge of her periphery. Dee closed her eyes, pictured herself back in Cassie's kitchen.

Jennifer! That was it.

Dee was part of a Facebook group for local women in business. Opening the Facebook app on her phone, she went to the group page. The group had over five thousand members. Undaunted, she started scrolling through the list of members. She found several women called Jennifer, but they all listed their occupations as something other than hairdresser. Dee would have to find Cassie's boss some other way.

She had joined this group shortly after moving back to Eastbourne. Louise had convinced her that networking was essential if Dee wanted to pick up freelance writing work. As it turned out, Dee had managed just fine without having to do any tedious networking. As a result, she rarely visited this group. Reading through some of the comments now, she saw a lot of the posts were from people asking for recommendations.

That gave her an idea. She created a new post and started typing:

> In need of a haircut and looking for recommendations. I'm sure I remember someone here mentioning a hairdresser called Jennifer. Any ideas?

By the time she'd finished her glass of wine, Dee's phone was already pinging with notifications. In no time at all, she had the name she needed – Jennifer Trevorrow, owner of Strands hairdressers in Polegate. The salon had its own Facebook page, which was perfect for what Dee needed.

A quick Google search gave her the salon's contact details, but when she dialled the number, she got a recording telling her the salon was closed and would reopen again on Tuesday morning.

Dee hung up and, when she checked the time, she realised with a jolt that Ed was now forty minutes late. The unease she'd felt earlier shifted and grew into something bigger and darker: fear. Because Dee knew Ed Mitchell and she knew he would never leave her sitting here alone without calling or texting to tell her why he was so late. Which meant there was only one possible explanation for why he hadn't turned up: something bad had happened.

Eighteen

Before

Cassie rang the doorbell, and waited. When Lizzie didn't appear, she rang it again. This time, keeping her finger pressed down so the bell carried on ringing. Even so, she had to wait another minute before the front door was finally flung open.

'I've already told you,' Lizzie said, 'I never want to see you again.'

'Please,' Cassie said. 'I'm so sorry for what happened, Lizzie. I was drunk and it was a mistake and I swear to you I've never regretted anything so much in my entire life.'

'I don't care how drunk you were, or how much you regret it,' Lizzie said. 'You know how I felt about him, but that didn't stop you having sex with him. I thought we were friends, but friends don't do that to each other.'

Cassie wanted to tell Lizzie that she deserved so much better than someone like that, but she didn't think Lizzie would appreciate the advice. Not after what Cassie had done.

'And now you're married with a kid and you've got everything you ever wanted,' Lizzie continued. 'And if you think turning up on my doorstep with Grace is going to soften me up, you're wrong. Yes, I love babies and I wish to hell I could pick her up because she is so goddamn cute, but even she's not enough to fix this.'

'Would it help if I told you marriage isn't all it's cracked up to be?'

'Is that why you're here?' Lizzie asked. 'Because you've had a row with Paul and you want a shoulder to cry on?'

'No. I'm here because I miss you, Liz. I miss hanging out with you and having a laugh. No one makes me laugh the way you do. I know it's completely my fault you're not in my life anymore, but tell me what I can do to fix it and I'll do it.'

'Cassie...' Lizzie paused and shook her head. 'What's the point? You already had your chance and you blew it.'

'What are you talking about?'

'Grace's present?'

Cassie cast her mind back over the months since Grace was born. Most of it was a blur of sleepless nights and long, lonely days. All of it punctuated with the gradual awareness that marrying Paul had been a monumental mistake.

'I have no idea what you're talking about.'

Cassie saw immediately it was the wrong thing to say. Lizzie's face hardened as she pointed at Grace, asleep in the buggy beside Cassie.

'Her blanket.'

Cassie looked down at the pink blanket, confused. The blanket had been a present from one of Paul's work colleagues. She remembered him handing the parcel to her, telling her they'd dropped it around while Cassie had been sleeping. She remembered this because the parcel didn't have a card with it. When she'd asked Paul who to send the thank you card to, he'd told her not to bother.

'I know things can be difficult after you have a baby,' Lizzie said. 'But I thought, after everything that had happened between us, you'd at least send me a text or something. Any acknowledgement would have been fine, but instead I got nothing. Not a single word. And you know what, Cassie? I don't even know why I bothered. I was still so angry with you. I *am* so angry with you, but you'd had a baby and that felt huge. Even though I hated you, I wanted to give you something for Grace. Don't ask me why, because I really have no idea.'

'There was no card with it,' Cassie said. 'So I didn't know who had given it to us. If I'd known it was you, God, Lizzie,

I would have called you right away. It would have meant so much, you've no idea.'

'I guess I don't,' Lizzie said. 'Anyway, it hardly matters now. Neither of us can undo the past. It's probably best for both of us if we get on with our lives and don't see each other anymore. You've got different priorities now. A husband and a baby. The perfect family you've always dreamed of. So, off you go and get on with your perfect life and leave me to work out what to do with mine.'

It's not perfect, Cassie wanted to scream, but Lizzie had already stepped back inside the house and closed the front door. Cassie put her finger on the bell to ring it again, then changed her mind. Maybe Lizzie was right. Cassie couldn't undo the past, no matter how much she might want to. What mattered now, the only thing that mattered, was Grace.

Cassie needed to stay focused, make more of an effort with Paul and their marriage. Because he'd promised her and her unborn child the security Cassie knew she'd never be able to provide by herself. Paul wasn't perfect, but she was stuck with him and she would have to find a way of making this marriage work. If not for herself, for Grace.

Nineteen

Ed lived in a red-bricked Victorian terraced house on Motcombe Lane in the Old Town area of Eastbourne. To get to the house, Dee had to pass the historic church of St Mary the Virgin, where the dead body of a young woman had been found last year. Normally when she passed the church, Dee made a point of asking whatever god was up there to take care of poor Lauren Shaw's immortal soul. This evening, as the taxi she was in drove past the church, the only thing on her mind was Ed.

After what felt like an interminable length of time, the taxi finally pulled up outside Ed's house. Thrusting a ten-pound note at the driver, Dee jumped out of the car and ran to the front door. They had keys to each other's houses and she already had Ed's key in her hand. Ringing the doorbell, she put the key in the lock and pushed open the door.

'Ed?'

She stepped inside, calling his name again.

No response.

She stood still, ears straining as she listened for any sign that Ed was here. But the only sounds were the thudding of her own heart and the ticking of the grandfather clock in the sitting room to her right. With a growing sense of trepidation, Dee pushed open the sitting-room door and looked inside. There was no one in there, and when she checked the rest of the rooms, he wasn't in any of those either.

Yet it was clear he'd been here recently. There was condensation on the windows in the bathroom, as if he'd just come out of the shower. When she breathed in, she smelled mandarin and sage – the scent of the fancy shower gel he liked.

She knew by now he wasn't here, but she kept looking because she had to make sure. Her mind had gone into over-drive as she pictured him lying injured, or worse, in some hidden corner she might miss if she wasn't very, very careful. She checked every single part of the house.

At his bedroom, she paused in the doorway. Something was wrong, although it took her a moment to work out what it was as she scanned the tidy rows of shoes on the rack, the neat pile of books by the unmade bed and the overturned bottle of cologne on the dressing-room table.

Ed was meticulously tidy. In Dee's opinion, this was one of the least attractive aspects of his personality. He liked order, everything neat and tidy and in its place. It drove Dee demented, because who on earth needed their CDs and books organised not only alphabetically but also by category? And she really could not see the point of wasting time making sure your collection of spices were lined up the right way so you didn't have to root through them to find the one you needed each time you were cooking. Surely the daily hunt for the right spices, and the thrill of finding something you didn't even realise was there, was half the fun of cooking?

If this was Dee's bedroom, she'd never have noticed anything out of the ordinary. But she knew Ed, and knew hell would freeze over before he would leave the house without first making his bed and putting the bottle of cologne back in its proper place alongside the other neatly-lined up items on the dressing table.

The sound of her phone ringing broke the still silence, making Dee jump.

'Hello?' She hadn't recognised the number on the screen, but her racing brain told her it could be Ed. That maybe he'd lost his phone and that's why he hadn't called before now. It didn't explain why he hadn't turned up at the wine bar, or why his bedroom looked the way it did, but Dee clung onto the hope there was a rational explanation for his disappearance.

'Dee? It's Nessa.'

Ed's sister. Dee's legs lost their ability to keep her upright. Pressing her back against the bedroom wall, she slid to the floor.

'I've just had a phone call from Eastbourne hospital,' Nessa continued. 'Ed was rushed in earlier this evening.'

Outside, a group of people walked past the house, their voices merging together in giddy anticipation of wherever they were going.

'They called me because I'm listed in his phone as his emergency contact. I asked them to go through his contacts and give me your number. I hope you don't mind. I didn't know who else to call.'

—

Suspected stroke. That's what the nurse had said when Dee finally tracked Ed down in the hospital. The doctors would know more after the series of tests they were currently running to try to identify exactly what had happened.

Stroke. A terrifying word that triggered memories of her father. He'd suffered a stroke in his mid-forties. Dee remembered walking into the kitchen one morning and finding him lying on the floor, his hands clutching his head and his face distorted in pain. Within a few months, her father had made a complete recovery, but Dee knew that wasn't always the case. She'd once worked with a woman who'd lost the ability to speak after a stroke. The woman had died three years later, never having learned to speak again.

Dee tried to imagine Ed, incapacitated and unable to get his words out, but the image was too terrible to contemplate. She wanted to sit with him, but the nurse had told her that wasn't possible. It was outside visiting hours and Dee's presence might disturb the other patients in the ward. Instead, she had to make do with waiting in the visitors' room, a faux-cheerful yellow and white square space with a heavy air of despair hanging over it.

The presence of other people in the room did nothing to improve Dee's spirits. If anything, their palpable grief made her feel even worse. Doing her best to avoid eye contact with the elderly couple in the corner and the three middle-aged women sitting in row beneath a TV with its volume on mute, she settled into one of the remaining chairs and took out her phone.

After half an hour on the internet reading about what could happen to someone if they had a stroke, Dee's anxiety levels had rocketed. Putting her phone away, she looked up and noticed one of the women by the TV was staring at her.

'Our father,' the woman said, 'triple bypass. We've been stuck here for five hours now and we still don't know whether he'll pull through or not.'

'I'm sorry to hear that,' Dee said.

'How about you?' the woman asked.

'I'm here with my friend,' Dee said. 'He may have had a stroke. We're waiting for the results of some tests.'

'Hear that?' the woman said, turning to her companions. 'Stroke. Isn't that what happened to your Arthur, Debs?'

One of the other women, presumably Debs, nodded morosely and looked across at Dee. 'Terrible business, love. I wouldn't wish it on anyone.'

Unable to think of a suitable response, Dee looked down at her phone. She couldn't continue reading about strokes or she'd risk having one herself. But she had to do something. She left the visitors' room and walked along the corridor to the ward where Ed was being looked after.

'There's no change,' the ward nurse said, recognising Dee from earlier. 'Probably won't be for the next few hours, at least. Best thing you can do for your husband is go home and get some sleep.'

When Dee had arrived at the hospital earlier, she'd lied and told this nurse that she was Ed's wife. In her panicked state, she'd worried she might not be allowed to see him if the hospital staff knew she wasn't family.

'I won't sleep if I go home,' she said. 'Besides, his sister is on her way down from Norfolk. I need to be here when she arrives.'

'Well, make sure you get something to eat and have a hot drink,' the nurse said. 'I promise if there are any changes I'll come and find you.'

'Thanks.' Dee managed a small smile before walking away. Unable to face going back into the visitors' room, she went down the stairs and outside. It was late, some time after midnight, but Dee felt wide awake.

A tree-lined path led from the hospital to the road. She walked along this and, when she reached the end, she crossed the road and kept walking. She had no idea where she was going, or how long she'd walk before turning back to the hospital. All she knew was that she had to walk, because if she didn't focus on putting one foot in front of another, over and over again, she wouldn't be able to ever go back into that hospital and face up to what was happening to Ed.

Twenty

The next days passed in a blur of hospital visits and meetings with consultants and acclimatising to a whole new vocabulary of medical terms and acronyms. Ed had suffered an ischaemic stroke, caused when the blood supply to the brain is stopped because of a blood clot. According to the consultant in charge of his care, Ed had been 'lucky'. The stroke had happened while his regular cleaner was at his house. The cleaner's husband had suffered a stroke last summer. When Ed collapsed in his bedroom, she recognised the signs immediately. She'd dialled 999 and an ambulance had been at the house within ten minutes. Thanks to her fast actions, the clot had been removed promptly, preventing further damage to Ed's brain.

Dee had tried not to think of what might have happened if Ed's stroke had happened on another day, when his cleaner wasn't there. It wasn't always easy; especially during the long nights when she couldn't sleep and her mind seemed intent on taking her to dark places she didn't want to be.

It was too early to know what the long-term effects of the stroke might be. Ed was still heavily sedated, unable to speak or swallow. The stroke had affected the right side of his brain, although he didn't appear to have suffered any weakness to the left side. The consultant had warned Dee and Nessa that people who survive a stroke are often left with long-term problems caused by the injury to their brain. At the very least, Ed would require a long period of rehabilitation when he came out of hospital.

Nessa, Ed's sister, had been staying with Dee since she'd arrived in Eastbourne five days ago. Five days of anxious worrying and bedside vigils while they waited for the consultant to give them a clearer idea of what to expect as Ed recovered. If he recovered.

Nessa and Dee had spent the first few days together in the hospital, before realising it made more sense for them to take turns. This morning, Nessa was there, so Dee had taken the opportunity to drive to Bexhill for her rescheduled meeting with David Verney, the retired police detective.

As she approached the cafe where they had arranged to meet, Dee could see David Verney sitting inside. She recognised him from the photo on his website, although he looked at least ten years older in real life.

He stood up as Dee pushed open the door and walked into the welcoming coolness of air conditioning.

'Dee?'

He held his hand out and gave her a smile that didn't reach his eyes, which were piercing blue and ice cold. His handshake was firm and confident. Much like the man himself, Dee suspected. He insisted on ordering coffee for both of them. When the drinks were ready, he carried them across to the table and sat down opposite Dee.

'So,' he said, when he was settled. 'This story you're writing. Remind me again what your angle is.'

Dee took a sip of her coffee, giving herself a moment before she answered his question.

'Nice coffee.' She smiled, pretending she hadn't noticed the hostile tone in his voice.

'Glad you like it. This place is like my second home. I come here most mornings.'

'I read on your website you do consultancy work these days,' Dee said. 'What does that involve?'

'I work with creators of fiction, providing expert advice on all areas of police work. It started as a hobby, really. After I retired, I was looking around for something to fill my days. A friend was midway through writing his first crime novel and he asked if I'd help him with the police procedural side of it. I was more than happy to offer my advice, and he was more than happy to take it. The author was William Langhorn.'

He looked meaningfully at Dee, clearly expecting some sort of reaction.

'Wow,' she managed, which must have been enough, because David beamed and continued speaking, visibly puffing up the more he spoke about himself.

'Back then, Bill wasn't the household name he is now. That book, the first in his Larry Legend series, was a bestseller and Bill's now one of the country's most respected and successful crime writers. We've collaborated on all his books and gradually my consultancy work has taken off. These days, I have a handful of successful writers I work with, but most of my time is taken up with TV. I've been chief advisor on several of the biggest shows of the last few years.'

While he listed the programmes he'd worked on, Dee worked hard to pretend she was interested.

'It's been great,' he said, 'a lot of hard work but hugely rewarding. Well, I don't need to tell you that. You know how the industry works.'

Dee blinked. She had no idea what 'industry' he was referring to.

'Your gig with Channel 4,' he continued. 'Any chance you could put me in touch with the producer? It's been great working behind the scenes, but I'd love a chance to get in front of the cameras. Joey's hooked me up with a few people, but nothing's come of those meetings so far. It's always good to make new connections.'

Dee decided she'd had enough. If she had to listen to one more second of his self-obsessed nonsense, she wouldn't be accountable for her actions.

'Why did you tell Joey Cavellini where I live?'

'Sorry?'

'You heard me,' Dee said. 'I want to know why you went to the effort of finding my address and then giving it to a man I barely know.'

David sat back and folded his hands behind his head before answering.

'Spur of the moment. I called Joey to see how he was doing. He said he was desperate to find Cassie and I thought of you. So while I was still speaking to him, I went online and found out where you lived.'

She didn't bother asking how he'd found out. He was an ex-detective and, even if he wasn't, Dee knew it was easy to find someone's address if you knew the right resources to use.

'Why?' she asked instead.

He laughed. 'Because I didn't buy your bullshit story about writing a "where are they now?" piece. You're an investigative journalist. There's only one reason you're looking into that murder. You're trying to prove I got it wrong, and Cassie didn't kill her husband. Once I'd worked that out, it was easy to work out the rest. You live in Eastbourne, so does Cassie. It's obvious you're doing this because she'd asked you to.'

'You're only partly right,' Dee said. 'It wasn't Cassie who asked me to look into Paul's murder.'

'If it wasn't Cassie, then who was it?'

'Well, David, I'm afraid I can't share that information with you.'

Dee drained her coffee and stood up. David Verney wasn't about to share any information with her, so there was no point staying here any longer.

'But I can tell you this,' she said. 'I don't believe Cassie killed Paul. I think you messed up and sent an innocent woman to jail. You might not want me looking into what really happened back then, but I'm afraid there's nothing you can do to stop me.'

It wasn't entirely true, but the man had pissed her off and she wanted to do the same to him.

He started to speak, but she was already walking away. She had heard enough to know he was a vain, self-obsessed idiot who cared more about his reputation than uncovering the truth. She had contacted David Verney hoping to find an ally; instead she suspected she'd just made herself a formidable enemy.

Twenty-one

'You're off out?' Joey asked, as Freya came down the stairs.

'Just going for a walk,' she said.

'Looking pretty fancy for someone who's going for a walk.'

Instinctively, she reached up to touch her hair that she'd just finished straightening.

'I'm glad I caught you, actually,' Joey said. 'I wanted to apologise.'

'What for?'

'For getting so angry when I found out you hadn't told us about Grace meeting up with her birth mother.'

'It's okay,' Freya said. 'You had every right to be angry about it.'

'I know you were only doing what Grace asked you.'

Freya's eyes filled with tears that she blinked away angrily. She had no right to cry. Joey had been right to be angry with her. It was her fault Cassie was missing. If she'd told the police the truth from the beginning, Cassie would probably have been arrested by now and this agony of waiting for her to be caught would be over.

'We'll get through this, Freya,' Joey said. 'As long as we stick together, we'll pull through.'

'Even Mum?'

'Yes,' Joey nodded. 'Her too.'

He was being so strong for all of them. Freya knew it couldn't be easy for him. He'd loved Grace as much as any of them. In fact, Joey had never hidden the fact that Grace was his favourite niece. The two of them had had a special bond that excluded the rest of the family. Grace used to say it was because they were both adopted. Freya's grandparents had adopted Joey because they thought they couldn't have children of their own. Two years after adopting him, Freya's mother was born. Then her uncle, Paul, came along a few years later.

'She seems like she's given up,' Freya said. 'You know that yesterday she didn't even get out of bed?'

'She's grieving,' Joey said. 'It's going to take time. Try to be patient with her. She's been through a lot, you know. We had a tough time growing up. Our parents were angry people who took their anger out on their kids. That sort of thing damages you.'

'You don't seem damaged,' Freya pointed out.

'Maybe I just do a better job of hiding it.' Joey smiled. 'Anyway, none of that matters now. What matters is you and the brilliant life you're going to have. You owe it to Grace, as well as yourself, to do all the things she will never be able to. You'll be off to university, before you know it. Economics, isn't it?'

The lump in her throat made it impossible to speak.

'At Cambridge University,' Joey continued. 'It will be amazing, Freya.'

He sounded so pleased that she couldn't tell him she'd already decided not to go. That she couldn't begin to think about leaving her mother after this. Because apart from Joey and Freya, Mum didn't have anyone else.

'I've got to go,' she said. 'See you later, maybe?'

'Sure. You take care of yourself, Freya. Bye.'

It was only a ten-minute walk from her house to Albertine's in the heart of Meads village. But ten minutes was plenty of time for Freya's carefully applied make-up to be melted away. The sun was beating down, hotter than any day so far this stinking summer. Freya couldn't see her hair, but she knew the time she'd spent straightening it would have been wasted. She only had to touch it to feel how the humidity had frizzed and curled it.

There was a girl Freya didn't recognise working behind the bar. Tall and rake-thin, with long dark hair and piercing blue eyes that bored into Freya.

'We've got an over-18 policy,' she informed Freya. 'You got any ID on you?'

'I'm not here to drink,' Freya said. 'I'm looking for Lloyd. Is he around?'

She'd worn her new dress, a fitted yellow dress from Urban Outfitters with a sunflower print on it. When she'd put it on earlier, she thought it was perfect. Now, she felt overdressed. Especially compared to the other girl, in her distressed denims and faded black Nirvana T-shirt. Grace had loved Nirvana, used to play their music all the time. Freya's breath caught in her throat as Kurt Cobain's voice filled every corner of her brain and Grace's ghost danced around her. *Hello, hello, hello.*

'Hey,' the girl was looking at her, frowning. 'Are you okay?'

Freya had never liked Nirvana. Their sound was all wrong, loud and raw and difficult. Freya preferred softer sounds like Lana del Rey and Mitski and Billie Eilish. Music that made sense and didn't make you want to rip your clothes off and howl at the moon before running naked into the freezing cold sea.

'I'm fine.'

The girl shrugged, like she didn't believe her but didn't care enough to argue about it either. 'Lloyd's out back,' she said, 'in the garden.'

Freya walked past her, through the door that led outside to the walled garden that had always been her favourite part of the wine bar. With its rustic tables, pots of colourful flowers and a canopy of vines, you could almost imagine you were in France out here.

Lloyd was sitting at a table in the far corner. He wasn't alone, as she'd expected. He was talking to a woman Freya had never seen before. There was something about the way they were sitting, their chairs close together, heads tilted towards each other, that made them look like a couple. Which couldn't be true, because the last time Freya had spoken to Lloyd, he'd been bereft.

She paused, unsure whether to walk across and say hi, or make a quick exit. In the end, the choice was taken out of her hands because Lloyd looked up and saw her. Something dark passed across his face, fear or guilt or anger, it was difficult to tell. He said something to the woman he was with, before standing up and walking across to Freya.

'Freya, what a surprise. Everything okay?'

'Fine,' she said, although the opposite was so clearly true she wondered why he'd bothered asking. 'I was just passing and thought I'd drop in and say hi.'

'Well, I'm glad you did.'

He was smiling, but it looked forced, like he'd fixed the smile onto his face and was working hard to keep it in place.

Lloyd's not the nice guy you think he is.

Grace's voice in her head, telling Freya something she hadn't wanted to hear then and didn't want to hear now.

Across the garden, the woman he'd been talking to was watching them, the scrutiny of her stare making Freya uncomfortable. She was older than Freya had first realised. Twenty-five, or maybe even a few years older, with glossy blonde hair and golden skin.

'That's Zoe,' Lloyd said. 'The DJ? She does all those wild club nights in Brighton.'

Freya shook her head. Wild club nights weren't exactly her scene.

'We're sort of in the middle of something actually,' Lloyd said. 'Normally, I'd suggest you hang around until we're finished, but I promised Zoe I'd drop her back home later. Her car's being serviced. Maybe we could catch up another time?'

'Sure.' Freya gave him a smile every bit as fake as the one plastered on his own face. 'No worries, Lloyd. See you later.'

He gave her a quick peck on the cheek, told her how great she was looking and then he was gone.

As Freya walked back through the bar, her cheeks burning with embarrassment, the Nirvana girl called out to her.

'Hey!'

Freya stopped walking and looked at her.

'Maybe you should call ahead the next time, so you don't get caught out like that again.'

'Drop dead,' she hissed, before pulling open the door and stepping outside into the blinding brightness of the day.

'Freya?'

She had walked straight into Patrick Keenan, who, for some bizarre reason, was standing right outside the entrance to the wine bar.

'Patrick, what are you playing at?'

'You're the one who practically ran me over,' Patrick said. 'I was just standing here minding my own business when you stormed out of there like you were being chased.'

'You're not stalking me, are you?'

'In your dreams.' Patrick grinned. 'I need a job and I heard this place is hiring at the moment.'

'You're joking.'

'Course not. Oh, I get it. You're here for the same reason, right?'

'Wrong. I'm here because this is the bar where my sister worked before she was murdered.'

Freya drew out the last word as much as possible, wanting him to realise what an idiot he'd been.

'Shit.' He put his hand over his mouth. 'I'm so sorry, Freya. I had no clue, I swear.'

'How could you not know? It's in every single story that's been written about her since she disappeared. *Missing bar girl.* Like that's the sum total of who she was. It's disgusting.'

'The press can be awful,' Patrick said. 'It's why I've avoided reading too much about your sister's murder. It feels a little salacious, you know?'

'I'm not sure I even know what salacious means.'

'Sure you do. Four A-stars predicted, one of them in English Lit? Of course you know what it means. Anyway, I didn't want to work there. I've heard the owner's a bit of a dick.'

'That's racist bullshit.'

'There's nothing racist about calling someone a dick if that's what they are.'

'Well, he's not a dick. He's lovely and kind and funny and I hate the way people think they can talk shit about him for no reason.'

'Sorry.' Patrick held his hands up. 'I didn't know you two were friends. Is he the reason you never want to see me anymore?'

'Who said I don't want to see you?'

'Me. Any time I ask if you want to do something, you always have some excuse. We used to hang out all the time, Freya. What happened?'

She'd lost interest in boys her own age, that's what had happened. She was on the verge of telling him this, but something in his face made her stop. The way he was looking at her, like a dog who'd just been kicked. He was pathetic, but she didn't have the heart to make him feel any worse than he clearly already did.

'I was focusing on my studies,' she said. 'I need those A-stars to get into Cambridge. There wasn't much time for anything else.'

She didn't say the whole idea of university seemed pointless now. She wouldn't know which university she had got into until she got her A-level results next month. A few weeks ago, those results seemed like the most important thing in the world. Now, she didn't care what she got. She didn't care about university or A-levels or any of the stuff that had once seemed so important.

'How are you doing?' he asked.

'How do you think?'

He winced. 'Stupid question. Sorry.'

'It's not stupid,' she said, relenting. 'You're talking to me about it, which is more than anyone else has tried to do. More, too, than I tried to do for you after your dad died.'

'That was a while ago now.'

'I know, but I should have got in touch. The truth is, even though I should have known what it was like for you, I didn't know what to say. So I stayed away and said nothing.'

'You weren't the only one,' Patrick replied. 'Most people didn't know how to talk to me about it.' He paused. 'Listen, I'm heading up to the beach for a few hours if you want to come along?'

She should get back home. Her mother would start worrying if she stayed out for too long. But there was something about the way Patrick was looking at her, his goofy grin and his blue eyes, that was making Freya feel a tiny bit less shit about herself. Before she knew it, she was smiling at him and saying that would be lovely.

As they walked away from the wine bar, Patrick reached out and took her hand in his. Normally, she would have pulled her hand away immediately. But today, she didn't do that. For the first time since Grace had disappeared, Freya felt that Joey might be right after all and she would find a way through this.

Twenty-two

That evening, Dee made pasta for herself and Nessa. Dee's go-to pasta sauce was normally carbonara, but Nessa was vegan, so Dee had gone with a tomato and chilli sauce tonight. Although when they sat down to eat, Nessa only ate a few mouthfuls before pushing the plate away.

'I'm sorry,' she said. 'It's delicious, but I don't have much appetite.'

They were sitting outside, on the deck. The sun had set and a fat white moon hovered over the black sea.

'It's really beautiful here,' Nessa said. 'Ed's told me about your home, but I wasn't prepared for the wow factor. You must love living here.'

'I do,' Dee said. 'Although if you'd told me ten years ago that I'd end up living back here, I'd have laughed and said over my dead body.'

'So what happened?' Nessa asked.

'I got divorced and lost my job. The two things happened pretty close together. After years in London, I found myself wondering what to do with myself. Then my dad got ill, my mum soon after that. I moved home to be close to them, thinking I'd go back to London one day, but it never happened.'

'If you'd told me ten years ago I'd be happily settled in rural Norfolk with a man I love, two kids and a load of rescue animals, I'd have laughed in your face,' Nessa said. 'It's funny how we think we're in control of our lives when really we're not.'

'You don't think we're in control of what happens to us?'

'We like to think we are,' Nessa said. 'But things happen that are completely out of our control. Like you and Ed. I bet after you got divorced you didn't think you'd end up being in a serious relationship again.'

'I suppose not.'

Dee thought this probably wasn't the right time to tell Nessa that she and Ed were not, in fact, in a serious relationship.

'I'm so glad he's got you,' Nessa said. 'I couldn't bear the thought of him coming out of hospital and trying to cope by himself.'

She reached across the table and squeezed Dee's hand.

'You won't let that happen, Dee, will you?'

'Of course not.'

Dee didn't know if Nessa was asking or telling. Either way, she wanted to put an end to this conversation before it got even more difficult. She stood up and started clearing the plates away.

–

An hour later, Nessa had gone to bed and Dee was sitting in front of her laptop reading everything she could find on the internet about Paul Cavellini's murder. She was tired to her bones, but knew if she went to bed now she wouldn't sleep. The truth was, she'd barely slept at all since Ed's stroke. Anxiety keeping her awake, night after endless night, as she worried about Ed's health and what their new future might look like.

So she spent her evenings like this, instead. Sitting at her laptop, working on her book or trying to build a narrative around the weeks leading up to Paul's murder. She made notes as she went along, but, without input from Cassie, it was a slow process. A frustrating one too, because if Dee could only speak with Cassie, she would get most of this information in a quarter the time it was taking her to collate it now. When her brain decided it had had enough for the evening, Dee shut down the internet and read back over the notes she'd made so far.

Eighteen years ago, Cassie McNamara got married and became Cassie Cavellini. Cassie and her new husband, Paul, rented a flat together in Croydon, south London, where they'd both grown up. Four months after the wedding, their daughter Grace was born. Paul was murdered a month before Grace's second birthday. Stabbed to death in the kitchen of the house he lived in with Cassie and Grace. It was Cassie who found his body and reported the murder to the police.

From everything Dee read, it seemed Cassie was the main suspect right from the start. A woman called Lizzie Collier came forward early in the police investigation, claiming that Cassie hated her husband and had spoken several times about wishing he was dead. Dee had already searched online for anyone called Lizzie Collier who had lived in Croydon at the time of Paul's murder. There were plenty of Lizzie Colliers out there but none of them were the one she was looking for.

Frustrated, Dee pushed her chair back and stood up. She slid open the bifold door and stepped onto the deck. She leaned against the wooden railings, taking deep breaths of sea air as she tried to think how else she could track down Lizzie Collier. But without Cassie, everything was so difficult. Dee was starting to think it was pointless going any further.

Down on the beach, a family of foxes ran along the edge of the water, silvery silhouettes captured in the light of the pale moon. Dee thought she saw something else out of the corner of her eye, another movement near the mobile home. But when she looked in that direction, the place was as dark and empty as it always was.

She remembered Nessa's comment earlier, about how none of us are really in control of our lives. Dee wondered if that was true and, if so, why she tried so bloody hard at everything all the time. Because if she couldn't control any of it, wasn't it better to simply sit back and wait to see what life threw at her?

On the beach, one of the foxes let out a shrill, high-pitched bark, the sound reverberating across the empty beach. Dee stayed outside, watching them, until they moved further along the beach and out of sight. When she went back inside, she checked the time. Five minutes to eleven. Late, but maybe not too late to send Joey Cavellini a text. He'd given Dee his number the other day, told her to call if she had any news about Cassie. Grabbing her phone now, she found his number and typed a quick message, asking him to call her back. A few seconds later, her phone started ringing and she saw Joey's name on the screen.

'It's good of you to call me back so late,' she said, once they'd got the greetings out of the way.

'I'm not sleeping too well at the moment,' he said. 'Anything that distracts me from my own thoughts is welcome. Have you got some news about Cassie?'

'Not yet, I'm afraid. I wanted to ask how well you knew her when she was married to Paul.'

'Hardly at all, really. We grew up in the same part of Croydon, but Cassie's eleven years younger than me. That's a big age difference when you're kids. Why do you want to know?'

'I'm trying to get a picture of what sort of person she was back then,' Dee said.

'David warned me to be careful about what I share with you,' Joey said. 'He seems to think you're hell-bent on proving someone else killed my brother.'

'You didn't have to call me back if you don't want to talk to me.'

'I know. The truth is, I was glad when I got your text. I enjoyed our chat the other day. If you're writing a story about Paul's murder, as long as it's respectful to my family, then I don't see the problem.'

'There's something you should know,' Dee said. 'The reason I know Cassie is because of Grace.'

'Excuse me?'

'A few months before she died, I got an email from Grace,' Dee said. 'She said she knew I was an investigative journalist and she had a story I might be interested in. We met, and she told me her mother had been the victim of a miscarriage of justice. She asked me if I'd help prove this.'

'I see.' There was a pause as Joey seemed to process this new information. 'I had no idea she'd been looking into her father's murder. I know she was very angry with Trish when she discovered what had happened. She felt Trish should have told her the truth. She couldn't see that all Trish was trying to do was protect her.'

'What about Trish's husband?' Dee asked. 'Where does he fit into all of this? You told me he walked out when the girls were little, but surely he stayed in touch with his daughters?'

'He never considered Grace was his daughter,' Joey said. 'It's one of the reasons the marriage broke up. Trish and I were determined that Grace wouldn't be taken into foster care. I wasn't in a position to adopt her myself, so it made sense for Trish and Conor to do it. Conor seemed okay about it, at first. But it didn't take long for him to start to resent Trish for it.'

'So what happened?'

'He had an affair with a much younger woman, ended up leaving his family for her. Last I heard, he's married for a second time and living in Australia with his new wife and their two kids.'

'Sounds as if Trish is better off without him,' Dee said.

'She is,' Joey agreed. 'Problem is, she's never seen it that way. She's always blamed herself for the marriage breaking up. Thinks she should have taken Conor's opinion into consideration a bit more. It's all bullshit, of course. Grace was just a kid, and she's family. We were never going to abandon her.'

'So how did Trish feel when she found out Grace wasn't Paul's child?'

'It's never made a blind bit of difference to either of us,' Joey said. 'Trish loved Grace just as much as she loves Freya. And so did I.'

'Did you or Trish ever have any ideas about who Grace's real father might be?'

'A girl like Cassie, I'm afraid there's quite a lot of guys to choose from.'

'I thought you barely knew her back then,' Dee said, biting down on her lip to stop herself saying anything else. The throwaway sexist remark rankled and told her something about the sort of man Joey was beneath all that easy charm.

'Well, enough to know she had a bit of a reputation.'

'Did you ever sleep with her?'

'Me? You've got to be kidding. No offence, Dee, but I've always gone for girls with a bit more class.'

Dee swallowed down a number of retorts that came to mind when he said that.

'The reason I was asking about Grace's father,' she said, 'is because I wonder if he might also be someone who had a motive for killing Paul. I'm guessing that, whoever he is, he was never a suspect because back then no one knew about him.'

She expected him to tell her this was a ridiculous idea. That Cassie had been convicted of Paul's murder because she was guilty, and Dee was wasting her time trying to prove anything else. Instead, he surprised her.

'You know, that has never actually occurred to me before now,' he said, after a moment. 'I mean, I just assumed all along that Cassie had killed him. I still think she did, but you're right. No one ever considered there might be someone else with a motive.'

'A shame you don't know who he is.'

'Actually, there was someone,' Joey said. 'A bloke called Mark Collier. Cassie and him were an item for quite a while, I seem to remember. I'm pretty sure Mark wasn't too happy when Cassie dumped him for Paul.'

'How did no one ever follow this up at the time?' Dee walked across to her laptop and scrolled through the notes she'd made earlier. She paused when she reached the name of the key witness in the police investigation: Lizzie Collier, the woman Dee had failed to track down earlier this evening.

'Like I said, no one knew Grace wasn't Paul's child.'

'Any idea where he is now?' Dee asked.

'Dead most likely. Mark Collier had a big drink problem. Probably the reason Cassie dumped him.'

'Did he have a sister?'

'I have no idea.'

'There was a woman called Lizzie Collier who gave evidence against Cassie during the trial,' Dee said. 'It's not a very common surname. She and Mark must be related.'

'Possibly,' Joey said. 'But like I've already told you, I didn't know any of them very much. Mark, Lizzie, Cassie, even Paul – as far as I was concerned, they were just kids.'

They ended the call soon after that, with Joey telling Dee if he thought of anything else he'd let her know. Dee knew it was a promise he had no intention of keeping. Lizzie Collier had been one of the key witnesses in Paul's murder trial. Yet Joey had acted as if he'd never heard of her. Which meant he had lied to Dee just now.

Twenty-three

Tuesday morning, two weeks and a day since Cassie disappeared, Dee finally made it out to Polegate to speak to Cassie's boss. Strands hair salon was located midway along a modern parade of shops on Polegate High Street, squeezed in between a Chinese restaurant and a newsagent's. Through the window, Dee could see the interior was more welcoming than it appeared on the outside. There was a reception area, where four women sat flicking through magazines while they waited to get their hair done. Behind the reception area, mirrored walls made the space seem bigger and brighter than it really was. Dee spotted three women getting their hair cut, and several others sitting alone, silver foil covering their hair as they spoke across the room to each other.

Jennifer Trevorrow was sitting behind the reception desk. When Dee pushed open the door and stepped inside, Jennifer looked up and frowned.

'I was wondering when you'd show up,' she said.

'Hello, Jennifer,' Dee said, 'you remember me, then.'

'Difficult woman to forget, aren't you?' Jennifer heaved herself out of the chair she'd been sitting on. 'I'm afraid you've had a wasted journey, Dee Doran. Oh don't look so surprised that I know your name. Cassie told me all about you. But Cassie's not here today and there's nothing I want to say to you.'

'Just ten minutes,' Dee said. 'That's all I need. Please, Jennifer?'

The radio was playing through a series of speakers fitted along the walls above the mirrors. While Dee was speaking, 'Lady in Red' by Chris de Burgh started up.

'Can't stand this song,' Jennifer muttered. 'Ten minutes, you say? Okay. Follow me.' She walked towards a door at the back of the salon. Dee hurried after her into a small kitchen.

'I'll put the kettle on,' Jennifer said. 'Tea or coffee?'

'Tea, please,' Dee said, noting the jar of supermarket-branded instant coffee on the shelf beside the kettle.

'Tea it is. Shut the door, would you? My girls are good at their jobs but they're all terrible gossips. They'll be desperate to hear what we're talking about. Not sure if you noticed, but Sonia nearly passed out when she saw you. She's a big fan of that TV show you're on. Never stops talking about the fact there's a woman from Eastbourne on it.'

Jennifer reached up to a speaker mounted on the wall and turned the volume down, silencing the music.

'That's better,' she said. 'At least now we can talk without my ears being traumatised by Chris de bloody Burgh. Right, Dee. I'll give you five minutes. What do you want?'

'Grace wanted me to help prove Cassie didn't kill Paul,' Dee said. 'She was convinced Cassie had been the victim of a miscarriage of justice. At the time, I thought she was wrong. Because how could she know what her mother was like? She wasn't supposed to have met her. But it turns out Cassie and Grace had been meeting secretly for months. And now I think that maybe Cassie told Grace something that convinced her she was innocent.'

She stopped speaking, aware she wasn't making much sense.

'You think it'll make you feel better if you can find something that proves Cassie's innocent?' Jennifer said.

'Maybe,' Dee acknowledged. 'I didn't do enough for Grace when she was alive. Now she's dead, I feel I need to make up for that.'

'And what if you don't find anything? Or you find something that proves, beyond doubt, that Cassie did it after all?'

'At least then I'll know I've tried,' Dee said.

Jennifer poured water from the kettle into two mugs that she'd already put teabags into.

'I'll leave the milk and sugar on the counter,' she said. 'Help yourself to whatever you want.'

'Thanks.' Dee used the teaspoon beside one of the mugs to squeeze out the teabag before throwing it in the bin. After adding some milk, she leaned back against the counter and asked Jennifer how long Cassie had worked for her.

'Ever since she got out of prison,' Jennifer said.

'You knew she'd been in prison when you hired her?'

'I started writing to Cassie when she was in prison,' Jennifer said. 'I'd followed the trial, and after she was convicted I couldn't stop thinking about her. So I wrote to her and, after a few months, she wrote back. We kept in touch after that. I started visiting her, too. We became friends, I'd like to think.'

'What made you want to write to her?' Dee asked.

'I was in an abusive relationship when I was young. I never killed the bloke, but there were times I thought of it. A lot of times. When I read about Cassie, I knew there's only one reason a woman would do something like that. I felt sorry for her, I suppose.'

'How did you get out of that relationship?'

'I got pregnant,' Jennifer said. 'The moment he found out about it, he beat me black and blue and then scarpered. I never saw him again.'

'How awful,' Dee said.

'It was a long time ago now. Whatever wounds I had have well and truly healed over the years. Anyway, you're here to talk about Cassie, not me. She didn't have the best start in life. Alcoholic mother, absent father. Cassie learned early to trade on her looks to get what she wanted. Her face was the one thing she could use to break free from the life she'd been born into. Unfortunately, she went straight from living with her alcoholic mother to living with an abusive husband. She had no skills or qualifications, nothing to fall back on when she left prison. I knew she'd have a hard time getting a job. So I took her on as an apprentice and trained her up. Turned her into a good little hairdresser.'

'Wow,' Dee said. 'That's pretty impressive.'

Jennifer shrugged. 'It felt like the right thing to do. And I never regretted it. Until recently. Now, I don't know what to think. She never told me about Grace, you know. I knew her baby girl had been given up for adoption, but I had no idea she was living here in Eastbourne.'

'It's a bit of a coincidence, isn't it?' Dee said. 'You and Cassie's daughter both living in the same town?'

'I doubt Cassie would have accepted my offer of a job if Grace had been living somewhere else,' Jennifer said. 'And maybe I'd never have made the offer in the first place if I'd known.'

'Why not?'

'I might have thought the temptation to contact Grace would have been too much for her. And I'd have been right, wouldn't I?'

'What about the other girls who work here?' Dee asked. 'Was Cassie friends with any of them?'

'Not really. Kept herself to herself, did Cassie. If you ask me, the other girls are a bit jealous of her.'

'Why?'

'Because she's my favourite. Or she used to be, at any rate. She's the best hairdresser I've got and until this business she's never caused me a moment's trouble.'

'Cassie's lucky she's had you to look out for her.'

'I'm the one that's lucky,' Jennifer said. 'At least, that's what I thought.'

'Do you have any idea where she might have gone?' Dee asked.

'None.'

There was a question circling at the back of Dee's mind, but each time she tried to focus on it, it slipped out of reach. So she asked another question instead.

'From your accent,' she said, 'I can tell you're from Liverpool or somewhere around there. How did you end up living in Eastbourne?'

'I've got family here,' Jennifer said. 'Moved here to be closer to them. Now then, I think I've given you enough of my time. I need to get back to work.'

'Of course.' Dee smiled and thanked Jennifer for her time.

She had missed something important, but each time she went back over the conversation she couldn't identify what that was. As she walked back through the salon, she felt herself edging closer to it. But then one of the hairdressers rushed over and asked for Dee's autograph and it was gone again.

Twenty-four

There was no silence in hospitals. Even here, in the stroke unit, where you'd think there would be peace and quiet, there was always something or someone making noise. Machines that bleeped and beeped, the shuffle of shoes on hard hospital floors, murmured voices from visitors and staff, the swishing of doors opening and closing, the endless sense of things happening that you had no control over. Dee remembered this from when her mother was in hospital, sitting by her bedside while the life gradually seeped out of her until there was nothing left. And now here she was again; this time with Ed. Except, unlike Dee's mother, Ed would get better. Dee held onto that belief, refusing to accept any other possible outcome.

'Hey.'

His voice was low, raspy and unrecognisable. The nurse who'd been here earlier said that was to be expected. He'd spent the last week with a tube down his throat. The tube had been taken out earlier today. He was breathing without the help of a machine, and had managed a few words of conversation before falling asleep. Now he was awake, and appeared to be trying to smile.

'Hey, yourself.' Dee reached out, wrapped her hand around his and squeezed gently. 'How you doing?'

'Great.' He made a hacking sound that sent Dee's anxiety spiking, until she realised he was laughing.

'Ness?' he asked, when the hacking stopped.

'I sent her home to get some rest,' Dee said. 'I hope that's okay.'

Ed said something but she couldn't make out the words.

'I didn't catch that,' she said, leaning in closer.

'She wants me to become vegan,' he rasped. 'Please don't let that happen.'

'Cross my heart,' Dee said, although part of her couldn't help thinking if Ed's diet had been a bit healthier this might never have happened.

'Thanks.'

He smiled at her before closing his eyes. She remained beside him, holding his hand, watching as he drifted into sleep again. Her chest ached with a complex mix of love and sadness and anxiety.

After a messy divorce, Dee had thought the romantic part of her life was over for good. Then she'd met Ed and, all over again, she'd got mixed up in a messy relationship that had left her feeling more emotionally bruised than ever. When they'd finally split up, she had vowed that was it. Ed was in her past and that was where he would remain. Somehow, it hadn't ended there. They had started seeing each other again, first as friends, but – maybe inevitably – it had rapidly become something more.

The problem was, she loved him. It wasn't ideal, and she had tried her damnedest not to let it happen. But it seemed that no matter how hard you tried not to love a person, sometimes you simply couldn't help it. Loving someone, being emotionally dependent on them for your happiness, was something Dee had fought hard against. She'd made that mistake with Billy, her ex-husband, and it had given her nothing but heartache. The thought of opening herself again to the risk of being hurt was terrifying.

She'd spent too much time over the last few days worrying about what would happen when Ed eventually got out of hospital – where he would live, how much care he would need, whether she had it in her to be his primary carer. Sitting here now, holding his hand and watching him sleep, she realised none of that mattered. He had woken up and he had smiled at her. He was alive.

Tears filled her eyes, spilling down her cheeks as it hit her – properly for the first time since she'd got Nessa's phone call – that Ed might have died. Dee had already lost too many people she cared about. She didn't want to lose someone else. Ed would recover from this. He had to.

She stayed with him for the rest of the afternoon. Nessa turned up, just as Dee was leaving.

'I'm heading straight back to Norfolk after this,' Nessa said. 'Javi says the kids are missing me. Although, I think the truth is, he's missing me more than they are. Either way, I can't stay here forever so I may as well head back tonight. I'll call you over the weekend to see how he's doing.'

'Please do,' Dee said, fighting down the surge of panic at having to deal with this by herself. Stupidly, it hadn't occurred to her that Nessa would go back home. It made sense for her to leave, Dee knew that. Nessa had her own life – a partner, two kids and an ever-growing collection of rescue animals. She couldn't stay here indefinitely, while Dee dithered over what to do when Ed finally came out of hospital.

Pulling up outside her home twenty minutes later, Dee realised she was relieved to have the place back to herself again. She enjoyed Nessa's company, and would be happy for her to come and stay whenever she wanted. But there was no denying the fact that Dee was looking forward to not having to care for anyone except herself. Especially if that wasn't going to be the case for much longer.

As she opened the front door, she heard a noise inside the house that made her pause.

'Hello?'

There was no response and she stepped into the house, closing the door behind her. In the living room, the bifold doors that led onto the deck were open. Nessa must have forgotten to close them before she left.

Leaving the doors as they were, Dee went into the kitchen to make herself a cup of tea. But when she checked her fridge, there was no milk. So much for Nessa's veganism, Dee thought, pouring herself a glass of sparkling water instead. Clearly, Dee wasn't the only one who couldn't face drinking tea without milk. In the absence of the oat milk Nessa usually drank, she had obviously decided to take the last of the cow's milk instead.

Smiling as she pictured herself telling Ed about Nessa's transgression, Dee carried the glass and her phone out to the deck. It was almost seven o'clock. Any visitors to the beach had gone home for the day and Dee had the place to herself. As she settled into one of the chairs, the anxiety that had been building up over the last week started to recede. She sipped her water, taking a moment to soak up the view and reflect on how very lucky she was to live somewhere so beautiful.

It was still warm, but without the intense heat of earlier. On the horizon, the sun was dipping down towards the flat blue sea. Apart from the squalling of seagulls and the sound of the water rolling in and out over the shingle, everything was still and peaceful. It was a welcome reprieve from the endless, industrial noise of the hospital.

When Ella and Jake had been living in the mobile home, Friday nights were when the neighbours got together. They would order pizzas and, on warm summer evenings like this one, they would sit on the deck while the sun went down, catching up on how their week had been. Now, Ella and Jake were in Canada with Jake's dad, and Dee spent her Friday nights either with Ed or by herself.

To stop herself becoming too gloomy, Dee picked up her phone and opened her internet browser. She typed Jennifer Trevorrow's name into the search engine, looking once again for anything she could find on Cassie's boss. She had already done this several times, but there was something about her meeting earlier that kept niggling at her. She had the annoying feeling she had missed something important. Yet each time she ran back over everything Jennifer had said, she couldn't pinpoint the exact moment she'd felt something was wrong.

As before, the internet search didn't throw up any new information. Dee opened Facebook and started scrolling through her news feed when her phone started ringing. The caller ID was withheld, and her first thought was that it must be the hospital calling. With her heart pounding in her chest and a roaring sound in her ears, she slid her thumb across the screen to accept the call.

'Hello?'

Nothing.

She tried again, louder this time. 'Hello? Who's there?'

This time she heard something. Breathing – a slow, heavy sound that made her skin crawl. She looked around, aware of how vulnerable she was out here alone on the edge of nowhere.

'Who is this?' She tried to make her voice strong but she came off sounding weak and more than a little bit scared.

The person on the other end of the line didn't speak. Just the breathing, loud and steady and lodging itself inside Dee's head.

Abruptly, she ended the call and stood up. It was getting dark, the pale grey evening light fading to an inky blackness.

Dee went inside and shut the doors, taking extra care to make sure they were locked. Most nights, she kept the blinds open so even when she was inside she could see the beach. Tonight, she pulled them down. But even after they had blocked out every bit of the outside world, she couldn't shake off the feeling that someone was out there, hidden in the darkness, watching her.

Twenty-five

Before

Sometimes, Cassie wondered if Paul knew the truth and was punishing her for what she'd done. His behaviour seemed to grow crueller with each passing week. She tried her best to keep him happy, never answering back or asking for money above the paltry weekly allowance he gave her. But no matter how hard she tried, he always found a reason to be angry with her.

Growing up, she'd imagined the perfect life she'd have as an adult. She would marry a man who loved her and earned enough money so she didn't have to work and could devote all her time to the children they'd have. They would live in a big house in the country, and they'd have animals and plenty of space for their children to run around. Her children would have all the things that Cassie herself never had. Lizzie would still be her friend, of course. They would live close to each other. Lizzie's husband and Paul would play golf together at weekends. Their children would become best friends, just like Lizzie and Cassie.

So far, Cassie thought bitterly, her dreams of married life were a long way from the reality.

Paul was late home again tonight. The third time this week he'd gone to the pub straight after work. She was trying hard not to let it get to her, but the anger was like a fire in her stomach, hot and burning and growing bigger until it felt as if her body would explode if she didn't do something. It wasn't that she minded him not being here. If anything, it was easier because it meant she didn't have to navigate his dark moods or make sure Grace's crying didn't make him say or do something nasty. But tonight there was no food in the house and she'd been sitting here all evening, waiting for him to come home to give her some money so she could go out and buy something to eat. She tried telling herself he worked hard and there was nothing wrong with going out for a few drinks after work. But then she would walk into the kitchen and look at the empty shelves and all reasoning disappeared.

It was almost ten o'clock and she had no idea when he'd be home. She had called him and sent him a text message, but he hadn't answered his phone and still hadn't replied to the text. She kept checking her phone, waiting for a reply that never came, and hating herself for doing it. She had changed, become needy and lonely and nothing like the Cassie she'd been before she got married and became a mother. That Cassie would never have sat here like some sad fifties' housewife, waiting for her man to come home. She would have been waiting with a knife in her hand, ready to plunge it into his black heart for the way he was treating her.

Grace was eighteen months, and still not sleeping through the night. Paul had made it clear that the night feeds were Cassie's responsibility. He had to be up early for work, he'd explained, whereas Cassie could lie in bed all day if she wanted. She hadn't told him that staying in bed was impossible with a young child. It wouldn't have made any difference, and besides, there was a part of her that didn't like the idea of him being alone with Grace. The underlying worry was always with her. The fear that, one day, he would realise how she had deceived him.

The desire to stay up and confront him battled with Cassie's need to sleep. She knew the only way to cope with the never-ending, low-level exhaustion that came from long-term sleep deprivation was to be in bed before ten. That way, if she was lucky, she got a few hours' sleep before Grace woke up.

Her stomach cramped, fear replacing anger at the idea that she might one day have to do this by herself. That she would end up being the one thing she'd dreaded becoming: a single mother with no money and no options. That she would end up just like her own mother, miserable and alone and utterly without hope.

'Marry money,' her mother had said, her words slurred and difficult to understand because she was drunk. 'Don't make the same mistakes I did.'

Not becoming her mother had been the single thing that had defined most of Cassie's life. It was Paul who'd first realised she was pregnant. Cassie's periods had always been irregular, and she hadn't noticed that she was two months late. She shivered, remembering the moment. Paul's hand running over the swell of her stomach, asking if there was anything she wanted to tell him. The cold fear, as it gradually dawned on her that she might be pregnant. Because that night, the one she would regret for the rest of her life, they hadn't been as careful as they should have been.

She had denied it, of course. But Paul insisted on buying a test and sitting with her while she peed on the stick. Her horror, when she saw the two blue lines that meant she was pregnant, was in complete contrast to his jubilation. When he got down on his knee later that morning and asked her to marry him, she'd said yes because she didn't know what else to do. He was so happy and she allowed herself to be swept up in the fantasy he created for her. Never once stopping to ask herself if this was what she really wanted.

She was in bed and asleep when Paul came home. She didn't wake up until he was in bed beside her. She was lying with her back to him and pretended she was still asleep. Even when he put his arms around her and started stroking her breast, she didn't move or give any indication she was awake. And when he pushed his erection against her and moved her until he was able to thrust himself inside her, she bit down on her lip to stop herself screaming out loud.

Twenty-six

'You don't need to stay,' Ed rasped. 'I know you've got other things to do.'

'I like it here.'

The comment triggered the hacking sound that Dee had come to recognise as Ed's laugh. She wanted to know when his voice and laugh would stop sounding the way they did now, but didn't know how to ask without embarrassing him.

'What's so funny?' she said instead.

'You are.' Ed coughed and Dee tried not to flinch. However bad his laugh was, it was nothing compared to his cough, which sounded like someone was scraping sandpaper along the inside of his throat. 'Has anyone ever told you what a terrible liar you are?'

'Okay, I'm not a fan of hospitals,' she admitted. 'But I'm not here for my love of hospitals. I'm here for you.'

'I love that you're here, but I don't expect it, Dee.'

'Where else would I be?'

'Oh, I don't know. Working on your book, or trying to find out who killed Paul Cavellini?'

'I'm not doing a very good job of that,' Dee said. 'It feels like no matter what direction I take, I hit a dead end sooner or later.'

'You'll get there eventually,' Ed said.

'How can you be so sure?'

'Because I know you. You're not someone who gives up on something once you've started it. You're the most determined person I've ever met.'

'Determined or pig-headed?' Dee said.

'Both.' Ed smiled. 'I remember when I first met you. Ella and Jake had disappeared, and Ella was the chief suspect in a murder investigation. You never once believed she was guilty. And you threw yourself into proving she hadn't killed that poor woman. In all the time I've known you, you've never given up on something until you've got to the truth.'

Unexpectedly, a lump appeared in Dee's throat and her vision blurred as tears filled her eyes and threatened to embarrass her.

'Thanks, Ed.' She put her hand on his and they stayed there like that for a long time, sitting together without saying anything.

He was still in the stroke unit, in a ward with a TV screen and seven other patients. Yesterday afternoon, the consultant looking after him had warned them both that Ed could expect to be in hospital for a while longer. When Ed had asked what happened after that, the consultant had smiled at Dee and said Ed was lucky he had someone to care for him when he was finally allowed home. So far, Dee hadn't found the courage to ask exactly what sort of care he was going to need.

'I'm getting sleepy,' Ed said. 'Mind if I close my eyes for a bit?'

His face was grey, his eyes drooping as if it was an effort to keep them open.

'Of course I don't mind,' Dee said. 'You get some rest. I'm going to go grab a coffee. Do you want me to get you anything?'

'I'm fine, thanks.'

While she queued up for coffee, Dee tried to contain the swell of grief as she thought of that lovely, vibrant man lying in bed unable to do anything for himself. She vowed she would do everything in her power to get him back to his old self as quickly as possible.

After paying for her coffee, she walked back to the ward full of fresh resolve. She was going to sit down with Ed, tell him he had to move into her house when he came out of hospital and, together, they would focus on his recovery to the exclusion of everything else.

But when she got back to the ward, Ed was already asleep. She sat by his bed and drank her coffee. By the time she'd finished it twenty minutes later, he was still asleep. After another twenty minutes, she kissed him gently on his forehead and whispered that she'd be back in later.

In her car, Dee thought about how she was going to spend the next few hours. She wanted to come back to see Ed this evening, but that gave her a bit of time to herself first.

Taking out her phone, she opened the internet and typed in 'Mark Collier' and 'Croydon'. The first search result was a website for a business called Picture This. The blurb on the website informed Dee that Picture This offered 'bespoke painting and decorating solutions' for domestic and commercial clients in Croydon and the south-east of England. The owner and founder of the company was a man called Mark Collier.

The website had a gallery of photos. Most of these were before and after shots of various projects Mark had completed. There was also a photo of Mark himself – a lean and healthy-looking man with cropped hair, who appeared to be around the same age as Cassie. Joey had described Cassie's ex as a loser, but it was quite possible he had turned his life around since then. If, of course, this was the right Mark Collier.

Dee examined his photo, searching his face for any similarities with the images she'd seen of Grace Parker. They both had brown eyes, but, apart from that, it was difficult to see any resemblance. The problem was, Grace looked so like her mother, it was impossible to see past that and find any trace of her father in her features.

Opening the page with the company's contact details, Dee found the phone number and called it. Almost immediately, a man answered.

'Hello?'

'Hi,' Dee said. 'Is this Mark?'

'That's right.'

'Great. I'm looking for a quote to get some work done on my house.'

'What sort of work are you thinking about?' Mark asked.

'Um, my kitchen needs updating. I haven't done anything to it in years. Maybe the rest of the house too. What sort of services do you offer?'

'General painting and decorating,' Mark said. 'But I could certainly help with a kitchen refit too, if that's what you're after. With my wife, we also offer an interior design service. I could give you a few different quotes and you could pick and choose which services you'd actually like.'

'That sounds perfect,' Dee said.

'Perfect's a good start.' He laughed and Dee found herself smiling too, even though she knew if this was Cassie's ex he wouldn't be laughing for much longer. 'When would be a good day for me to pop around and see what you're thinking about?'

'Any day,' Dee said. 'I work from home so I'm pretty flexible.'

'Where do you live? I'm finishing a job in Three Bridges tomorrow. If you're near there, I can drop by yours in the evening after work.'

'I actually live in Croydon,' Dee said. 'You were recommended by a friend.'

'Which friend?'

Dee squeezed her eyes shut before answering.

'Her name's Cassie MacNamara.'

She heard a sharp intake of breath just before he ended the call. When she tried calling him back, she got his voicemail. Dee didn't bother leaving a message. There was no need. She'd got exactly what she wanted.

Twenty-seven

Dee woke early Friday morning and sat on the deck, drinking coffee while an orange sun rose on the horizon and the world turned from grey to burning ochre before the colours flattened out again and dawn became day.

It was three weeks today since Grace's body had been discovered. Two weeks and four days since Cassie had gone missing. With every day that passed, there seemed to be another story in the press about Cassie MacNamara. Between them, the nation's journalists appeared to have tracked down every person who'd ever known Cassie when she was growing up in Croydon, as well as several women who'd been in prison at the same time as her. None of the people chosen to be interviewed had a good word to say about Cassie. Presumably, Dee thought bitterly, that's exactly why they'd been chosen.

She had finished her coffee and was planning out her day, when she heard a car pulling up at the front of the house. She rarely had visitors, and certainly didn't feel like seeing anyone this early.

Her mood didn't improve when she walked around to the front of the house and saw Joey Cavellini hauling himself out of a white sports car.

'Dee, glad I caught you.'

He gave her the benefit of his hundred-watt smile as he walked towards her, clearly under the misguided belief that she was pleased to see him.

'I'm afraid you've caught me at a bad time,' Dee said. 'I can spare you a few minutes, but no more than that.'

The smile faltered but didn't slip.

'A few minutes is more than generous,' he said. 'I'm so sorry. I should have called first. My head's all over the place at the moment, I'm not thinking straight. Actually, you know what? If this is a bad time, why don't I just go and come back some other time?'

The prospect of him coming back again was even less appealing than having to deal with him now, so Dee shook her head and told him it was okay.

'I can give you half an hour,' she said. 'But that's absolutely as much time as I can spare. And if you're lucky, I may even offer you a cup of coffee.'

'Thanks, Dee.' He took a deep breath, and closed his eyes briefly. 'I'm really grateful.'

She felt bad then, as she reminded herself that this was a man dealing with a terrible tragedy. She mightn't like him very much, but the least she could do was show him some basic courtesy.

'Is it okay if we sit on your lovely deck?' he asked, as he followed her around to the beach side of the house. 'It seems a shame to be here and not make the most of these amazing views.'

'Of course,' Dee said. 'You go and sit down while I make a fresh pot of coffee. Unless you'd prefer a cup of tea?'

'Coffee sounds great,' he said. 'Thanks.'

It was the second time he'd thanked her since he'd been here. His gratitude made Dee feel doubly shitty as she set about preparing the coffee.

'How's your investigation going?' Joey asked, when she came back outside a few minutes later.

'Slowly,' Dee said, pouring a mug of coffee and handing it to him before sitting down. 'Is that what you've come out here for – an update?'

'Not really,' he said. 'I'm trying to keep on top of everything, that's all. Trish isn't coping. Freya is doing her best, but I can see she's struggling as well. The police aren't exactly helping, either. How hard can it be to find Cassie and get this case wrapped up once and for all?'

'Rachel Lewis is a good detective,' Dee said. 'I'm sure she's doing her best.'

Although in truth, Dee had heard no more about the case and had no idea how the investigation was progressing.

'If that's her best,' Joey said, 'I'd hate to see her on a bad day. You know they still haven't managed to find Grace's cardigan or necklace? They're vital clues, but when I phoned Lewis yesterday to ask about them, she honestly sounded like she didn't know what I was talking about.'

The white cardigan and the silver pendant necklace Grace had been wearing the night she disappeared were missing when the police found Grace's body, and there'd been widespread speculation that the killer had taken them. Although no one seemed clear on why the killer would do that.

'Joey, I don't mean to be rude, but do you want to tell me why you're really here? A friend of mine is in hospital and I'm hoping to get across to see him this morning.'

'What's wrong with your friend?' Joey asked.

'He's had a stroke. Luckily, it wasn't a bad one. At least, it doesn't seem to be. But he's still got a long recovery ahead of him. He's in hospital here in Eastbourne, but I'm hoping he'll be able to come home soon.'

'Okay.' Joey nodded. 'The last thing I want to do is hold you up any longer than necessary.'

'So tell me why you're here and then we can both get on with our days.'

'I'm worried about you.'

Joey reached across the table and took Dee's hand. The gesture was overly intimate and made her feel deeply uncomfortable.

'Forgive me,' he said, when she pulled her hand away. 'I shouldn't have done that.'

Dee stood up, pushing her chair back so hard it fell over. 'I think you should go.'

'Of course.' He stood up as well. 'I didn't mean to upset you, Dee. Just hear me out. I've been thinking about this, going over and over it, trying to work out if I should say anything. But I know if I don't and something happened to you, I'd never forgive myself. When you told Grace you couldn't help her, she decided to go it alone. She started looking into Paul's murder, speaking to anyone who knew Cassie and Grace at the time. You don't know her, but when she got her teeth into something she wouldn't give up. She was relentless.'

'Why are you telling me this?'

Dee was breathing too fast, but she couldn't help it. Fear and anger causing her adrenaline to spike.

'Because if Grace's death was connected to whatever she found out about Paul's murder, you could be next.'

'You need to leave.' She took a step back, suddenly aware of the overpowering stink of his cologne clogging the insides of her nose and mouth.

'I'm not trying to scare you, Dee. I could have said nothing, but I felt I needed to tell you what I'm thinking. If I didn't, and something happened to you, I'd never be able to forgive myself.'

Twenty-eight

Freya was scrolling through Instagram looking at posts from Zoe, the DJ Lloyd had been talking to at the wine bar. Zoe posted several times a day. Lots of the posts were about her music, photos of her behind a DJ deck in front of hundreds of people. Lloyd had been tagged in three recent posts, although they were all from the weeks before Grace had disappeared. He hadn't responded to the posts, but he must have seen them because you always got a notification from Instagram when someone tagged you in a post. Freya zoomed in on the photos, searching for her sister's face in the dancing crowds. But if Grace was there, she couldn't see her.

She was listening to music through her headphones. Mitski's pure and haunting voice filling her head. A hand on her shoulder jerked her away from a world of losing dogs and crushed little stars. When she looked up, she saw her mother's face, eyes red-rimmed and watery, a frown creasing the centre of her forehead.

Reluctantly, Freya hit pause and removed the headphones.

'I knocked,' Mum said, 'but you didn't answer.'

'Is everything okay?' Freya asked.

'Joey's on the phone to the police, so I thought I'd come and see how you're doing.' She sat down heavily on the side of the bed.

Breathing in her mother's smells of stale alcohol and days'-old sweat, a wave of sadness washed over Freya. Until a few months ago, Mum had been the most glamorous of all her friends' mothers. Then all this business with Grace had kicked off and the mum Freya had known her entire life seemed to disappear overnight. Replaced with this shell who stayed up late drinking too much wine and didn't shower for days on end. Some part of Freya knew that her mum might have recovered eventually from her big falling out with Grace, but she would never recover from this.

'Joey's obsessed,' Freya said. 'Why can't he leave the police to get on with their job? I'm sure they're doing the best they can. Calling them every day is a waste of time.'

'He's sad,' Mum replied. 'You know how close he was to your sister. He feels helpless, and I suppose calling the police at least makes it feel like he's doing something.'

'What if Cassie didn't do it?' Freya said.

Mum's whole body stiffened, and when she spoke again, her voice was cold and angry-sounding.

'Your dad and I put that court protection order in place to keep Grace safe. Cassie broke that order, and now Grace is dead. You can't seriously believe the two things are unconnected?'

The truth was, Freya didn't know what to believe. She knew, because to think otherwise was inconceivable, that Lloyd hadn't done it. But she couldn't understand why her mother and her uncle were so convinced Grace's killer had to be Cassie.

'Not that your dad ever gave a damn about her,' Mum continued. 'He never wanted us to adopt her, you know. He was willing to let my brother's child, my own niece, go into foster care. But that's your father for you. A selfish bastard who never thinks of anyone except himself.'

Freya's hands clenched into fists. Moments like this, she hated her mother. All through her life, Freya had tried to work out why he'd left. She had times when she blamed Grace, believing if her parents had never adopted her then their marriage would never have broken up. Other times, she blamed her mother. If Mum had been a better wife, he might have stayed. But these moments always passed and, inevitably, Freya always came back to the single fact she couldn't ignore: her father had left because he didn't love her enough to stay. She could dance around that fact all she liked, try to find other reasons for his absence in her life, but deep down she knew this was the real reason.

'Will you come downstairs?' Mum said suddenly. 'Joey's keen to speak to you.'

Freya's stomach clenched. She couldn't face another conversation with her uncle, going back over the same thing again and again. Freya had lost count of the number of times Joey had sat her down and made her tell him every detail of Grace's secret meetings with her birth mother. He acted like he thought Freya was holding something back and if he asked her enough times she would eventually crack and tell him everything. Except there wasn't anything else to tell him. She wished she could get him to believe that.

'Please?' Mum said, when Freya didn't answer. 'He wants to ask you about Lloyd. Because the police have let him go again, and Joey isn't convinced that's a good idea.'

'You just told me you think Cassie killed her,' Freya said. 'So what does it matter if the police have let Lloyd go or not?'

'Joey's just trying to make sure the police do their job properly. Until someone is arrested and charged with Grace's murder, we have to assume everyone's a suspect.'

'Even me?'

'Of course not.' Mum stood up. 'Me, you and Joey – we all loved your sister. But outside this family, we can't trust anyone. Now do me a favour, darling, and come downstairs?'

'I'll be there in a few minutes,' Freya said.

'Thank you.'

After a long drawn-out moment, Mum left, staggering slightly as she closed the bedroom door behind her.

Freya tried to focus on her breathing the way her counsellor had taught her. It was important to do this because when the anxious thoughts started, Freya had always found it too easy to let them take over until they blocked out everything else and she became submerged beneath a dark, suffocating cloud.

When her phone pinged with an incoming message, it was a relief to have something else to focus on. The message was from Patrick.

> I'm outside. Fancy a picnic on the beach?

Somehow, they'd ended up meeting every day since she'd bumped into him outside the wine bar. He would message her, with an invitation to do something like go for a swim or a walk up the Downs. Freya found herself always saying yes to whatever he was suggesting. Probably because Marissa and everyone else seemed to have dropped her without a second thought. If it wasn't for Patrick, she literally wouldn't be seeing anyone from school at the moment.

Before she could reply, he sent another message.

> I've got gluten-free crackers and vegan chocolate (which tastes DISGUSTING, btw)

She smiled, couldn't help herself.

You've got no taste, she typed, *c u in 5*

She almost typed an *x* at the end, but managed to stop herself just in time. The last thing she wanted to do was give him the wrong idea about why she was hanging out with him.

Twenty-nine

The conversation with Joey had left Dee unsettled and on edge. She couldn't work out if he'd been genuinely concerned for her welfare or trying to scare her off. She kept remembering the sensation of his damp hand on hers, bigger and stronger. The underlying sense that, somehow, she could be in danger. If he'd been hoping to put her off, he was out of luck. The encounter had made her more determined than ever to uncover the truth about Paul's murder.

She spent the morning with Ed at the hospital and the afternoon working on her book. After that, she went for a swim before getting changed and driving to Caterham. Mark Collier had told her he was free this evening, which meant she had a good chance of finding him at home.

There'd been an address on the Picture This website. Following the directions on her satnav, Dee found herself driving down a wide, tree-lined street of detached, red-brick Victorian houses. The house she wanted was midway down the street. She parked a little way further along, got out of her car and started walking.

The house had a gravelled driveway, bordered on either side by a bed of red roses and purple dahlias. As she approached the front door, Dee had to step around two vehicles parked in front of the house: a silver-grey Mazda and a white van with the words *Picture This* on the side of it.

She rang the doorbell and waited. Moments later, the door was opened by a woman with wavy, honey-blonde hair and the lean physique of someone who spent long hours in a gym.

'Hello.' The woman smiled expectantly at Dee.

'I'm looking for Mark,' Dee said. 'I hope I've come to the right place.'

'Right place, but wrong time, I'm afraid. He's not here. Is this about work? If it is, the best thing to do is leave me your number and I'll get him to call you back.'

'Maybe I could wait for him?'

'Sorry, I'm on my way out. You just caught me. Leave me your details and I'll pass them on. What's your name?'

'Dee. I'm a friend of someone Mark used to know when he lived in Croydon.'

The woman's eyes narrowed as she took another look at Dee. 'Mark doesn't have anything to do with his old life. Whoever you are, he won't want to see you. I think you should leave now.'

'Please,' Dee said. 'It's important. I really need to see him. It's about Cassie MacNamara.

'Nina?'

Dee turned around to see Mark Collier walking towards the house, two young boys running ahead of him.

'Mummy!' one of them shouted. 'Daddy bought us ice creams after swimming.'

'Is everything okay?' Mark asked, looking between Dee and the woman called Nina.

'She says she wants to speak to you about Cassie,' Nina said.

A flash of pain across his face, gone so quickly Dee might have imagined it.

'Take the boys inside,' he said to Nina. 'I'll deal with this.'

She opened her mouth to speak, then seemed to change her mind.

'Come on,' she said, speaking to the boys. 'Let's get you into the bath and ready for bed.'

As the boys and their mother retreated inside, Mark stepped towards Dee. There was something in his face she didn't like, and it took all her courage to stand her ground as he moved so close she could feel the heat of his body and smell the bitter stink of nicotine on his breath.

'You're the woman who called yesterday,' he said.

'I'm not here to cause trouble,' Dee said. 'I'm a friend of Cassie's and I really do need to speak to you.'

'You think I'm stupid?'

She could feel his breath on her skin, damp drops of spittle landing on her cheeks.

'I've seen the news. I know what's happened, and why you're here. You want to see what dirt you can dig up on her. So you turned up at my house where my wife and children live, trying to get me to speak about a time in my life I never want to think about. How dare you?'

'Dad?' One of the boys appeared at the front door. 'I left my bag at the swimming pool.'

'It's all right, Dylan,' Mark said, not taking his eyes off Dee. 'I'll go back and get it for you. I'll be with you in a few minutes, okay?'

The little boy started to speak, but his father held his hand up.

'Inside, Dylan. Now.'

'I'm not here to hurt Cassie,' Dee said. 'I want to help her. I think she's been the victim of a terrible miscarriage of justice and I'm trying to put that right.'

Not exactly true, but Dee figured it was the best way to get him to open up to her.

'Cassie didn't kill Paul,' he said vehemently. 'She was stitched up.'

'Who killed him, then?' Dee asked.

'You need to go.'

Anger radiated off him and Dee found herself stepping back, needing to put some space between them. 'You've got exactly two seconds to get the fuck out of here, before I grab you and drag you out myself.'

'I think you might be Grace's father,' Dee blurted.

'How dare you?'

She saw his hand lift, as if he was going to hit her. Dee would never know if he'd actually have gone through with it, because suddenly his wife was there, throwing herself in between them.

'Get away from us,' Nina shouted. 'Leave my family alone. We've already been through too much. We don't need this as well. Leave, or I'll call the police.'

Before Dee could say anything else, Nina Collier had grabbed her husband by the arm and dragged him inside the house, slamming the door in Dee's face.

Thirty

Night was drawing in across the sky when Dee arrived home. At this time in the evening, the beach was deserted and the sense of peace was like a balm as she stepped out of the car and breathed in the warm, salty air.

Pulling her key out of her bag, she pushed open the front door and paused. Someone was inside the house. She heard footsteps, and the clink of a glass being placed on the kitchen worktop.

'Hello?'

Silence, then the click of the bifold doors closing and the patter of more footsteps, this time on the outside deck at the back of the house. Dee held her breath and waited, listening for other sounds. But there was nothing, apart from the usual rumble of the sea rolling in and out over the shingle beach and the screeching of seagulls criss-crossing the pink-tinted sky.

She walked slowly through the house. When she reached the open-plan living area, the smell hit her. Familiar, but so utterly out of place it took a moment for her brain to register what it was. When it did, she felt the first tingle of fear.

The smell was cigarettes. Dee didn't smoke, but her ex-husband had been a smoker. One of the few concessions he'd made was to never smoke inside their London home. Yet somehow, the smell of the cigarettes he smoked had managed to permeate every corner of the house. It stuck to Billy's body and he brought it with him everywhere he went, until the entire house stank of old cigarettes. Now the same smell was here, inside her house.

Pushing down the panic that was making her heart beat too fast and her cheeks flush with heat, Dee scanned every corner of the room, looking for signs of a break-in. But everything seemed in its right place. Her laptop was open on the small table by the window. The TV and stereo were exactly where they were supposed to be. The oversized painting she'd purchased last summer was hanging where it always hung over the low bookcase that ran along the far wall.

The bifold doors were closed but not locked. Dee slid them open and stepped outside as she remembered telling Cassie about the empty mobile home. And then she remembered other things too: Cassie smoking on the beach; Cassie walking out of Dee's house and disappearing; the missing milk from Dee's fridge, the same evening as Dee had found the back door open. She'd thought that was Nessa's doing, but she'd been wrong. Apart from the fact that Nessa was vegan and wouldn't touch cow's milk, she was also extremely conscientious. There was no way she'd have left Dee's house without checking everything was securely locked up.

When Dee went into the hall and checked the rack where she kept her keys, the one for the mobile home was missing. It wasn't a problem. There was another set of keys in her mother's old office. Dee went in there now, got the spare key and hurried along the beach.

As she drew closer to the mobile home, she saw immediately that her suspicions were correct. Someone had been here. The curtains in the front living room were slightly open. Dee knew, with absolute certainty, that the last time she'd been in there she had closed them completely, keeping the light out so it couldn't fade Jake's beautiful drawings.

Inside, she flicked on the light and looked around.

'Cassie?'

The small sitting room opened onto an even smaller kitchen. A corridor led to two bedrooms and a bathroom. The doors to all the rooms were open. From where Dee stood, she could see the entire mobile home. It was possible someone was hiding behind one of the doors or in the tiny wardrobe in the main bedroom, but the place was so small she would have heard them fidgeting or breathing.

The open doors and the gap in the curtains were proof, however, that someone had been here recently. Dee always kept the doors closed when the place was empty. If a fire broke out, open doors meant a much greater risk of the fire spreading.

The fridge and kitchen units were covered in Jake's drawings. The same drawings Dee had tried to protect from the sun by keeping the curtains drawn. They symbolised the different things in Jake's life that were important to him when he'd lived here. The beach and the sea. Stick drawings of his parents – Ella with her long, dark hair; Tom towering over her with legs that were too long, just as in real life. And another person in almost all the drawings. A woman with a frizz of dark hair and a wide smile, holding the hand of a smaller figure who Dee knew was meant to be Jake. Her name scrawled across the bottom of the drawing in his barely legible writing: *Dee*.

Swallowing down the hard lump in her throat, she opened the fridge door. A half-finished loaf of sourdough from the Poppyseed bakery, and some cheddar cheese wrapped in cling film. Dee knew the bread was from the Poppyseed bakery, because she'd bought it last Thursday evening. When she'd noticed it was missing, she'd assumed Nessa had eaten it. Just as she'd assumed Nessa had drunk the milk and left her back door open.

There were other signs that someone had been here recently. Drops of water in the shower tray, condensation on the window in the tiny bathroom. An indented pillow on the double bed, and a crease in the duvet cover as if it had been quickly pulled up without being smoothed out properly.

A sudden shrill sound made her yelp in fear, until she realised it was her phone ringing. When she went to answer it, she saw the call was from a withheld number.

'Hello?'

Silence, then the unmistakable sound of someone breathing.

A shiver of fear, as she realised she was completely alone. Normally, the silence and emptiness of this stretch of beach gave her comfort. Right now, with some stranger breathing in her ear, it had the opposite effect.

'Who the hell is this?' she said, hoping she sounded braver than she felt.

Keeping the phone pressed to her ear, she moved back through the mobile home, closing all the doors as she went.

She stepped outside, relieved to be out in the open with no small rooms to make her feel trapped.

'Cassie, is that you? Are you okay?'

A click, and the line went dead.

'Shit!' Dee kicked the side of the mobile home. Pain shot through the tip of her big toe and up her foot, causing her to curse again.

The sun was setting, as she hobbled back along the beach. Shots of orange streaking the sky and sea, while the shingle glowed as if there was a fire burning beneath it. Normally, Dee would have paused and taken a moment to simply watch it all, losing herself in the explosion of colour and light and the sheer perfection of the natural world.

This evening, her attention was drawn instead to the sound of a car driving towards her house. For a split second, she thought about turning around and running away, trying to find somewhere to hide. But rage replaced common sense and she hurried forward. She'd already been messed around enough. Whoever this was now, they had better have a good reason for being here or they would have a very angry Dee Doran to deal with.

Thirty-one

Before

Cassie had left her phone on the sofa when she'd heard Grace waking from her afternoon nap. If she hadn't, then maybe everything would have been all right. Paul wouldn't have found her phone and started looking through her messages, and now he was holding her by the collar of her shirt and smacking her face and asking her why there were so many messages from Mark.

'You're my wife,' he hissed, pushing his face into hers so that her head was pressed against the wall. 'So what the fuck are you doing sending messages to that scumbag lowlife? And why is he saying he's worried about you? What does he need to worry about? You live here with me in this lovely house and I provide for you and our child, and that good-for-nothing piece of shit thinks he has the right to worry about you?'

She saw his fist out of the corner of her eye, but he was holding her and she couldn't move. He punched her in the stomach, knocking all the air out of her body, leaving her wheezing and gasping for breath. She was whimpering, a pathetic sound that she couldn't control. Her bladder ached with a sudden need to wee, but she knew she had to hold it in. If she wet herself it would make him angrier than he already was.

'You've been calling him too,' Paul shouted. 'Six phone calls over the last three weeks. Are you sleeping with him? Is that what this is?'

'No,' she managed. 'I swear to you, Paul. I wouldn't do that to you.'

'Liar.'

He was right. She deserved his anger and his rage and his violence because she was a terrible person who had done a terrible thing and it was right she should be punished.

'I'm sorry,' she said. 'I'm so sorry. He calls me sometimes and I feel bad, so I call him back. It's only because I know he doesn't have anyone else. I won't ever call him again. I swear.'

She thought he was going to hit her again and she flinched, anticipating the punch. But he let her go, shoving her from him so forcefully that she fell to the ground. She scrabbled forward, needing to get away from him, but he put his foot on her back, the pressure forcing her flat onto her stomach.

'You won't ever phone him again.'

'No. I promise. I'm so sorry, Paul. I really am.'

She saw her phone land on the ground by her face. He lifted his foot off her back and stamped down on the phone. The crunch of broken plastic loud and final. She could feel the carpet against her face, the rough texture scratching her cheek. She could sense him standing over her, watching her, waiting for her to do or say anything that would give him a reason to hurt her again. So she stayed completely still, barely breathing in case it angered him.

She could hear Grace through the baby monitor, grizzling and growing impatient. Fully awake now. In a few seconds, she would start screaming for someone to come and lift her out of the cot. The need to go and get her, to pick her up and hold her and breathe in her soft baby smell, was strong. But Cassie was too scared to move.

'Don't fucking move.'

He started to walk away. The sitting-room door creaked as he pulled it open and, a moment later, his voice was coming through the baby monitor.

Bile rose up the back of Cassie's throat as she realised where he was. She lifted her head, looking through the open door and down the corridor. From here, she could see straight into Grace's bedroom. There he was, leaning into the cot and lifting Grace out. Her baby looked tiny in his arms that were big and muscled from hours spent in the gym. A gym he somehow still had the money to pay for, despite always telling her they needed to find a way of spending less.

She couldn't see his face, but she could hear his voice.

'Mummy's been a naughty girl,' he said. 'What are we going to do with her, Grace?'

Her daughter gurgled and giggled, and Cassie's hands curled into fists.

'Shall we go out somewhere?' he said. 'Just you and me. We'll leave naughty Mummy here so she's got time to think about what she's done.'

Cassie growled at the thought of him taking Grace away from her. She wanted to jump up, rip her baby from his arms and make sure he could never touch her again. But she knew the best thing to do, for now, was to stay still and let him think he'd won.

She'd married him for the security she'd never had as a child. He'd filled her head with empty promises and she had believed everything he'd said. But not any longer. He was the devil. An evil and cruel man who needed to be cut out of her life for good. He'd already told her, more than once, that he wouldn't ever let her leave him. He'd said he would kill her if she ever tried.

She stayed still and quiet while she listened to him change Grace's nappy, put her in the buggy and leave the house. She stood up as soon as she was sure he was gone. There was a mirror over the fireplace in the sitting room. Her mother's face stared back at her. White cheeks and a haunted look in the eyes that Cassie had never seen before.

Paul had done this to her. If she stayed with him, she would turn into the person she had always been scared of becoming. Her mother. She couldn't let that happen. She would kill him first, if that's what it took.

Thirty-two

As Dee got closer to the house, she saw Louise climbing out of her car and walking towards her.

'This is a nice surprise,' she said, relieved to see a friendly face after the evening she'd just had.

'You didn't get my text?' Louise said.

Dee had, in fact, received a text from Louise earlier. But she'd been driving when it came through. She'd meant to read it when she got home, but had forgotten.

'I haven't read it yet,' Dee admitted. 'Is everything okay?'

'I'm on my way back from Hastings,' Louise replied. 'As I was passing your place, I thought I'd drop in and see how you're doing. Any chance of a glass of wine? Just a small one, obviously, as I'm driving.'

Dee cast her mind back to last Saturday, sitting in Louise's garden drinking wine with her cousin who rarely drank any alcohol. Here she was again, asking for more wine. Dee promised herself she wouldn't let Louise leave this evening until she found out what was going on with her. First, however, she needed to call Rachel Lewis and tell her she thought Cassie had been hiding out in her mobile home.

'I need to make a quick phone call,' she said to Louise. 'Wine's in the fridge, help yourself. I'll be with you in a few minutes.'

While Louise went in to get some wine, Dee called Rachel, who answered almost immediately.

'Dee,' Rachel said, 'I've just been in to see Ed. He's doing pretty well, isn't he?'

'Not bad considering,' Dee said. 'Although the doctors still haven't given any idea of how much longer he'll have to be in hospital.'

'I'm sure they'll be keen to discharge him as soon as possible,' Rachel said. 'NHS waiting lists are horrendous at the moment. Will he move in with you when he comes out, or back to his own place?'

'We haven't worked out any of that yet.'

'It can't be easy for you,' Rachel added, her voice softening a little. 'Listen, it's not really any of my business, but make sure that whatever you decide is the right thing for both of you, not just Ed.'

'What do you mean?' Dee asked.

'When something like this happens, it's easy to think the only thing that matters is Ed's well-being. Don't get me wrong, he's one of my closest friends and his well-being is very important to me. But you need to think of yourself too. It won't do either of you any good in the long run if you move in together before you're ready for that.'

Part of Dee wanted to tell Rachel to mind her own business. But another, more mature, part of her knew Rachel was talking sense. So she thanked Rachel for the advice, before moving on to the reason for her phone call.

'I think I know where Cassie's been hiding,' she said, before going on to tell Rachel about what she'd found in the mobile home this evening. 'She was here the day she disappeared,' she explained. 'She left really suddenly. At the time, I didn't know why, but when I think back on it, I'm pretty sure she left because I started talking about the child protection order. She already knew the mobile home was empty. I keep the key in the hall, with a tag on it, so it's easy to see what it's for. I imagine she grabbed it on impulse and later, when everything became too much, she went there to hide away from it all.'

'Any idea where she might have gone now?' Rachel asked.

'None, I'm afraid. She might come back, but I doubt it. I'm worried about her, Rachel.'

'How long since she was there, do you think?'

'Half an hour,' Dee said. 'Forty-five minutes at the most.'

'Well she doesn't drive, so she can't have gone too far. Try not to worry, Dee. We'll find her. As soon as we do, I'll call to let you know.'

Louise had come out while Dee was on the phone to Rachel. She had two glasses of wine in her hand and handed one to Dee when she hung up.

'Cassie was here all this time?' Louise said.

'Looks that way.'

Louise looked along the beach towards the mobile home. 'I hope they find her.'

'Why? So they can arrest her and lock her up?'

'No.' Louise frowned. 'Don't be such a bitch, Dee. I mean for her own sake. She must be going through hell right now.'

'Sorry.' Dee sat down on one of the rattan chairs and took a deep slug of wine. 'It's been a long day.'

'Tell me about it,' Louise said, sitting down as well.

'I was hoping you'd do that,' Dee said.

'What do you mean?'

'Tell me what's going on with you at the moment.'

'How do you know something's going on with me?' Louise said.

'Because I know you,' Dee said. 'Now, come on. Spit it out.'

'Oh, okay then. If you must know, I handed my notice in this week.'

'You what?' Dee sat up straighter in her chair while she waited for this news to sink in. Louise had worked for the *Eastbourne Recorder* ever since leaving school. She had never gone to university, choosing instead to stay here in Eastbourne and carve a career for herself in local journalism. For the last twenty years, Louise had been the paper's editor. Her whole identity was so intractably tied up with the paper, Dee couldn't imagine Louise ever doing anything else.

'No need to sound so surprised,' Louise said, 'you've known for a while I haven't been happy there.'

Dee knew Louise bitched about her job a lot. And, now she thought about it, there had been a bit more bitching of late. But she'd never thought it was anything more than the general moaning people did about their jobs. She'd never thought Louise had been serious when she'd spoken about leaving some day to do something different.

'What are you going to do?' she asked.

'Nothing for a bit,' Louise said. 'Take some time out, think about who I am and what I want do to with the rest of my life. I've devoted so much of my life to that job, Dee. I barely know who I am without it, but I'm looking forward to finding out.'

'Well, congratulations,' Dee said, raising her glass in Louise's direction. 'It takes a lot of guts to make a decision like that.'

'I don't think I had a choice,' Louise said. 'It wasn't making me happy, anymore. All the cutbacks, the lack of resources to do anything properly. I hate what's happened to local journalism in this country. I stayed because I felt I hadn't got a choice. Then I realised a few weeks ago, that was rubbish. The system's broken. I can't change that, no matter how much I want to. But I can change myself. I'm fifty-one years old, Dee. I've probably lived over half my life already. I want to make sure I make the most of whatever time I have left.'

Unexpected tears pricked Dee's eyes. She thought of Ed and his plans to go travelling in a campervan. Now he was lying in a hospital bed, his future far less certain than it had been a few weeks ago. For all she knew, he might never get to travel again.

'You're absolutely right,' she said.

'You think so?'

'Yes.' Dee reached out, took Louise's hand and squeezed it tight. 'I really do, Lou.'

Thirty-three

Dee spent the next morning in the hospital with Ed. While she was there, the consultant in charge of his care came to tell them how well Ed was doing. If things continued like this, Ed would be allowed home at some point next week.

'Don't look so scared,' Ed said, after the consultant left. 'I have no intention of asking you to move in to be some sort of glorified nurse. I'm more than capable of looking after myself.'

'I'm not scared,' Dee said. 'And we both know you'd hate me living in your house, messing up all your stuff and putting your CDs back in the wrong order.'

'Good. I'm glad we both know where we stand.'

The conversation she'd had with Rachel last night replayed inside Dee's head.

Blocking out Rachel's voice, Dee smiled at Ed. 'That's why I want you to move in with me,' she said.

'No.'

'Yes.'

'Dee.' He reached out and took her hand. 'It's very lovely of you, but I can't do that.'

'You don't have a choice,' she said. 'It's not like I'm suggesting we live together permanently. This would be a temporary arrangement, until you're back on your feet again. If you say no, I'll end up spending all my time driving between both our houses to check you're okay.'

'Not if I go to Norfolk.'

'There's no need for that. I have more than enough room at mine. It makes perfect sense, Ed.'

'I've already spoken to Nessa,' he said. 'She's happy for me to stay with her for a few weeks. She said the kids would love it, and I'd love spending some time with them. In a few years, they won't want to hang out with their uncle. I may as well make the most of this opportunity to get to know them a bit more before that happens.'

Dee pulled her hand away, angry that he seemed to have made his mind up without bothering to consult her first.

'Don't be like that,' Ed said.

'Like what?' she snapped. 'Hurt and upset because you don't want me to be there when you need me? I don't understand you. A couple of weeks ago, you were telling me you want to hire a camper van and go travelling around Europe with me. Now you're saying you can't bear to spend a few weeks with me when you come out of hospital?'

'I don't want to be with you when I'm like this,' he said. 'It's not fair on you.'

'Even if it's what I want?'

'You might think it's what you want,' he replied, 'but you're not being honest with yourself. Look at how busy you are right now. You're really going places with your career, you're consumed with the work you're doing for Cassie. If I move in, how are you going to find time to do all that? The simple answer is, you won't. Something will have to give and I don't want to be the reason for that.'

'You really think I'd put my job ahead of you?'

Part of her knew she was being unreasonable. He was only voicing the concerns she'd had herself. Yet hearing him say them made her realise how selfish she'd been. This was Ed, one of the few constants in her life these days. She owed it to herself, as much as to him, to be there when he most needed her.

After Louise left last night, Dee had sat up late reflecting on the choices she'd made in her own life. Like Louise, most of Dee's life had been devoted to her job. Unlike Louise, Dee had never had children of her own to bring some much-needed balance to her life. There'd been the few years of caring for her mother, but Dee went straight back to work after that. She had, she realised, defined herself by the jobs she'd done and she wasn't sure, when she was lying on her deathbed, if that was going to be enough.

She had known for a long time that she loved Ed, yet she had been more than willing to keep him at arm's length. This was her chance to change that, to be brave like Louise and take a jump into the unknown.

'What about your follow-on appointments?' she said. 'They'll all be here in Eastbourne.'

'I've spoken with the consultant and he's happy to transfer my outpatient care to a hospital up there.'

'Even though there's no need for that because you can stay here in Eastbourne with me?'

'I don't want to talk about this anymore,' Ed said.

'Well I do. There's a whole lot more I have to say to you.'

But Ed had already turned his head away and closed his eyes, making it clear he wasn't going to listen.

'Is that it?' she said.

When Dee got no reply, she grabbed her bag and left. Outside the hospital, standing in the glaring heat of another scorching day, she felt exhausted. And angry. With herself for being a naïve fool, and with him for refusing to believe they could make this relationship work.

She marched across the car park to her car, mentally running through the conversation she'd have with him the next time she came in, planning the different things she could say to get him to change her mind. She was so involved in this imaginary argument that she barely noticed when her phone started ringing.

When she eventually heard it and saw who was calling, her anger faded.

'Rachel,' she said, as she took the call. 'Any news?'

'We got a call from the Beachy Head chaplains early this morning,' Rachel said.

Dee couldn't breathe. The Beachy Head chaplains were a team of volunteers who patrolled the white cliffs, watching out for people who had gone there to end their lives. The chaplains spent hours talking to these poor souls, trying to draw them back from the edge of the cliff and give life another chance.

'One of them found Cassie up there around 3am. She was in a bad way, but after a tricky few hours, the chaplain managed to talk her down. She's currently at the DGH undergoing a mental health assessment.'

'I'm at the hospital now,' Dee said. 'Can I go and see her?'

'I'm afraid not,' Rachel said. 'She's under police protection.'

'She's what?'

'It's for her own safety,' Rachel said. 'She nearly took her own life, Dee.'

'Because she's in unbearable pain.'

'I know that. Believe it or not, I really am aware how fragile Cassie is. I promise you I'll make sure she's treated with the kindness and respect she deserves.'

'Sorry,' Dee said. 'You got me at a bad time. I'm glad Cassie's okay, and I'm grateful to you for calling to let me know.'

'That's okay,' Rachel said. 'Just promise me you won't go into the hospital trying to find her?'

'You can trust me.'

She thanked Rachel again before hanging up, turning around and walking back towards the hospital. The staff in the main reception told her Cassie wasn't being treated as an inpatient and suggested Dee tried Accident and Emergency.

Sure enough, that's where Dee found her. Looking tiny and lost, sitting between two female police officers who clearly weren't happy to see Dee.

'Please,' Dee said, giving them her best smile, 'I'm a friend. I just want to check she's okay.'

Not giving them a chance to speak, Dee crouched down in front of Cassie and took her hand.

'You shouldn't have to do this alone,' she said. 'I'm here for you, Cassie.'

Tears started falling down Cassie's cheeks. When she did nothing to stop them, Dee reached up and wiped them away with her thumb.

'I took your spare key,' Cassie said. 'I shouldn't have done that. I'm sorry. I needed a place to hide and the mobile home seemed perfect. But when I realised you knew I was there, I freaked out and ran away. I wanted it all to be over. It's too hard, Dee. I can't do this.'

'Yes you can,' Dee said. 'You've got to keep going, for Grace's sake.'

She would have said more, but one of the police officers intervened and told Dee she had to leave. Reluctantly, Dee stood up to go.

'Hang in there, Cassie,' she said, walking away. 'I won't let you down.'

She had barely left the hospital when she got a text from Rachel:

> Do you deliberately try to piss off everyone around you or is this something you can't help?

Dee tapped a quick reply:

> Just you, Rachel. X

Unsurprisingly, she didn't get any reply.

Thirty-four

Dee couldn't relax. She'd spent the rest of the day working on her book and trying not to think about the row with Ed. She kept checking her phone for a message from him that never came.

Later that evening, after the sun had set, she poured herself a glass of wine and paced restlessly around the downstairs of her house. She tried to imagine Ed here with her, allowing herself to admit how she really felt about it. Scared, of course. But something else too. Optimistic. She really believed they could make it work. If only she could get him to see this too.

Her anger had faded and she felt bad about how the conversation had ended. Ed was a proud man and Dee could understand why he wouldn't want her looking after him. He would worry, she knew, that it would change the balance of their relationship, making him more dependent on her than he would feel comfortable with. She needed to speak to him, tell him she understood and apologise for being such a pig-headed idiot earlier. But when she called his phone, she got his voicemail.

'It's me,' she said. 'I wanted to apologise for earlier. Call me when you get this?'

She hung up and considered what she should do now. She hadn't eaten, but the tight knot in her stomach meant she wasn't hungry. It was tempting to pour herself another glass of wine, but the way she was feeling meant she wouldn't stop at just one more tonight. She would keep going until the entire bottle was empty.

So she made a cup of tea instead. When it was ready, she sat on the living-room floor with a sheet of A3 paper in front of her. This was how she liked to work: creating a mind map of all the information inside her head, laying everything out visually until she started to see the threads that connected it all. She used lines to indicate a connection – a dotted line for a possible link between two things or people and an unbroken line where there was a definite link. If there was no connection, there was no line.

She started with the things she knew, drawing two circles in the middle of the page and writing a name inside each one: 'Paul Cavellini' in the circle on the left; 'Grace Parker' in the circle on the right. Slightly beneath them, and halfway between each, she wrote Cassie's name inside another circle. Then she drew a straight line between each of the circles.

Half an hour later, the page was covered in writing and Dee's back was starting to ache. She sat back, looking at what she'd written so far. There were too many people she hadn't been able to speak to yet. Using her pen, she circled each of their names in turn. Lizzie Collier, who had testified against Cassie during the trial. Trish Parker, Joey's sister and Grace's adopted mother. And Grace's boyfriend, Lloyd Armstrong.

Joey seemed to think Grace was killed because she'd been looking into her father's murder. If that was the case, then Dee needed to find what connected the two murders. Apart from the obvious fact that both victims were related to each other.

David Verney's name was on the list. Dee had drawn a dotted line between his name and Grace. But if Grace had been investigating her father's murder, she might well have spoken to David. Dee wondered if the dotted line should be a solid one instead.

Picking up her phone, Dee scrolled through her list of contacts until she found David's name, and called him.

'Dee Doran,' he said, 'to what do I owe this dubious pleasure?'

'A very quick question,' Dee said. 'Did you ever meet Grace Parker?'

He waited a beat before answering.

'I'm sure the detectives leading the investigation into her murder wouldn't be too happy to hear you're trying to do their job for them.'

'You haven't answered my question,' Dee said. 'Did she contact you?'

'I thought I made it clear, the last time we spoke, that I have no interest in helping you waste your time trying to prove a guilty woman is innocent.'

'It's true then,' Dee said. 'You did speak to her.'

'I didn't say that.'

'You didn't have to. If you hadn't met her, you'd have told me. The fact you haven't tells me all I need to know.'

She picked up her pen and changed the dotted line between his name and Grace's to an unbroken line.

'I'm going to hang up now,' David said.

'Before you go, I thought you should know I've spoken to Mark Collier.'

'He still drinking these days?'

'Doesn't seem to be,' Dee said. 'He told me Cassie didn't kill Paul.'

'Oh yeah? He give you any reason why he thinks that?'

'He said she was stitched up.'

'Sounds to me as if he's filling you with a load of crap, love. I wouldn't believe a word that man says. Back then, he spent most of his time drunk, or high on drugs. I'm surprised he can remember anything from that time.'

Dee stood up, feeling the need to move. She walked onto the deck and scanned the beach, unsure what she was searching for in the darkness.

'Let me give you a piece of advice, Dee. Mark Collier is bad news. You need to be more careful, love. A woman like you, living by yourself with no neighbours around, that makes you vulnerable. You'd do well to remember that.'

'What do you mean?'

'You're not as safe as you think you are.'

She hung up then. And when he called her back a moment later, she switched her phone off so he couldn't get through. The knot of tension in her stomach was so bad, she thought she might throw up. David Verney's words seemed to reverberate around the empty beach.

A woman like you, living by yourself with no neighbours around, that makes you vulnerable.

She'd never told him she lived alone. Yet somehow, he'd found this out. Yesterday, Joey Cavellini had told her she was putting herself in danger. Now, David Verney had implied the same thing. They wouldn't be trying to scare her unless there was something they didn't want her to find.

Thirty-five

Ed called the following morning while Dee was eating her breakfast.

'I've only just heard your message,' he said. 'My charger died and I had to wait until today to borrow one from one of the nurses. I'm so sorry about yesterday, Dee.'

'I'm sorry too,' Dee said. 'I haven't given enough thought to how difficult this must be for you.'

'It's difficult for both of us. Listen, I've got to see the occupational therapist in a minute. Any chance you might drop in later?'

'Try and stop me,' Dee replied.

She was smiling when she hung up, her spirits instantly lifted. She had slept badly, anxious thoughts keeping her awake half the night. She had woken in a foul mood, but, after hearing from Ed, she resolved to make the most of the sunshine and try to enjoy the day.

Her resolve lasted all of half an hour, when another phone call sent her mood spiralling back down again. The call was from Rachel.

'Have you got a moment?' she asked.

'If this is about yesterday,' Dee said, 'I'm sorry, Rachel. I shouldn't have gone to see Cassie. I was worried about her, that's all.'

'That's not why I'm calling, actually. Although Cassie is the reason I need to speak to you. I've got some news, and you're not going to like it very much.'

'Go on,' Dee said.

'We charged Cassie with Grace's murder earlier this morning. She's being held in custody and will appear before the magistrate tomorrow.'

'You did what?' Anger, combined with a crushing sense of failure, made Dee speak without thinking first. 'Yesterday, you told me not to worry. You said you knew she was fragile and you'd take care of her. What was that, Rachel? A load of bullshit to sweeten me up so I wouldn't cause a scene at the hospital?'

'It wasn't bullshit,' Rachel said. 'Cassie's being properly looked after. But the facts speak for themselves. We have enough evidence to charge Cassie so that's what we've done.'

'Even if you know she loved Grace and would never have done anything to harm her?'

'Listen to me,' Rachel said. 'I called because I know you care about Cassie and I thought you deserved to hear this news from me. You should be thanking me, instead of speaking to me like I'm a piece of dirt. Not once, in all the time we've known each other, have I ever criticised you for the way you go about your work. Yet you seem to think it's okay to tell me I'm not doing my job properly?'

Some part of Dee's mind knew that Rachel was right, but anger won out over logic and she ploughed on regardless. 'If you don't like hearing my opinion, then you shouldn't have called.'

'You're damn right I shouldn't have called,' Rachel snapped, ending the call before Dee had a chance to say anything else.

–

Thirty minutes later, Dee was in her car driving back to Caterham. Mark Collier was the one person she'd met who didn't believe Cassie had killed Paul. Dee needed to speak to him again and find out why he was so convinced she hadn't done it. The prospect of another encounter with Mark wasn't something Dee relished but, right now, Cassie needed all the help she could get.

When Dee arrived at Mark's house in Caterham, however, she was out of luck.

'He's gone out for the day with the kids,' his wife – if that's who she was – informed Dee. 'You should be glad he's not here too. He was very angry after you left the other night.'

'I didn't come here to cause trouble for either of you,' Dee said. 'I'm just trying to find out the truth, that's all.'

'The truth about Paul Cavellini's murder, you mean?'

'And Grace Parker's murder too.'

So far, the press hadn't got hold of the news that Cassie had been charged, but it was only a matter of time before the police released a statement to that effect.

'I recognise you from the TV,' Nina said. 'Me and the kids love *The Big Chat*. Mark can't stand it, but you shouldn't take that personally. He rarely watches TV.'

'Any chance we could talk?' Dee asked.

'I'm not sure Mark would like you being here.'

'I don't have to come inside,' Dee said. 'I can stay out here or we can go for a walk. Whatever you think is best.'

She thought Nina might say no, but after a moment she nodded her head.

'There's a coffee shop a few streets from here,' she said. 'We can go there. This time on a Sunday it should be pretty quiet.'

At the coffee shop, Dee bought the drinks – coffee for her, green tea for Nina – and they sat at a table in the small garden at the back.

'What do you want to talk to me about?' Nina asked.

'I'm trying to get a sense of what Cassie was like back then,' Dee said. 'I know Mark and her used to go out together.'

'You asked Mark if Grace was his daughter,' Nina said. 'He doesn't know I heard you ask him that.'

'Do you think she might be?'

'I don't know. Since your visit, he's completely shut down. I can't get through to him, and that scares me. He's trying to process this by himself. Whatever "this" is. He's a typical man and still hasn't worked out that the best way to deal with the bad stuff is to talk it through with someone you trust, not bottle it up until it breaks you.'

'Did you know about him and Cassie before all this?' Dee asked.

'I knew they used to go out with each other,' Nina said. 'And I knew Mark was really cut up when she ended things between them. But he's never mentioned anything about Grace being his daughter. Which makes me think he never knew. Can you imagine what it was like for him when you turned up and told him she could be his? In a single moment, he finds out he might have a daughter he never knew about, but she's dead so he'll never get a chance to meet her. It's awful.'

Dee's cheeks burned with shame. 'I'm sorry,' she said. 'I should have thought before I opened my big mouth.'

Nina waved away the apology. 'I hoped I'd never have to hear that woman's name again. Cassie was his first love, the one that got away. Don't get me wrong, I'm not jealous. When you meet someone in your mid-thirties, they're bound to have baggage. God knows, I had plenty of it by the time we met.'

She smiled and, for the first time, Dee saw how beautiful she was. She had the sort of classic good looks that lasted with age. Delicate bone structure, naturally wavy blonde hair, clear skin and slate grey eyes that reminded Dee of the sea on a calm winter's day.

'We met in AA,' Nina continued. 'Two ex-alkies, trying to start over. My sponsor was really against Mark and I getting together. It's not always a good idea to date another alcoholic, because both of you have issues to deal with. More often than not, it can be a recipe for disaster. That's not how it was for us, though. Somehow, we saved each other.'

'My ex-husband was an alcoholic,' Dee said, feeling the need to give something in return for Nina's honesty. 'It destroyed our marriage.'

'So you know what it's like, then. And you must also realise how scared I am right now. I'm terrified Mark won't be able to cope and he'll start drinking again.'

'Tell me a bit more about Cassie and Mark,' Dee said.

'Not much more to tell, really. She dumped Mark and married Paul. After Paul was murdered, she tried to convince the police that Mark had killed him.'

'She what?'

'When the police turned up at the house the night Paul was killed,' Nina said, 'Cassie told them Mark had killed him. I think she truly believed he would take the hit. That he would hold his hands up and say *yes it was me. I killed him.* Luckily for Mark, the police had enough evidence against Cassie to charge her. She was convicted and that was the end of it. Or so we thought.'

'Hang on,' Dee said. 'This doesn't make any sense. Mark told me he doesn't believe Cassie killed Paul. He said something about a stitch-up.'

'I know.' Nina sighed. 'All these years he's been convinced she was set up. He doesn't think she's capable of doing something like that. But just because it's what Mark thinks, it doesn't mean he's right.'

'During the trial, a woman called Lizzie Collier gave evidence against Cassie. I assume she and Mark are related?'

'Lizzie's his sister,' Nina said.

'Is it possible she was trying to take police attention away from Mark?' Dee asked.

'I doubt it. Lizzie and Mark were never close, even before Paul's murder.'

'I've been trying to find her,' Dee said. 'Any chance you could give me an address or phone number?'

'Sorry,' Nina replied. 'Mark and Lizzie lost touch years ago. She moved away from Croydon soon after the trial. Went to university in Manchester and cut off all contact with her family. I couldn't tell you where she is now.'

Another dead end. Dee was getting sick of them. She left soon after that, giving Nina her phone number and asking her to call if she thought of anything else. Nina said she would, but Dee doubted she'd ever hear from her again. As Nina herself had said, her family was her world. She was a formidable woman, and Dee suspected she'd do whatever it took to keep her husband as far from Cassie MacNamara as she possibly could.

Thirty-six

Dee spent the rest of the day working on her book. In the early evening, she drove across to see Ed. When she entered his room, the first thing she noticed was that he was looking particularly pleased with himself.

'I've found Lizzie Collier.'

'You've what?' She pulled out the chair by his bed and sat down.

'Here.' He handed her his phone.

Dee found herself looking at a photo on Facebook of a couple on their wedding day. A tall, stooped man wearing a morning suit was holding hands with a woman dressed in a cream silk dress that looked like it had cost a lot of money. The photo had been posted four years earlier by someone called Marsha Adams. Underneath the photo, Marsha had typed *Liz and Neil's big day out.*

'His name's Neil Havers,' Ed said. 'He works with Marsha Adams for a German hedge fund company. The woman he married is your Lizzie Collier. Only she calls herself Liz these days. I've got an address too if you want it. The happy couple are living in Bray, a poncy commuter town in Berkshire.'

'Bray's not poncy,' Dee said. 'It's rather lovely, actually.'

'If you say so.'

'How did you find this? More important, why? You're meant to be resting, not doing work on my behalf.'

'I knew you were upset about Cassie,' Ed said. 'So when you called earlier and told me Lizzie had gone to Manchester University, I decided to try to find her. I called an old pal in

Greater Manchester and asked him to check the records for the university. Turns out Lizzie Collier studied law there. Graduated with a 2:1, and spent a few years working in the city until she had her first kid. Now, she's a full-time housewife.'

'Thank you.' Dee leaned forward and kissed him.

'Does this mean we're okay now?' he asked.

'I'll feel terrible if you don't come and stay with me,' Dee said. 'Plus, I don't think it's fair on Nessa and Javier. Their lives are busy enough already.'

'So is yours.'

'But I can shift some things around,' Dee said. 'It's easier for me. Besides, if you go to Norfolk, I'll miss you.'

'I'd miss you too. How about this? I'll think about it over the next few days and maybe we could chat again then?'

'Okay.' Dee smiled. 'Thanks.'

It wasn't ideal, because in Dee's mind there was nothing to think about. But if it made him feel better about it, then she was happy to give him more time to get used to the idea.

'Did Rachel tell you what evidence they've found against Cassie?' she asked.

'You know better than to ask me that, Dee. Rachel did you a favour calling to let you know Cassie had been charged. She didn't have to do that.'

'I guess not.' Dee knew she would have to call Rachel and apologise. Now that her anger had dissipated, she felt bad for the way she'd spoken to her. She'd always had a lot of time for Ed's partner. Given the fact that Dee could count on one hand the number of people she called a friend these days, she wasn't in any position to alienate someone who had always been good to her. 'I need to see Cassie,' she said. 'How do I go about doing that?'

'Emailaprisoner.com. You need to set up an account and then you can send an email to any prisoner in the UK.'

'It's that simple?'

'It really is.' Ed took her hand. 'It's so good having you here, Dee. I was wondering, do you fancy a walk down to the canteen?'

What she actually wanted to do was take out her phone there and then and email Cassie. Instead, Dee put on her brightest smile, squeezed Ed's hand and told him she'd love to go to the canteen with him.

–

That night, Dee had scheduled a Zoom catch-up with Ella, Jake and Tom. She poured herself a glass of wine, set up her laptop on the deck and sat down to join the meeting. Twenty minutes later, Dee's glass was nearly empty and no one else had joined the call. She was about to give up, when she saw Ella's face appearing on her screen.

'Sorry I'm so late,' Ella said. 'We were at the lake this morning and the traffic on the way back was terrible. It took me ages. How are you, Dee? It feels like forever since we've had a proper catch-up.'

'I'm good,' Dee said. 'Well, I'm okay. Ed's not been very well.'

She started to tell Ella about Ed's stroke, all the while waiting for Ella to be joined by the others. Most of the time, she was able to repress her longing to see Jake. Now, sitting in front of her laptop knowing that any moment he would make an appearance, she let some of those feelings of loss and longing come to the surface.

'I'm so sorry to hear about Ed,' Ella said. 'I'll get Jake to make him a card. He'll be sad when I tell him Ed hasn't been well. You remember how those two used to have such fun together?'

Dee remembered. She remembered all of it. Every big moment and all the small, insignificant ones too. Little Jake who had filled a hole in her life she hadn't realised was there.

'Ed would like that,' she said. Then, taking care not to sound too desperate, 'How's Jake doing? The seal is out today. I was going to take my laptop down to the water and see if we could find it together.'

'Oh Dee.' Ella's smile disappeared. For a short, sharp moment, Dee hated her because she knew what she was about to say. 'He was having such fun at the lake, he didn't want to come back home. We went with a group of his classmates. It didn't seem fair to drag him away. He'll be gutted not to have seen you, but I knew you'd understand. Plus, I figured it would give us a chance to catch up properly. There's so much I want to tell you. I haven't been able to the last few times, because Tom and Jake are always here.'

'That sounds great.' Dee smiled and hoped it was enough to convince Ella. The disappointment was so crushing she was struggling to catch her breath. 'Just let me go and get some more wine,' she said. 'I'll only be a sec.'

She stood up, grabbed her glass and hurried away before Ella could see how close to tears she was. In the kitchen, she splashed water on her face and told herself not to be so stupid. Of course Jake would want to be with his friends instead of being stuck in front of a laptop making awkward small talk with a woman he'd probably already started to forget all about. He was doing the right thing, moving on with his life. It was time Dee followed his example and moved on too.

Despite her disappointment at not speaking to Jake, Dee spent an enjoyable forty minutes chatting with Ella and catching up with everything that was going on in Canada. When they'd finished talking, it was late and Dee went into her bedroom to get ready for bed.

Before turning her phone off for the night, she sent Ed a text message telling him she'd see him tomorrow.

I'm looking forward to it, he wrote back.

Good, Dee replied. *See you then. Everything okay with you?*

A few seconds later, her phone pinged with his reply.

> A laugh a minute. Man in the next bed keeps farting. How are you?

Her fingers moved quickly over her phone keyboard as she tapped her answer:

> Good thx. I'll call in tomorrow. In the meantime, try not to breathe through your nose. Xxxx

She could see the three dots on her phone screen that told her he was typing back. After a few seconds, his message came through:

> Sleep tight, DD. Love you xxx

She blinked twice, then re-read the text. But the words didn't change, even when she read them a third time. She started to reply that she loved him too, before changing her mind and replacing the words with a simple *xxxx*.

Dee waited for him to reply, but, after a few minutes, it was obvious he wasn't going to. She switched her phone off, connected it to the charger, lay down and closed her eyes.

As her body started to relax, the thoughts swirling around her head slowed and settled. Her breathing grew deeper and she could feel sleep wrapping its warm embrace around her, ready to claim her for the night. And right then, as her mind slipped down into the darkness, she heard someone running along the beach outside the house.

Dee sat up, her heart beating fast and hard in her chest. A flash of light on the other side of the curtains. Footsteps sliding over stones, followed by an explosion of sound too loud and sudden as something huge and dark came hurtling towards her.

Thirty-seven

A rock. Not one of the white and grey stones from the beach. This was bigger, and infinitely more dangerous according to the Police Community Support Officers who had responded to Dee's 999 call. They asked Dee if she could think of anyone who might want to fire a rock through her bedroom window. She gave them two names: Joey Cavellini and David Verney, adding that she didn't really believe either man disliked her enough to throw a rock through her window. In return, the PCSOs had given Dee a crime reference number for her insurance company and told her they'd be in touch if they needed to ask her any further questions.

After clearing away the broken glass and covering the window with sellotaped pieces of bin liner, Dee spent the rest of the long night sitting on the deck watching daylight gradually move in across the sky as dawn announced the start of a new day.

As the orange sun crept up over the silver horizon, she ran across the shingle to the silent sea, stripped off and went for a swim. After that, there was nothing but water and sky and the golden splashes of sunshine trapped in the droplets of salty sea that exploded in the still air as Dee swam.

But the moment she was out of the water, the anxiety came rushing back. A black, heavy weight in the pit of her stomach that seemed to grow bigger as she walked up towards the house and saw the black plastic flapping in the gentle morning breeze.

She wanted Ed. She missed his wise words and his steadiness. If he was here now, he would know what to say to make her feel better. It was one of the reasons he'd become so special to her. Corny as it sounded, Ed filled in the missing parts of her and made her feel complete in a way she hadn't since the break-up of her marriage and the deaths of her parents.

By the time she'd finished showering and getting dressed, it was still early. Six thirty-five. Too early to call Ed. Instead, she decided to try to get some work done. She was sitting on the deck, drinking coffee and scrolling through her emails, when Louise phoned.

'Hey, Lou, is everything okay?'

'Where are you?' Louise said.

'At home. Where else would I be at this time?'

'With me,' Louise said. 'We were meant to be walking this morning.'

'Oh God, I completely forgot. Sorry.'

They tried to meet one morning a week to have a walk and a catch-up before the demands of work and, in Louise's case, family, took up the rest of their day. This morning, Dee remembered now, they had arranged to meet on the beach at Holywell.

'Give me fifteen minutes,' she said. 'I'll jump in the car and drive straight over.'

'It's almost seven,' Louise said. 'I promised Martin I'd be back home by eight.'

'That gives us an hour,' Dee said. 'See you soon.'

With its ornate Italian Gardens, quaint tea room and a stunning location at the western end of the seafront nestling beneath the white cliffs, Holywell was a popular spot with locals and tourists alike. During the summer season, the beach got very busy, but at this time in the morning there were very few people about.

It was already warm, despite the early hour. As they walked along the seafront, Dee had to take off the cardigan she'd put on and tie it around her waist. She had told Louise about the rock through her window and now was dealing with Louise's constant stream of questions and theories about who might have done it and why.

'Drunken yobs,' Louise said. 'We're getting so many reports of young people roaming the town in gangs at night. The situation's completely out of control. The police need to address the problem, before it damages our tourist industry. This town is getting more like Brighton and Hastings every day.'

Dee supressed a snort of laughter. Despite Louise's dark pronouncements, Eastbourne still had a decidedly genteel air about it. Like all English seaside towns, it had its fair share of poverty and associated problems. But it remained one of the safest and loveliest places Dee had ever lived in. On mornings like this, strolling along the seafront under a clear blue sky, it was impossible to imagine anything bad could ever happen in a place like this. Except, of course, bad things happened everywhere. Living somewhere pretty didn't change that. Grace's death proved that even the most beautiful places could be deadly.

'If it was some random gang, you'd have heard them, though. You said there was only one set of footsteps, which means there was just one person. Any ideas, Dee?'

'Not really.'

She didn't want to tell Louise her suspicions about David Verney and Joey Cavellini. If she did, Louise would try to lecture her on all sorts of things Dee didn't want lecturing about. Like being told to put her own safety first instead of trying to uncover the truth about a historical murder case.

'Maybe you should move out for a bit,' Louise said. 'At least until the police find out who did it.'

'I'm not leaving my home.'

'You could stay with us,' Louise offered. 'The kids would love it.'

'That's very kind,' Dee said, 'but we both know that wouldn't work.'

'Why not?'

'Lou, one of the reasons we still love each other is exactly because we've never lived together. I'm a messy, disorganised slob, whereas you're super organised and obsessively tidy. We'd end up arguing all the time.'

'Ed's obsessively tidy and that doesn't seem to worry you.'

'It's one of the reasons we don't live together,' Dee said.

'How's he doing?' Louise asked. 'I thought he seemed a lot better when I popped in to see him the other day.'

'He might be allowed home soon,' Dee said.

'That's fantastic news! You must be so relieved.'

'I am.' She smiled and linked arms with Louise. 'Although our conversation just now has reminded me it's not all going to be plain sailing when he comes out.'

'What do you mean?'

'I've asked him to move in with me,' Dee said. 'Not forever, just while he recuperates.'

'You sure that's what you want?'

'Of course I'm sure. Why do you ask?'

'Because you have this terrible habit of putting other people before yourself. It's lovely that you want to look after Ed, but you need to think about yourself too. Ed Mitchell isn't your responsibility.'

'I know that. Anyway, you don't need to worry. He's told me it's not going to happen.'

'Maybe that's for the best.'

'It's not,' Dee said. 'You're as bad as him. Why do you both seem to think I'm incapable of looking after him for a few weeks?'

A seagull flew towards them along the promenade, squawking angrily as it skimmed over the tops of their heads. Louise said something, but her words were lost beneath the seagull's screams. When Dee asked her to repeat what she'd said, Louise said it didn't matter.

'We should start heading back,' Louise said.

'We've got another ten minutes before we have to turn around.'

But Louise had already turned back and was walking fast along the promenade, as if she was trying to put as much space as possible between herself and Dee.

Thirty-eight

Dee spent a chunk of the rest of the morning phoning around, getting quotes for a replacement window. She eventually found someone willing to do the job this week, although the person she spoke to said it would likely be towards the end of the week. As today was only Monday, this wasn't ideal, but it was the best Dee was able to find.

To take her mind off the whole business, after lunch she drove across to Meads. She had never been to Albertine's before, although she'd passed it enough times and had often wondered what it was like inside. Her first impressions were that it was as close to France as you got on this side of the Channel. Decorated in shabby-chic style, with mismatched chairs and tables, stripped wooden flooring and Edith Piaf playing on a vintage turntable in the corner, Dee thought it was rather lovely.

Early on a Monday afternoon, the wine bar was quiet. A man Dee recognised from the news as Lloyd Armstrong was working behind the bar. As Dee approached, he smiled and asked how she was doing.

'Not too bad.' Dee opted for one of the tall stools at the bar, sliding her backside onto the seat.

'What can I get you?' he asked.

'A coffee, please.'

She watched him as he prepared the coffee. According to the news stories, Lloyd Armstrong was eleven years older than Grace. Dee wondered what Trish Parker had thought about her seventeen-year-old daughter dating an older man who had also happened to be her boss. The age difference and the fact he'd been Grace's boss hinted at an imbalance of power that didn't sit easily with Dee.

When the coffee was made, he placed the cup in front of her.

'Enjoy.' He gave Dee a smile that she was sure worked wonders on lots of his female customers, but did nothing for her.

While she waited for the coffee to cool, she took out her phone and pretended to look at it while she secretly observed Lloyd. A handful of other customers came into the bar. A couple of women wearing Lycra, and a group of older women who settled themselves at a table in the corner with much chat and laughter.

The Lycra women disappeared through a door at the back of the bar that seemed to lead to an outside area. Intrigued, Dee stood up to follow them and found herself in a pretty walled garden. As she settled herself at one of the tables out here, Lloyd came out and made a beeline for the women. They all clearly knew each other, because he greeted the women by their names and asked about their families before taking their drinks order.

On his way back inside, he stopped at Dee's table to ask if her coffee was okay.

'It's lovely,' she said. 'So is this place, actually.'

'I don't think I've seen you here before,' Lloyd said. 'Are you visiting Eastbourne or do you live locally?'

'I'm a local,' Dee replied. 'I've heard of Albertine's, but never had the chance to drop in before this morning.'

'I hope it doesn't disappoint,' Lloyd said, 'and that this won't be the last time you visit.'

He gave her another one of his smiles before turning to go.

'Actually,' Dee said, 'there's something I wanted to ask you.'

His shoulders visibly tensed, but he was still smiling when he turned back to her. 'Sure, what can I do for you?'

'I know Cassie,' Dee said, speaking fast so she could tell him why she was here before he kicked her out. 'I know she and

Grace had been meeting up. Cassie told me Grace was looking into her father's murder. Cassie thinks maybe that's why Grace was killed.'

The smile had vanished from his face while Dee was speaking. He looked like he was angry, but doing his best to hide it.

'I don't know anything about that.'

'You were her boyfriend,' Dee said, 'she must have spoken to you about what she was doing.'

There was no hiding the anger now. He leaned down, so his face was close to Dee's. 'What are you implying?'

'Nothing.' Dee pulled her chair back, putting some space between them.

'Yes you are. You're saying I knew Grace was putting herself into a dangerous situation, but I did nothing to protect her. You're wrong, lady. Grace didn't tell me about her secret meetings with her birth mother. Or about her father and what had happened. Turns out there was a whole side to that girl I knew nothing about. Now, if you'll excuse me, I have other customers to serve.'

He straightened up, ready to go again.

'Is that why you two split up?' Dee said. 'Because you found out she'd been keeping secrets from you?'

'We didn't split up.'

'Grace told Cassie she'd broken up with you.'

It wasn't exactly what Cassie had said, but it was close enough. In fact, she'd told Dee that Lloyd and Grace had split up, but she hadn't said who had ended things between them.

'Cassie said that?' He snorted. 'You're a fool if you believe anything that crazy bitch tells you. She killed her husband, you know. She's lying to you about me and Grace. We were solid. I loved her and now she's gone and my heart is broken. You have no right to come into my bar making allegations about our relationship. I think you should finish up your coffee and get the hell out of here before I call the police. Because this is harassment, plain and simple.'

'Sorry.' Dee put her cup down and stood up. 'I only came here today, because I'm trying to help my friend. I didn't mean to cause any upset.'

'You need to choose better friends,' Lloyd said. 'You can't go around telling lies about me. That's not right. If people think Grace finished things with me, then they'll start to assume all sorts of stuff about me. This is hard enough, without me having to cope with that shit too.'

'But if Grace was looking into her father's murder and that's why she was killed,' Dee said, 'don't you want to know about it?'

'I want her not to be dead,' Lloyd replied. 'Unless you can do that for me, there's no point talking.'

This time, when he turned to go, Dee didn't call him back. She'd got as much as she was going to from Lloyd Armstrong.

Thirty-nine

'That's where I'd like to be.' Freya pointed at the sailing boat moving across the surface of the water. 'Out on the ocean, putting as much distance between myself and this place as possible.'

She imagined what it would feel like, the tension lifting from her body as she breathed in the clean sea air and held her face up to the warm sunshine. The freedom that would come from knowing she didn't have to keep track of every word that came out of her mouth for fear of saying the wrong thing and upsetting Mum or Joey.

'My dad had a boat,' Patrick said. 'We sold it after he died. Mum said we needed the money.'

'That must have been hard,' Freya said.

'Everything's hard when someone dies.'

They were at Falling Sands, a stretch of moss-covered rocks and golden sand nestled into a quiet cove beneath the cliffs. Hidden away from the main beach, few people ever came to this quiet little haven. Freya used to come here with Grace. For years, they would celebrate each of their birthdays with an early-morning skinny dip in the clear water. Until this summer when Grace had changed so much it was difficult to remember what she'd been like before she'd discovered the truth about her parents and her world was ripped apart.

'My mother isn't coping too well,' Freya said. An understatement, but she didn't know how to explain what it felt like to see your own mother falling apart.

'Losing a child is the worst thing,' Patrick said. 'My mum says it's worse than when a parent or a friend dies.'

'She wasn't the easiest person, even before this,' Freya admitted. 'My uncle Joey says that Mum never really recovered from my dad walking out on us.'

'Do you still see him?' Patrick asked.

'My dad?' Freya shook her head. 'He's living in Australia now. He doesn't have anything to do with us. I'm not even sure if he knows about Grace.'

'Your mum would have told him, surely?'

'Maybe.'

The truth was, Freya was too scared to mention her father in any conversation with her mother, who was so unpredictable at the moment. There had been times over the last few days when Freya felt as if she was going to snap in two from the pressure of dealing with her own grief while also trying to stop her mother from going off the rails.

Her mum had properly lost it last night after dinner. Freya still didn't know what had started it, but she knew how it had ended. Broken plates in the kitchen and Mum storming out of the house in a haze of alcohol and fury. Freya had spent the next few hours in a suspended state of impending doom, worrying Mum wouldn't come home and it would be like Grace all over again. It was after three in the morning when she finally heard the front door opening and the unsteady shuffle of her mother's feet as she crossed the hall into the sitting room, where she'd fallen asleep. She'd still been there when Freya left earlier, her mouth open and a trickle of saliva running down her chin.

'I thought it would help after Cassie was charged,' Freya said, 'but it doesn't seem to have made any difference.'

'Maybe it'll get easier after the trial,' Patrick said.

'Except that's ages away.'

According to the police, they might have to wait nine months or longer. Freya's mind couldn't process that concept. Nine months, or more, of living at home watching her mother's mental health get worse as each day passed.

'Look at that,' Patrick whispered suddenly, grabbing Freya's arm and pointing at the grey heron that had landed on one of the rocks near to where they were sitting. 'Isn't he beautiful?'

Freya hadn't ever looked at a bird in any detail before, but now he said it, she saw he was right. The heron was, indeed, a thing of beauty. Long, slender neck, orange beak and yellow eyes that seemed to be observing Freya every bit as intently as she was observing it.

'He's looking for food,' Patrick said. 'That's why his neck is out like that. When they're resting, they hunch down much lower. See how still he is, waiting for his next snack to swim past.'

'I think it might be my fault Grace died.'

There. She'd said it. Finally let it out. She held her breath, waiting for Patrick to look at her differently, to see her for what she really was.

'You know it's only natural to feel guilty when someone dies?' he said.

'This is more than that.'

'So tell me.'

'Before she went out, she asked if she could call me later for a lift. I told her I had plans that night so I wouldn't be able to. It wasn't true. I lied because I was angry with her about something.'

She stopped there, scared to look at him and see the expression of loathing she was sure would be on his face.

'Oh Freya, you poor thing,' he said. 'It's not your fault. The person who killed her is responsible for her death. Not you.'

It was kind of him to say so, but Freya knew he was wrong. She had let her sister down at the exact moment she'd needed her most.

'Why were you angry with her?' Patrick asked.

'It doesn't matter.'

She couldn't tell him that the real reason she'd left her sister to die that night was down to selfish jealousy, caused by a lifetime of watching Grace get whatever she wanted without having to work at it. Unlike Freya, who had to work so hard for everything. It wasn't fair and the thing she'd hated most was how Grace never even noticed.

'Losing Grace is hard enough,' Patrick said. 'Don't start blaming yourself for what happened. You don't deserve that.'

Before she could answer, her phone pinged with an incoming message. It was from Lloyd, asking how she was and if they could meet up soon. Her cheeks flushed with pleasure as she typed a quick message back, telling him that would be lovely.

'Everything okay?' Patrick asked.

'Fine.'

The heron lifted away from the water, grey wings beating silently as it skimmed the surface of the sea without once touching it.

Forty

After Albertine's, Dee drove out to Polegate to see Jennifer Trevorrow. She hadn't spoken to Cassie's boss in a while, and she wanted to know what Jennifer thought about Cassie being arrested. But when she arrived at the salon half an hour later, there was no sign of Jennifer.

'Dee!' The young woman who'd asked Dee for her autograph practically skipped across the salon to greet her. 'Jennifer's not in today, I'm afraid. Is there anything I can help with? I don't have a client for another half-hour, so I'm free and I'd be happy to answer any questions you have. I've heard that Cassie's been arrested. I can't believe it. None of us can. I mean, it's just awful to think that all this time we've been working with a murderer. I've barely been able to sleep the last few nights, thinking about it.'

The whole time she was talking, Dee was wracking her brains to remember the girl's name. Finally, it came to her.

'Tell you what, Sonia,' she said, when the girl paused for breath. 'Why don't we go in the back and have a cup of tea? We can have a proper chat then.'

'Great.' Sonia beamed at Dee before turning to one of the other young women working here.

'Char, I'm taking a break. I've got Mrs Simons in half an hour. Call me when she comes in, would you?'

Without waiting for a reply, Sonia strutted off to the small kitchen at the back and gestured for Dee to follow her.

'Are you writing about Cassie?' Sonia asked, while she prepared a cup of tea for herself and Dee. 'Is that why you're here?'

'I'm trying to build up a profile of the sort of person she is,' Dee said. 'You must know her quite well, I imagine?'

'Not really,' Sonia said. 'Cassie keeps herself to herself, you know? We normally go out on a Friday night. Head to Brighton or Hastings for a bit of a night. She never comes with us, even though we used to invite her. She's a bit older than the rest of us, but that shouldn't stop her having a night out every now and then. Especially as she hasn't got kids. I mean, if you're married with kids it's different, right? But she hasn't any... Or so we thought.'

'You didn't know she had a daughter?' Dee asked.

'We knew she had a kid she'd given up for adoption,' Sonia said. 'Milk and sugar?'

'Milk, no sugar,' Dee said. 'Thanks.'

'But we didn't know any of the details. We sure didn't know that Cassie was an ex-con who'd killed her own husband.'

Sonia shivered dramatically before continuing.

'I always thought she didn't want to come out with us, because she thought she was better than the rest of us. Didn't help that she's always been Jen's favourite. The two of them are like this.' Sonia linked the index and middle fingers of her right hand together. Then, before Dee had a chance to ask her next question, 'What's it like being on TV? Is it really cool? I bet you know loads of famous people. I love Daisy and Dan. What are they like? Do you guys all hang out together?'

Daisy and Dan were the regular presenters of *The Big Chat*, the TV programme Dee appeared on every fortnight.

'They're lovely,' she said, after she'd managed to catch up with the barrage of questions being fired at her. 'But no, we don't hang out much. For starters, I'm old enough to be their mother. I'm sure the last thing they want to do is spend time with an old fogie like me.'

'Yeah, probably.' Sonia looked at Dee sympathetically, before perking up again. 'Still, at least you get to see them when you're making the show.'

'Indeed. Sonia, what did you mean when you said Cassie was Jennifer's favourite?' Dee asked, keen to move the conversation away from the show and back to Cassie.

'Just that,' Sonia said. 'It's not just me who thinks it, either. All the girls have noticed it. Drives us mad, if I'm honest. Cassie gets to pick and choose her shifts and never has to deal with some of our more difficult clients. And believe me, we've got a few of those. Cassie talks to Jen in a way she never does to the rest of us. It's because they've got a common bond, see?'

'They have?'

'They both had kids that were given up for adoption.'

'Jennifer had a child?' Dee said, wondering if she'd misunderstood what Sonia was telling her.

'She doesn't talk about him much,' Sonia said. 'Only after she's had a few drinks. It's how I know about Cassie. Jen got pissed one night and started going on about how none of us realised how difficult Cassie's life had been. She said being forced to give a child up for adoption is one of the worst things that can happen to a person.'

Dee remembered Jen mentioning she'd got pregnant and that was the reason her abusive relationship had ended. She hadn't said a word about having to give the baby away. Then again, Dee reasoned, why would she want to share something that personal with someone she'd only just met? She wouldn't.

'Anyway,' Sonia continued, 'that's why they had this special bond. Because they both lost their babies. Well, I assume that's the reason. I wouldn't know for sure, because Cassie never talks about stuff like that. Not to us, at least. She'll talk to Jen but not anyone else. To be honest, Dee, the only time I really talk to Cassie is the nights Jen takes us all out.'

'Does that happen often?' Dee asked.

'Every couple of months she books a restaurant and treats us all to a nice meal. Cassie comes along for those nights.'

'When was the last time you all went out together?'

Dee didn't know why she asked the question. Maybe she just wanted to know a bit more about Cassie's friendship with her boss.

'Well,' Sonia said, 'me and the girls have been talking about that. It was a few weeks ago. Jen booked Picasso's because it's her favourite place to eat. Cassie was meant to be coming and I know this for a fact, because she turned up to work that day wearing this black top that she only ever wears for going out. I suppose it's her special top or something.

'About halfway through the morning, Cassie got a phone call. I don't know who called her, but afterwards I heard her telling Jen she needed to speak to her. They both came in here and were whispering away together. The next thing we knew, Cassie was heading off home. She didn't even finish her shift and she didn't join us for dinner.'

'Is that really so weird?' Dee asked. 'There could be all sorts of reasons why she didn't want to go out that night.'

'Ah, but I haven't told you the rest of it,' Sonia said. 'So we went out, right? All of us together. First to Bibendum's, then on to Picasso's. I'd had a few glasses of wine so I was a bit tipsy, but not so much I can't remember what happened. We'd barely sat down to eat, when the next thing, Jennifer's phone starts ringing and she goes outside to take the call. A few minutes later, she comes back inside and she's, like, really flustered. We could all see something was wrong. She said she had to go, that something had turned up. She left her card details with the restaurant and told us to eat and drink whatever we liked.'

'And you think the call came from Cassie,' Dee guessed.

'Exactly.' Sonia beamed.

'Okay,' Dee said, trying to work out what this might mean, before she noticed Sonia was watching her carefully, as if there was something Dee should have worked out but hadn't. 'When was this exactly?' Dee asked.

'I was wondering when you'd ask that,' Sonia said. 'Because that's the really weird part of this. Dee. That night, it was the same night Grace Parker disappeared.'

Forty-one

With the help of her car's satnav, Dee spent two and a half hours the following morning driving to Bray in Berkshire. She had been to Bray only once before, on a boozy weekend with Billy. They'd stayed in a fancy inn with a Michelin-starred restaurant and sumptuous bedrooms. Billy had got so drunk during dinner he couldn't remember what he'd eaten the following day. Something Dee had taken as perfectly acceptable behaviour at the time. It was only later, when her husband had reached a point of being unable to leave the house in the morning without 'a quick snifter', that Dee had realised the extent of his problem.

As she approached the village, Dee's phone started ringing. Although her phone was connected to the car system via Bluetooth, Dee preferred not to take calls while she was driving. But when she saw Jennifer's name flash up on the digital display unit, she made an exception. After her conversation with Sonia yesterday, Dee was very keen to speak to Cassie's boss.

'Hello, Jennifer. What can I do for you?'

'Heard you dropped by the salon yesterday,' Jennifer said. 'Any reason for that?'

'I wanted to see how you felt about Cassie being charged with Grace's murder.'

'Feel pretty shit about it, if I'm honest,' Jennifer said.

'The police think Grace was hit by a car,' Dee said. 'I know Cassie doesn't have a car, but the police must think she had access to one. Do you know if she could drive?'

'She could drive all right. I used to let her borrow my car from time to time. If she needed to go somewhere and it was going to be difficult to get there by public transport. Does this mean they found the car that killed Grace?'

'I don't know,' Dee said.

She had passed through the village and, according to her satnav, she was less than five minutes from Neil and Liz Havers' house.

'I suppose there's no chance the police have made a mistake?' Jennifer said.

'I don't know,' Dee said. 'They must have some pretty solid evidence against her. They wouldn't have arrested her otherwise.'

'I'm starting to think I got Cassie all wrong,' Jennifer said. 'I really wanted to help her. But now I wonder if I was just a foolish old woman looking for something to give my life a bit of meaning. I let myself believe she saw me as a surrogate mother. I thought she trusted me, but she never did.

'And you want to know the worst of it, Dee? I can't help thinking that if I'd never given Cassie a job, that poor young girl would still be alive.'

Dee turned left and found herself on a winding, tree-lined road a couple of miles outside the village.

'None of this is your fault,' she said. 'Listen, Jennifer, I've got to go now, but would you like to meet up for a drink later in the week?'

'I could do Sunday,' Jennifer said. 'Have to be early evening, though, as I've got something else on later.'

'Sunday should be fine,' Dee said. 'I'll text you later in the week to firm up a time and place.'

A few seconds after hanging up, the automated voice on her satnav informed her she had reached her destination. She pulled up at the side of the road and got out of the car. She could see the house up ahead, standing in its own grounds down a gravelled driveway behind wrought-iron gates. The main gates were closed, but there was another, smaller gate for pedestrians which stood open.

Dee walked up the driveway until she reached the house. It was huge and beautiful, with white brickwork, a red-tiled roof, and a deep front porch framed with wisteria. The manicured gardens included a tennis court and a river flowing along the borders of the property.

Dee had taken a risk driving here without calling ahead. She'd had a vague idea that if the house was empty, she might be able to speak to the neighbours and get some information on the Havers family. But the nearest house was at least half a mile further along the road and this didn't strike Dee as the sort of neighbourhood where people would welcome strangers asking intrusive questions.

There was a silver SUV parked in the driveway. The sort of car favoured by yummy mummies everywhere.

Stepping into the cavernous front porch, Dee pulled the brass handle for the doorbell and waited. After a few seconds, the door was opened by the woman Dee had seen in the photo on Facebook. She was every bit as striking in real life. Pale skin, the same brown eyes as her brother, and glossy dark hair tied back in a sleek ponytail. Dressed head to toe in black Lycra, she looked as if she'd just been working out. Her cheeks were flushed and Dee spotted tiny dots of sweat on her flawless forehead.

'Liz Havers?'

'Who wants to know?'

'My name is Dee Doran. I'm a friend of Cassie MacNamara's.'

Something flickered across the woman's face, rapidly replaced by the cool, calm gaze she'd had when she first opened the door.

'I have no idea who that is.'

'That's strange,' Dee said, 'considering you gave evidence against her when she was accused of murdering her husband.'

'I think you should leave.' The expression on Liz's face didn't change, but there was a definite tremor in her voice when she said this.

'I'm not here to cause any trouble,' Dee said. 'I just want to ask you a few questions about Cassie.'

'You're a journalist,' Liz said. 'Good God, you people are unbelievable. Don't you think Cassie has suffered enough? She's just lost her daughter. Why on earth can't you leave her in peace?'

It wasn't the reaction Dee was expecting. This, after all, was the woman responsible for Cassie being convicted of murder.

'You're right,' Dee said, 'I am a journalist. But I'm not here to dig up dirt on Cassie. I wasn't lying when I said she's my friend. And right now, I'm one of the few friends she's got.'

'Why should I believe you?'

'Because I've got no reason to lie to you.'

Lizzie shook her head. 'I really don't want to talk to you. Sorry.'

'Just tell me why you testified against her,' Dee said. 'Please?'

'Why should I?'

'Because I met Grace before she was killed, and she asked me to help prove Cassie didn't kill Paul. She believed her mother was innocent. Now Grace is dead, I feel like I owe it to her to at least look into Paul's murder and see what I can find out.'

'Well I'm sorry,' Liz said, 'it's not me you need to speak to.'

She started to shut the door, and Dee put out her hand.

'Just one more question,' Dee said, 'and then I promise I'll leave you in peace.'

Liz waited.

'Did you know the truth about Grace?'

'I don't know what you're talking about.'

But her cheeks had flushed red and she looked scared.

'Paul wasn't Grace's father,' Dee said. 'Is that why you fell out? Because you knew Cassie had lied to Paul about the baby?'

'Please,' Liz said, 'I really need you to go now.'

Dee had already taken out a business card, ready to hand it over. She thrust it into Liz's hand, asking her to call if she thought of anything else. But Liz didn't answer. She stepped back inside the house and slammed the door in Dee's face, leaving her in no doubt that she had overstayed her welcome.

Forty-two

Before

Paul was asleep on the sofa, his mouth hanging open. He was snoring, the sound reverberating around the sitting room, bouncing off the walls and drilling into Cassie's head. He'd fallen asleep with his arm draped around Cassie's shoulder. As quietly as she could, she removed the arm and slid off the sofa.

She felt light-headed as she stood up, the pain in her jaw unbalancing her. As if one side of her face was heavier than the other. She caught a glimpse of herself in the mirror and looked away quickly. But not quick enough to miss the swelling or the start of a bruise, red and angry-looking and spreading up her cheek, so that she knew she would have to avoid going outside the house for the next few days.

She looked down at Paul, hate spreading through every cell in her body. She hadn't known it was possible to feel this way towards another human being. She hated him so much it was literally making her ill. She couldn't eat or sleep, because the mere presence of him in her life turned her stomach and sent her mind spiralling during the long nights as she imagined the different ways she could escape from this intolerable life they shared together.

It was all-consuming, this revulsion she felt towards him and towards herself. Because she was as much to blame as he was. She should have been braver, never let herself be talked into a marriage she hadn't wanted with a man she had never really loved. Yet somehow, she had let it happen. Now she spent her days thinking of escape, and her evenings in a limbo world of fear while she tried to anticipate his moods and do all she could to stop him hurting her.

Escape. The magical word that filled her with hope whenever she allowed herself to imagine a different sort of life. The problem was, for all her thinking about it, she didn't know how to make it happen. She wanted, more than anything, to walk away from this marriage, but she had nowhere to go and no means of doing it.

If she had her own money, it would be different. She could pack up while he was at work, and take a train or a bus or a taxi to some other part of the country far from here where he would never find her. But Paul controlled their money, along with everything else.

When they'd first married, his sister had been kind to Cassie and welcomed her new sister-in-law into the family. But all that had changed when Trish decided she needed the money she had given Paul for their wedding. Cassie knew, because Trish kept calling and leaving messages that Cassie deleted before Paul could hear them, that Trish blamed Cassie for the loan not being paid back.

As if Trish somehow knew that Cassie was thinking about her, the phone started to ring. Trish was the only person who ever rang the landline so Cassie knew this would be her. Normally, Cassie let the answer machine pick up the calls. Tonight she was more worried about Paul waking up than having to talk to his sister, so she ran into the hall and picked up the receiver.

'Hello?'

The throbbing in her jaw was worse when she tried to speak. When she put her hand up to touch it, she was surprised by how hot and swollen it felt.

'Cassie? It's Trish. I've spoken with Joey and he agrees it's not fair what you and Paul are doing. When I lent Paul that money, he promised he'd pay it back immediately. That hasn't happened yet, so I've been forced to ask Joey for help. From next month, he's going to start docking money from Paul's wages and paying me the money directly.'

At the mention of Joey's name, Cassie tasted bile at the back of her throat. That bastard. This wasn't about the money Paul owed Trish. This was about her. Joey wanted her to know he could still control her life, any time he wanted to.

'He can't do that,' she whispered.

'He's Paul's boss,' Trish said. 'He can do whatever he wants.'

Cassie closed her eyes. If only her sister-in-law knew how true that was.

'I'll let you pass on the news to Paul,' Trish said.

Cassie hung up without answering.

She couldn't tell him. She wouldn't tell him. Somehow, she had to find a way to stop Joey docking Paul's wages. She ran her finger along her jaw, lightly touching the tender skin and bruised bone, her mind working through her options. There was one thing she could do, of course. But she'd sworn to herself, the day her daughter was born and she'd first held her in her arms, she would never do that. Maybe it was time to reconsider and tell her in-laws the truth.

In the sitting room, Paul was still snoring. Sound asleep and oblivious to the mess he'd created. Cassie couldn't think through the noise he was making. Her skin itched, her chest was so tight she could barely breathe, and her head felt like it was about to spin right off her neck. She needed to get out of here before everything inside her exploded.

Pulling open the front door, she stepped out into the cool night. There was a fat white moon in the sky, hanging low over the roofs of the houses as she walked to the end of the road. If it wasn't for Grace, back in her room and fast asleep, Cassie would have kept on walking until her legs ached and her feet throbbed and she was as far away from that house and that man as she could possibly get.

'Cassie?'

Warmth filled her chest as she turned around, smiling even though it made the throbbing in her jaw worse.

'Mark. What are you doing here?'

He gave her a lopsided smile that told her he was embarrassed by the question. 'I walk home this way sometimes. I like to pass your house and think of you and Grace in there, safe and loved.'

Tears pricked her eyes, blurring her vision.

He took a step towards her, unsteady on his feet but not yet falling over drunk. That would happen later, when he was alone in his bedsit facing into the long, dark night. She knew this because she knew him as much as any person can ever know someone else.

'Hey.' He frowned as he looked at her face. 'What the fuck, Cassie? Did he do this to you?'

She shook her head, but couldn't speak because she knew if she did, she would start to cry and she couldn't let him see her crying.

'He hit you?' His voice almost broke her, soft and incredulous and immeasurably sad.

'I fell,' she said.

'Bullshit.' He touched her cheek, gently. So, so gently. 'That fucking bastard.'

He turned abruptly and she grabbed his arm, because she knew where he was going and she couldn't let that happen.

'No.' Her voice was loud, too loud for the quiet of the still night. 'Don't, Mark. Please. I want you to go home. Paul hasn't been hitting me. I really did fall. I was in the park earlier and I tripped and hit the ground face first.'

'I don't believe you.'

'It doesn't matter whether you believe me or not,' she said. 'I'm telling the truth.'

He was just drunk enough not to be able to judge if she was lying or not. If he'd been sober, she knew, it wouldn't be this easy.

He put his hands on her shoulders and looked down at her. There was something in his eyes, a darkness she had never seen before that scared her. 'If he ever lays a finger on you again,' Mark whispered, 'I swear to God I will kill him, Cassie.'

'It's okay,' she said. 'Really, Mark. You don't need to worry about me.'

But later that night, as she lay in bed unable to sleep because even here in the bedroom, she could hear Paul snoring, she thought again about what Mark had said. And she realised, with a shock of cold fear, how desperately she wished for her husband to be dead.

Forty-three

Dee had finally received a reply from the email she'd sent to Cassie through the Email a Prisoner website. The email had included a visitor's request from the prison. Dee had filled it in and managed to get a slot to see Cassie on Wednesday morning.

The drive from Eastbourne to HMP Bronzefield was one Dee was very familiar with. Ella, Dee's ex-neighbour, had spent nine months in the prison a few years earlier for her involvement in a cold case murder that had nearly ruined her life. When Ella came back home, Dee had hoped she'd never have to visit that dismal place again.

Yet today, here she was again. Worse this time than when she'd been visiting Ella. Because with Ella, there had been no doubt in anyone's mind – least of all Ella's – that she deserved to be punished for the crime she'd committed. Ella had spent a long time running from her past. When it had caught up with her, Dee suspected there was a part of her that was relieved. It meant she could finally face up to what she'd done. Today, all Dee felt was a deep sadness as she sat on one of the plastic chairs alongside the other visitors and waited for the prisoners to be led into the room.

She barely recognised Cassie at first. She had lost weight. Her gorgeous hair hung in lank strands around her gaunt face. Her skin was grey and dull. She looked emptied out, as if the essence of her personality had been extinguished.

'Thank you for agreeing to see me,' Dee said. 'I've been so worried about you.'

She didn't ask Cassie how she was doing, because it was obvious. She looked as if she was barely holding herself together.

'I didn't kill her,' Cassie said. 'I don't care anymore what happens to me. I may as well be here as anywhere else, because no matter where I am, it's not going to bring her back. But I am not going to let her killer walk free.'

For the first time, Dee saw a flash of emotion in Cassie's face, a raw combination of anger and grief.

'What can I do?' Dee said.

'I've been set up,' Cassie replied. 'When they searched my house, they found Grace's cardigan. It was the one she was wearing the night she was killed. It had her blood on it. But I didn't see her that night, so how did her cardigan end up in my house?'

'Do you remember the day I met you on the beach and took you back to my place?' Dee asked. 'I told you I'd been at your house that morning, and that I thought someone else was there too.'

'I remember.' Cassie frowned. 'You didn't see who it was?'

'No, but whoever it was must have known it was your house,' Dee said. 'Do you see?'

'Lots of people know where I live. The girls in the salon and Jennifer, obviously. My landlord, Clive. Grace, which means Lloyd probably knew. And Freya. Maybe Trish, too, if Freya told her about me and Grace meeting in secret.'

'If Trish knew, she could have told Joey,' Dee said.

Cassie blinked twice. 'Joey?'

'It's possible,' Dee said. 'Anyone else you can think of?'

But Cassie didn't answer. Her face had turned red, and her breath was coming in short, sharp bursts like she was struggling to breathe.

'Cassie?' Dee leaned across the table and touched Cassie's arm. 'What's the matter?'

'Nothing.' Cassie pulled her arm back, like she'd been burned. 'I'm fine. Just a bit too hot, that's all.'

It didn't look like nothing to Dee, however.

'Is there something I should know about Joey?' she asked.

'No.' Cassie shook her head. 'Why would you ask that?'

'Because when I mentioned his name, you looked like you might have a panic attack.'

'I told you,' Cassie said. 'I'm just hot. It's nothing to do with Joey.'

Dee didn't believe her, but it was clear Cassie wasn't going to tell her any more than that so she pressed on.

'Tell me what happened the night Grace disappeared,' she said. 'I know you were meant to be going out for dinner, but you cancelled. Why was that?'

'Grace called and said she needed to see me. She had something important to tell me. I was thrilled to hear from her. So I cancelled my plans and invited Grace to come over to my house instead. But she never showed up.'

'She was on her way to see you when she was killed?'

Cassie nodded. 'The police found traces of her blood on the gatepost outside my house. They think she hit her head against it. That's probably where she was killed. Whoever killed her knew two things: they knew where I live, and they knew she'd planned to visit me.'

'So,' Dee said. 'Who knew?'

'I don't know who Grace would have told,' Cassie said. 'Maybe Freya. Not Lloyd, because they'd recently had a row and she didn't want anything to do with him. Jennifer knew, of course, but she had no reason to tell anyone else.'

'Jennifer knew you'd been meeting up with Grace?' Dee asked, not bothering to hide her surprise.

'Yes she did.' Cassie frowned. 'Why do you look so surprised, Dee? I had to tell someone and I knew Jen would understand because she'd also had a baby that she'd given up for adoption. She knew what it felt like.'

Dee ran back over every conversation she'd had with Jennifer Trevorrow. Jennifer had claimed she'd never even known Grace was living in Eastbourne. Yet if Cassie was telling the truth – and Dee thought she was – it seemed Jennifer knew a whole lot more than she'd been letting on.

'Did you tell Jennifer about your plans to see Grace that night?' Dee asked.

'I had to,' Cassie said. 'She was worried when I told her I wasn't going to come to dinner. But when I told her why, she was fine about it.'

'What car does Jennifer drive?'

'A white Mazda,' Cassie said. 'Why? Oh God. You think Jennifer could have killed her? No way. Jennifer's a friend. One of the few people who've treated me right. I owe her a lot.'

Dee nodded while she thought about this. The car that had killed Grace was a silver Nissan Juke, but if Jennifer drove a white Mazda, it couldn't have been her car.

'You know she gave me a job when I got out of prison,' Cassie said, 'trained me up and everything. She's a good woman, Dee. Whoever killed my Grace, it wasn't Jennifer.'

Forty-four

Dee sat on her deck, drinking wine and watching the sun go down behind the horizon. The sea reflected the burning red sky, making it look as if the whole world was on fire. It was beautiful, and Dee never tired of watching this nightly display of nature in all its glory. Her phone was on the table in front of her. When it started ringing and she saw Joey Cavellini's name on the screen, she was tempted to let it go to voicemail. He'd called a few times since she'd given his name to the police on Monday. She knew why he was calling, and she didn't want to have that conversation now. Eventually, however, curiosity got the better of her. She picked the phone off the table and answered the call.

'You told the police I threw a rock through your window?' he said, getting straight to the point. 'Are you for real, Dee?'

'Good evening to you too,' Dee said.

'Why would you tell the police something like that?'

'The last time we spoke, you threatened me.'

'I told you I was worried about you,' Joey said. 'That's slightly different, don't you think?'

'Maybe.'

'So,' he said, after a pause that she didn't feel like filling, 'what actually happened?'

'I was lying in bed and someone fired a great big rock through my bedroom window.'

'How awful. Were you injured?'

He sounded genuinely concerned, but for all Dee knew he was a good actor.

'It didn't hit me,' Dee said. 'But it might have.'

'Well, believe it or not, I'm sorry to hear that,' he said. 'I hope the police have told you it couldn't possibly have been me, because I was with my sister and my niece when it happened.'

The police had, indeed, already passed on this information. Along with the news that David Verney also had an alibi for Sunday night. He'd been visiting an ex-colleague in Whitstable. They'd gone for dinner, then stayed up late drinking whisky. All of which meant whoever had thrown that rock through Dee's window was still out there somewhere. Could even be there now, watching her as she sat on her deck speaking to Joey Cavellini.

'Actually,' Joey said, 'I was wondering if you might fancy meeting up. I'm in London at the moment. I've been working on a new series of *Millionaire*. But I'm travelling down to East-bourne tomorrow and wondered if you'd like to meet for a coffee.'

'I'm busy tomorrow,' Dee said. 'My friend's still in hospital. I'm planning to spend most of the day with him.'

'How about tomorrow evening, then?'

'I can't do that either, I'm afraid.'

The truth was, she didn't want to see him. Since leaving Cassie yesterday, Dee kept remembering how she'd reacted when Dee had mentioned Joey's name. The more she'd thought about it, the more convinced Dee became that Cassie had been frightened.

'Well maybe another time, then?' he said.

Or maybe not, Dee thought.

'I went to see Cassie yesterday,' she said.

'Why would you do that?'

His voice, so appeasing a few seconds earlier had turned decidedly hostile.

'Because I don't think she killed Grace and I want to find out who did.'

'You barely know Cassie,' Joey said. 'Why do you care so much about what happens to her?'

'She's been through a lot, and she doesn't have many people watching out for her,' Dee said. 'I'm only doing what I think is right.'

'What happens when she's found guilty of Grace's murder? Will you stop then, or will you keep going with this pointless crusade?'

'I'll keep going until I get to the truth.'

'The truth's already there,' Joey said, 'staring you in the face. You're just refusing to see it. Listen Dee, it's clear to me that you're a good person, but you're wasting your time with this. Cassie killed Paul, and now she's killed Grace. That's all you need to know.'

'Why did she do it?' Dee asked. 'Grace was her daughter and she loved her. What possible reason could she have for wanting her dead?'

'We've already gone over all this.' Joey sighed. 'It's pointless going over it again, if you're not going to listen. I'm going to say goodbye now and I wish you a pleasant evening. I hope things go well at the hospital tomorrow.'

'Just one thing before you go,' Dee said. 'You told me that you barely knew Cassie, but I've since learned that's not exactly true.'

This was a lie, but she wanted to push him and see what happened.

'Who told you that?' he said, the hostile tone back again.

'Does it matter who told me? What matters is that you lied to me about how well you knew her.'

'How well I knew – or didn't know – Cassie is absolutely none of your business.'

'It is now,' Dee said, 'because I think you lied for a reason. I'm curious to know what that is. You're hiding something, Joey. I'm not going to give up until I find out what that is.'

He hung up without another word. Dee smiled. She had rattled him, got beneath that sickly smooth exterior, and it felt good. She wasn't finished yet, either. After pouring herself another glass of wine, she went onto Facebook and joined several local Crawley groups. In each one, she posted a message saying she was trying to contact anyone who had worked at Cavellini Construction in the early days before the company – and its founder – had become a household name.

When she was finished, she sent a text to Jennifer Trevorrow reminding her that they'd agreed to meet on Sunday. Jennifer was another person who had been keeping secrets from Dee. It was time, Dee decided, to find out what exactly Jennifer had been lying to her about. And why.

Forty-five

Running was the single thing that kept Freya going. When she wasn't running, the anxious thoughts built up inside her until the noise inside her head became unbearable. Each morning, she woke up and remembered that Grace was dead. The only thing that got her out of bed was the prospect of getting into her running gear and going for a run. She ran every day. Chasing her fear over the top of the Downs and along the edge of the white cliffs where her sister had died. Racing faster and faster until there was nothing left except the pounding of her feet on the ground, the thumping of her heart inside her chest and the freedom that she only ever felt when she was running.

Today, she'd woken early and gone for a 20K circular run over the Downs. By the time she'd finished, it was mid-morning. She wasn't ready to go home yet, so she bought a bottle of water in the kiosk at the bottom of the Downs and drank from it as she walked along the seafront. She felt loose and relaxed, a feeling she wanted to savour while it lasted.

She was just passing the building where her uncle lived when she saw Patrick walking towards her, his face breaking into a big stupid grin.

'Hey,' he said, stopping in front of her. 'You've been for a run?'

'No shit, Sherlock.'

It came out snarkier than she'd meant it to, because she was embarrassed he'd seen her like this – sweaty and red-faced. She probably stank as well.

'Sorry,' he said. 'Stupid question.'

'Just a bit.' She smiled to show him she didn't mean it.

'I've been worried about you,' he said.

She felt guilty, thinking of the messages he'd sent her over the last few days that she hadn't replied to. 'I've just been busy, you know?'

'I'm free later,' he said, 'if you fancy hanging out for a bit?'

'I can't. I promised my mum I'd spend the day with her.'

'No worries. See you later, then.' He tipped the side of his forehead with his finger and started walking away.

'Patrick?'

He turned back.

'I'm free tomorrow. Maybe we could do something then?'

'I'm working tomorrow.'

'Oh, okay. Never mind. It was just, you know… It doesn't matter.'

'The new Marvel movie's out this week,' he said. 'I was going to go and see it at the Depot in Lewes. We could go together if you'd like?'

'Sounds good.'

'Great.' He smiled and she smiled back and she felt a sudden surge of unexpected joy that took the breath right out of her lungs, making her feel dizzy and delirious.

She was about to ask if he wanted to hang out now, when she caught sight of Joey on the other side of the road. He was speaking to a woman Freya didn't recognise. She wondered if the woman might be her uncle's latest girlfriend. As far as Freya knew, Joey had never had a serious relationship. He was a serial womaniser who seemed like he would never settle down.

This woman certainly looked his type: petite and pretty with a figure to die for. Although if they were a couple, Freya had clearly caught them in the middle of a lovers' tiff. Their voices were raised, not loud enough for her to hear what they were saying, but it was clear they weren't whispering sweet nothings to each other.

Joey wagged his finger at the woman, as if he was issuing a warning. She said something in response before abruptly walking away from him. When he started to go after her, she spun around and held her hand up in warning. She pointed a fob at a silver car, clicked it open and climbed in.

As Freya crossed the road, the car roared away from the kerb and sped too fast down the road.

'Who was that?' Freya asked, when she'd reached Joey.

'No one,' he said, keeping his eyes on the road long after the car had disappeared.

'Are you okay, Joey?'

'Fine. Why wouldn't I be?'

'You two looked as if you were having a row,' she said.

'It was nothing, Freya. Really.'

But he didn't sound as if he meant it and when he finally looked at her, Freya thought he looked scared.

Forty-six

The following morning, Dee sat on her deck drinking coffee and scrolling through Facebook. She'd had a few replies to her posts asking about anyone who'd worked in Joey's company when it was first set up, but none of them had anything tangible Dee could follow up.

While she made a pot of coffee, she tried to think what other avenues she could explore. She was on her second cup of coffee when she got an idea. Taking her mug with her, she went outside and called David Verney.

'David, I know we got off to a bad start, but I'd really appreciate another chat,' she said. Eating humble pie was never pleasant, especially when the apology wasn't sincere, but Dee needed more information and David was the only person who could give her that.

'You still looking into Paul's murder?' David said. 'I thought you'd have given up by now.'

'I'm changing my focus,' Dee said. 'I want to do an in-depth profile piece on Cassie. I'm thinking it could be the first in a series of articles on women killers. I won't be able to publish anything until after the trial, but it seems sensible to start doing my research now so I can have the piece ready to publish as soon as she's convicted.'

'You've changed your tune since the last time we spoke,' David said.

'I'm big enough to admit when I've been wrong about something.'

'You told the police I threw a rock through your bedroom window,' David said.

'Sorry about that. They asked me for a list of names. You were one of the people I thought of.'

'Why me?'

'The last time we spoke,' Dec said, 'I thought you were trying to scare me off.'

'I wouldn't do that.'

'No, I realise that now. I'm sorry, David. I was scared and overreacted.'

She wasn't sorry, not really, but she had phoned to make amends not start another argument.

'I can understand that. A rock through your bedroom window isn't pleasant. I hope they catch whoever did it.'

'Yes, let's hope so.'

'So this piece you're writing, where do I fit in?'

Dee allowed herself a small smile, before she continued speaking.

'As the detective who caught her, you're pretty central to the whole story.'

She was glad she was doing this over the phone. If he could see her, she suspected he'd see straight through her lies. Or maybe not. Because David Verney was a man with a huge ego. On another day, Dee might have amused herself with musings about his ego compensating for some of his physical attributes, but she didn't have time for that today. She was a woman on a mission, full of refreshed energy, drive and determination.

'Interesting,' he said. 'You know, I like the sound of this. Do you remember that film a while back with Charlize Theron? I reckon you could get a film studio interested.'

'You think so?' Dee rolled her eyes, but managed to make herself sound a lot more enthusiastic than she felt.

'I do. Tell you what,' David said. 'I'm not someone to hold a grudge. You've apologised and I accept your apology. Why don't we arrange to meet over the next few days? You can tell me your ideas and let me know how I can help. In the meantime, do you want me to put out some feelers to my contacts in the industry?'

'It's a bit early for that,' Dee said. 'Let's meet first and make a plan. But I love the idea of a screen adaptation. We can definitely keep that in mind for later.'

They arranged to meet on Saturday morning in the same coffee shop as the last time. Dee made a note not to have breakfast beforehand. David Verney was so nauseating, she didn't want to risk meeting him on a full stomach in case she was unable to keep her breakfast down.

She had just hung up from David when she got a call from Ed.

'I was wondering if I'm going to see you today,' he said.

'Definitely. In fact, I was planning to pop over there later this morning.'

–

Ed was waiting for her inside the entrance to the hospital when she arrived. Fully dressed and, for the first time since his stroke, looking more like his old self.

'Look at you,' she said, kissing his cheek. 'Up and dressed and ready for anything.'

'I feel great,' he said. 'Well, certainly a lot better. I've just been with the occupational therapist. She says I'm doing really well. Doesn't even think she'll need to see me once I'm discharged.'

'Any idea when that will be?'

'Hopefully end of tomorrow at the latest,' he said. 'Do you mind if we sit outside for a bit? It's a beautiful day and I'm desperate for a bit of fresh air. I'm starting to think I must smell of hospital. Here.' He held his arm out. 'Smell my shirt. Does it reek of sick people and antiseptic?'

'You smell fine.' Dee linked her arm in his. 'Come on. Let's find a bench to rest our old bodies on.'

They sat on a rotting wooden bench, located beneath some trees at the side of the car park. It wasn't the loveliest place they had ever been together, but Dee felt happier than she had in weeks. Especially when Ed took her hand and told her he had decided to take up her offer of moving in with her when he was discharged.

'Only if you're absolutely sure about it,' he said.

'I am,' she said. 'And I'm so happy you've finally agreed it's a good idea.'

'After my session with the occupational therapist, I feel more confident about how much I'll be able to do.'

'Now hang on a second,' Dee said. 'You're not moving in unless you agree to fully rest up and do everything the doctors tell you.'

'I'm not stupid,' he said. 'I'll be careful, Dee. I promise.'

'Good.'

'You're off to London to record your TV show tomorrow?' Ed said. 'What's this week's big topic?'

'No baby on board.' Dee groaned. 'It's about women who choose careers over parenthood. Can you believe that in the twenty-first century women are still being defined by something as narrow and sexist as whether they have children or not?'

'Is that what you'll tell them?'

'Damn right.'

'That's my girl.' Ed smiled and they sat side by side on the bench, talking about everything and nothing, until Ed said he was feeling tired and they should probably go back inside.

Later that evening, Dee sat out on her deck thinking about how things finally felt like they were coming together. Every time she thought about Ed moving in with her, she felt a giddy sense of excitement. All her earlier worries and concerns had disappeared. He was a good man – one of the best she'd ever met – and she knew, deeply and completely, that she was lucky to have him in her life. They had almost lost each other once before. Now they were back together, Dee was going to work at things this time around. Whether that included taking time out to go travelling around Europe in a camper van was yet to be seen. But she certainly wasn't ruling it out.

She had left her phone inside, giving herself an enforced break from scrolling through the internet and social media. She didn't look at it again until she was in bed. She had several new text messages, all from a withheld number. Each message had a photo attached. Dee assumed, at first, the messages were spam. Scrolling through them, she saw that only the first one had any text with it. The rest were all blank, just the attachment but with no text explaining what it was.

Curious, Dee clicked on the first message and read the text:

> Love makes fools of all of us.

She didn't understand what it meant, until she opened the photo. It showed a middle-aged man, and a woman about the same age. They were sitting on a bench, their faces hidden by the long shadows thrown from the trees above. Dee didn't need to see their faces to know who they were. Her and Ed, sitting outside the hospital.

She clicked on the next photo, her heart thumping too loud and too fast. Then the next and the one after that too. Six photos in total. Dee was in all of them except the last one. While the first five had been taken outside the hospital, this final one was different. It showed Ed, sitting in the chair by his hospital bed. From the angle of the chair, Dee guessed he had been watching TV when the photo was taken. Which probably explained why he hadn't noticed the person taking the photo.

Fear wrapped itself around her chest and squeezed tight. This couldn't be happening. Hospital was meant to be a safe place. The wards all had intercom systems. You had to press a button and say who you were and why you were there. No one could simply walk in off the street and get into a ward without having to do that. Yet that's exactly what someone had done.

They might still be there. The thought sent Dee out of her chair and racing around the house to her car, parked at the front. As she pulled on her seat belt, she called Ed's phone. The call went straight to voicemail, and the one after that as well. Picking up her phone, not caring that she shouldn't be looking at it while she was driving, Dee found the phone number for the hospital. After what seemed like a lifetime, she was finally put through to the ward where she'd left Ed earlier this evening.

'I need someone to check on Ed Mitchell,' she said.

'Who is this?' the nurse asked.

'I'm his girlfriend. I was with him earlier today and he seemed okay, but I got an odd message just now and I'm worried about him.'

'Is this Dee?'

'Yes.'

'I was about to call you,' the nurse said. 'It's a bit strange, to be honest. He left the ward earlier, told me he was going for a walk and he hasn't come back. I'm afraid we don't know where he is.'

Dee hung up, swearing under her breath, pushed her foot down on the accelerator and promised herself if anything bad had happened to Ed she wouldn't rest until she had hunted down the person who had harmed him.

Forty-seven

By the time Dee arrived at the hospital, Ed had been found. Alive, but not well. Unable to sleep, he had told the ward nurse he was going to get himself a cup of tea from the vending machine. Instead, he'd gone outside for some fresh air. Walking around the side of the hospital, someone had rushed past him from behind and knocked him over. Ed had fallen against the wall and been unable to get back up. He'd been lying there for over an hour before he was found by a paramedic who'd slipped out for a sneaky cigarette in the middle of her shift.

While Ed was being check over by the doctors, Dee phoned Rachel.

'Dee? What's the matter? It's the middle of the night.'

'Hardly,' Dee said. Then, remembering she had vowed to make more of an effort not to piss Rachel off, 'Sorry for calling so late. It's Ed. Something's happened.'

As quicky as she could, she told Rachel about the photos she'd received earlier and Ed's fall.

'It was deliberate,' Dee concluded. 'He thinks it was an accident, but it wasn't. He was pushed on purpose. I'm scared, Rachel. What if they come back and try to hurt him again?'

'Stay there,' Rachel said. 'I'll be with you as quickly as it will take me to get across from Brighton. In the meantime, I'll send someone over to check the hospital CCTV footage.'

The next few hours passed in a blur. Two uniformed officers turned up within ten minutes of Dee hanging up from Rachel. They took statements from Dee, the ward nurse and – once they were given the all-clear from the doctor – Ed.

'It was an accident,' Ed told them. 'It was dark and I was in the wrong place, that's all. I suspect whoever ran into me didn't even realise I'd fallen. If they had done, I'm sure they'd have stopped to check I was okay.'

'How can you say that?' Dee said. 'You've seen the photos. Someone was here, watching you. The same person who took those photos pushed you over. They're trying to use you to stop me helping Cassie.'

She had shown the photos to the two police officers as soon as they'd arrived, but she could see they weren't sure what to make of them. It was only when Rachel turned up, demanding to ask why they hadn't already examined the CCTV footage, that they seemed to take the whole thing a bit more seriously.

After checking on Ed, Rachel asked Dee to walk with her to the vending machine.

'You need to tell me everything,' Rachel said, as soon as they were out of Ed's hearing. 'That man in there is one of my closest friends. If someone is out to get him, then I need to know about it. Who sent those photos? More to the point, why? What the hell have you got yourself into this time, Dee?'

Normally, Dee would have bristled at Rachel's tone, but tonight she was too exhausted and scared to react. 'Someone wants me to stop looking into Paul Cavellini's murder,' she said.

'Show me the photos.' Rachel held out her hand.

Dee opened the text messages and handed the phone to Rachel.

'I thought hospitals are meant to be secure,' Rachel said, as she looked at the photos. 'How did someone get into the ward to take this?'

'It's actually very easy,' Dee said. 'If someone rings the buzzer, all you need to do is follow them in. I've done it loads of times over the last few weeks. People want to be helpful. If you're going into a ward and someone's right behind you, you're not going to shut the door in their face.'

'Why are you so sure this is connected to Paul Cavellini?' Rachel asked, handing the phone back to Dee.

'I can't think of any other reason someone would be trying to scare me.'

'I made a few calls on the way over,' Rachel said. 'This is the second time someone's tried to intimidate you. Last Sunday night, two PCSOs responded to a call at your house after someone threw a rock through your bedroom window. You gave them Joey Cavellini's name. David Verney's, as well.'

'They both have alibis for that night,' Dee said. 'Neither of them know about me and Ed.'

'So who does know about you?'

'Louise and Martin, obviously. I guess some people would have seen us together before his stroke. I don't know, Rachel. I'm sorry. I shouldn't have showed him the photos. He didn't need to know about that. I thought he should know, but it's only going to stress him out and the last thing he needs is stress at the moment. He's meant to be focusing all his energy on getting better, not looking over his shoulder all the time.'

'Dee, stop talking. You look exhausted. I think you should go home.'

'I can't do that,' Dee said. 'I need to stay here with Ed. He's meant to be moving in with me when he gets out. Do you think that's a good idea? If someone is watching us, or trying to hurt him, it might be putting him in danger. He was going to go to Nessa's, but I persuaded him not to. I wanted to prove that I could look after him, but I can't. It's my fault this has happened. He needs to stay as far away from me as possible, not move in with me where he won't be safe.'

'Calm down,' Rachel said. 'Take some deep breaths and try to stop that adrenaline spiking any worse than it already is.'

Dee did as she was told and, gradually, the worst of the panic started to subside.

'You're no good to anyone like this,' Rachel said. 'Especially not Ed. There's nothing more you can do for him this evening. I'll keep an officer here for the rest of the night just in case. Although I'm pretty sure whoever took those photos is long gone.'

'What happens next?' Dee asked. 'How will you find who did this to him?'

'We still don't know that the person who ran into him is the same person who took the photos,' Rachel said. 'We'll know a lot more once we've been through the CCTV footage. In the meantime, I want you to stop any work you're doing on Paul Cavellini until I know more about what's going on here.'

'I can't do that,' Dee said. 'That's giving whoever did this to Ed exactly what they want.'

'You don't have a choice,' Rachel said. 'Ed's very lucky he wasn't seriously injured tonight, or worse. You called me because you were scared and you want me to take this seriously. That's exactly what I'm doing. Now you need to do the same. If you don't stop, and something else happens to Ed, I will hold you accountable. Do I make myself clear?'

'One hundred percent.'

Rachel was right. Nothing was more important than making sure Ed was safe.

As Dee drove home, she vowed she would stop all work on Paul Cavellini for now. It was a resolution she had every intention of keeping. Until she woke up the following morning and realised, with the blinding clarity that only comes in the moments before sleep and wakefulness, that she knew who had sent those photos.

Forty-eight

The first thing Dee did, even before getting out of bed, was call Rachel.

'I told Joey Cavellini about Ed being in hospital.'

She heard Rachel sigh, and could perfectly picture the sceptical expression on her face. 'Please tell me you're not saying you think he sent those photos and attacked Ed?'

'That's exactly what I'm saying.'

'I assume you're also able to tell me why he'd do something like that,' Rachel said.

'He knows I've been looking into his brother's murder,' Dee said. 'Cassie is scared of him, although she won't tell me why. And Joey has already tried to warn me off looking into Paul's murder. When that didn't work, he took things a step further.'

'I can't see him for this,' Rachel said, 'but I'll have a word with him just in case.'

'Thank you, Rachel. I really appreciate it.'

'I'm not doing it for you,' Rachel said. 'This is for Ed.'

The next thing on Dee's list was to cancel her visit to London. She felt terrible letting the TV people down at the last moment, but the only thing she wanted to do this morning was be with Ed.

When she turned up at the hospital an hour later, he was in good spirits and seemed remarkably unbothered by what had happened to him the previous evening.

'I've never had police protection before,' he said. 'It makes me feel quite special. Hey, shouldn't you be on your way to London now?'

'I cancelled,' Dee said.

Ed frowned. 'You didn't have to do that. As you can see, I'm perfectly fine.'

'I don't think you should stay at mine when you come out of hospital.'

She realised, when she saw the hurt look on his face, that she could have found a more tactful way of telling him this.

'It's not that I don't want you there,' she added, 'but after last night, I'm worried you won't be safe.'

'What about you?'

'What do you mean?' Dee said.

'If it's not safe for me to stay at your house, how is it possibly safe for you?'

'That's different.'

'And that's bullshit.'

'I'm only thinking about what's best for you,' Dee said.

'Because I'm an old man who's incapable of taking care of himself?'

'No.'

'I don't believe you,' Ed said. 'I'd let myself believe that the stroke wasn't going to change how you felt, but that's exactly what it's done. You know what? You're probably right. I'll call Nessa this morning and ask if her offer still stands. I'm not sure being with you at the moment is what I need.'

'You think my feelings for you have changed?' Dee was angry now, her voice rising at the same pace as her temper. 'Well yes, they have changed. But not in the way you're implying. If anything, these last few weeks have made me realise how much you mean to me. You can't get angry with me for wanting to protect you. You've been through a huge trauma and you need time to recuperate properly. If something happened to you while you were staying with me, I'd never forgive myself.'

'Tell you what then.' He looked at her and she saw the challenge behind his eyes. 'How about we go somewhere together?

Let's hire a house where no one will be able to find us. That way both of us will be safe.'

'No,' she said too quickly. 'I'm not going to let anyone chase me out of my own house. If I move out now, it will seem like I'm giving up.'

'Yet you're happy for me to give up,' Ed said quietly. 'That's all I needed to hear. I want you to go now.'

'It's not what I meant,' Dee said. But Ed had turned his face away from her, and when she begged him to look at her and talk to her, he didn't move. In the end, she had no choice but to stand up and leave.

Outside, she went back over the conversation, growing angrier the more she analysed what he'd said. He had no right, she told herself, to judge her for wanting to protect him. In fact, his attitude reeked of sexism. Because why was it okay for him to always do things for her and take care of her and look out for her, yet when she tried to do the same for him he threw it back in her face? She would never, she realised, as long as she lived, understand the workings of the male mind.

Dee went home, determined to spend the rest of the morning focusing on the book she was writing and doing everything she could to put Ed Mitchell out of her head. But when she sat down to write, her mind kept wandering. It was a relief, therefore, when her phone rang and she had an excuse to do something different. She didn't recognise the caller's phone number, but that didn't stop her taking the call.

'Dee? It's Liz Havers. You came to see me on Sunday.'

'Hello.' Dee pushed open the bifold doors and stepped outside. 'How are you?'

Unlike almost every other day this summer, today was grey and overcast. There was no breeze and the air felt muggy and heavy. As soon as this phone call was over, Dee decided, she would put her swimsuit on and go for a swim. She needed something to clear her head and help her focus.

'Not good,' Liz said. 'Ever since we spoke, I haven't been able to stop thinking about Cassie. Do you know how she's doing?'

'She's coping,' Dee said, 'for now, at least.'

'In the papers, they're making her out to be some sort of monster,' Liz said. 'The Cassie I knew was nothing like the woman they're describing.'

'What was she like then?' Dee asked.

'Complicated,' Liz said, 'but not bad. There's a difference. She was kind and funny too, someone who'd do anything for the people she loved. And there was no one in the world she loved more than her daughter.'

A white seagull dived down towards the metal-coloured sea. Far out on the horizon, Dee could see the faint outline of a container ship, misted grey like a ghost ship. She remembered Ed telling her he had an app that identified what ship you could see at any given time. If he was here now, he could use his app to tell her the name of the ship, as well as where it had come from and where it was going. The anger she'd been holding onto all morning disappeared. In its place, there was an aching sense of regret. It seemed that no matter how hard they tried, they always ended up back in the same place.

'Hello?' Liz said. 'Are you still there?'

'The way you speak about her,' Dee said, 'it sounds as if you two were quite close.'

'We were best friends once.'

'What happened?'

'Cassie did something that I couldn't forgive her for.'

'Is that why you testified against her?' Dee asked.

'No, of course not.'

'So why are you calling?' Dee said. 'You made it pretty clear the other day that you didn't want to talk to me.'

'You asked me if I knew about Grace,' Liz said. 'What did you mean by that?'

'I think you know exactly what I meant.'

'Maybe.'

'Why don't we meet?' Dee said.

'I'm not sure that's a good idea.'

'Liz,' Dee said, 'I think you're scared. I don't know who or what has you so frightened, but I promise you I don't want to cause you any harm. But if you know something – anything – that can help me prove Cassie didn't kill Paul, I need to know.'

'Do you promise,' Liz said, after a moment, 'if I tell you, that you'll find a way to keep me out of it?'

'I swear,' Dee said, because she didn't see there was any other choice. Liz Havers might be her final chance of clearing Cassie's name.

Forty-nine

Freya rubbed her palms down the sides of her skirt, but it made no difference. She couldn't keep them dry. She was giddy with nerves. Giddy and sweaty. She'd spent ages putting on her make-up, but it had been a waste of time. Her face was practically dripping. She tried fanning the collar of her vest top, but that didn't seem to make any difference. She was a hot, messy blob. Not the look she'd been aiming for, but there wasn't much she could do about it.

She was in Sovereign Harbour, standing outside an apartment building on the waterfront. Lloyd lived in one of the penthouse apartments at the top with sweeping views across the English Channel. She pressed the buzzer for his apartment and, a few seconds later, he was speaking to her and buzzing her into the building.

Freya stepped out of the heat into the air-conditioned lobby. She watched her reflection flicker along the mirrored wall as her feet clattered over the marble-tiled floor to the row of lifts. Flashes of black and red and yellow – her dress, her lips, her hair. The blackberry and lavender scent of her perfume filling the air around her.

Grace had told her that Lloyd's parents were loaded, which is why he'd been able to open his wine bar and also afford a fancy apartment in the harbour. According to Grace, Lloyd's parents spoiled him rotten. Grace had said some other stuff too then, about Lloyd being so used to getting what he wanted he didn't like it when people said no to him. But Freya didn't want to think about that now.

She had been here once before, and remembered the over-whelming sense of space as she'd walked out of the lift that led directly into the apartment. The last time, she'd been with Grace. It was before things between Grace and Lloyd had started to go wrong. Stepping into the lift now, Freya had a flashback to that night. Herself and Grace giggling together from the bottle of Prosecco they'd shared before coming out. Tonight, Freya was alone and sober.

As the lift doors slid open, she saw Lloyd, standing in the middle of the apartment, his back to the wall of windows, waiting for her.

'Hi.' She stepped out of the lift, shy and self-conscious.

He smiled, looking genuinely pleased to see her. As she walked towards him, he handed her a glass of something pink and sparkling.

'Chapel Down champagne,' he said. 'Not strictly cham-pagne, of course, because it's English, not French. But it's pretty good.'

She took a sip and smiled. 'More than pretty good. Thanks.'

Lloyd had called her yesterday to invite her over for dinner this evening. Freya had already arranged to go to the cinema with Patrick, but after telling Lloyd she'd love to see him, she'd called Patrick and told him they'd have to do it another time. She felt bad cancelling, but she knew Patrick wouldn't mind.

Lloyd had set the small table by the window. Silver cutlery, crisp white napkins and a narrow vase with a single red rose in it. The sun was starting to set. Freya sat down and watched the colours. Shades of orange and pale pink and rich, burning ombre. All of it duplicated across the surface of the sea. Three freighter ships were moving slowly along the edge of the horizon. Freya wondered what it would be like, all the way out there, midway between two countries, nothing but sea all around you.

'Food will be ready in a sec,' Lloyd said.

'You didn't have to go to so much effort,' Freya said. It was a bit more formal than she'd expected, increasing her sense of discomfort.

'It's no effort,' he called over his shoulder on the way to the kitchen. 'Besides, you're worth it.'

By the time she'd finished her drink, Lloyd was carrying plates of food over to the table. 'Grilled salmon with asparagus and sauteed new potatoes,' he said unnecessarily, because she was more than capable of seeing for herself what was on the plate. He topped up their glasses before sitting down opposite from her. 'I hope it's okay,' he said. 'I remember you telling me you like salmon?'

'I love it,' Freya said, picking up her knife and fork.

The truth was, she didn't like fish very much. She only ate it because it was better for her than meat. She didn't remember ever telling Lloyd she liked salmon, and wondered if he was confusing her with someone else.

'I was always trying to get Grace to eat less meat and more fish,' Lloyd said. 'But she didn't care, did she?'

Freya chewed the piece of salmon in her mouth, trying to make it small enough to swallow. She wished Lloyd hadn't mentioned Grace, because now her sister was all she could think of.

Grace had loved her food, refusing to watch her diet the way Freya and Mum did. Given a choice, she'd always choose a burger and chips, with extra mayonnaise and ketchup on the side, over fish and sauteed potatoes and stringy asparagus. She had been so full of life and laughter that no one ever seemed to care about the extra pounds she carried on her hips or the excessive hair around her bikini line because she'd refused – point blank – to wax it off, claiming it was an abomination to expect any woman to do that to their body. Freya's chest ached thinking about her.

'You okay?' Lloyd asked.

'Fine.' She took a swig of the pink drink and tried to smile. 'I just miss her, you know?'

'Yeah.' Lloyd put down his knife and fork. 'I still can't believe she's gone. I thought after they found the killer it would get easier, but it doesn't really change anything, does it?'

'Not really.'

'I've been contacted by a national paper,' Lloyd said. 'They want to do an interview with me. It will be all about me and Grace and how much we loved each other. Because you know we loved each other, right?'

'Yeah, of course.'

'Good. It's just, I'm a bit worried some people are trying to say things about us that aren't true. This woman turned up at the bar earlier in the week. She seemed to think Grace and I had broken up. It freaked me out, Freya.'

He leaned across the table, looked at her intently.

'You haven't been telling people we split up, have you? Because it's not true, you know. Whatever Grace might have said, we were well and truly together right to the end.'

So that's why he'd invited her over. He wanted to make money out of this by selling his story, probably for lots of money. And he wanted to make sure Freya didn't tell anyone that his relationship with Grace wasn't as perfect as he was going to say it had been.

Freya had barely touched her food, but suddenly she didn't want to be her any longer. 'Can I use your toilet?' she said.

'Sure. Down the hall and on the left, beside the bedroom.'

In the bathroom, she splashed water on her face and looked at her reflection in the mirror. Flashes of memory played through her head, things she had pushed to the back of her mind because they were too difficult to think about. Grace coming home one night a few months ago, her eyes bloodshot and red blotches on her cheek from crying. Another time, a row of purple bruises on Grace's arm like someone had held it too tight. Grace's voice, slurring after too much wine, telling Freya she was going to leave him because he wasn't the lovely guy everyone thought he was.

'You okay in there?' Lloyd shouted.

'Fine,' she called back. 'I'll be out in a minute.'

She washed her hands, holding her wrists under the cold tap and splashing more water on her face. When she'd finished, she looked for a towel, but there wasn't one. She could probably dry her face and hands with toilet paper, but the idea wasn't very appealing.

There was a cupboard beneath the sink. When she crouched down and opened it, she found two rows of neatly folded hand towels. As she reached in to take one of them, her fingers brushed against something hidden between two piles of towels. She put her hand in further, her fingers wrapping around the metal chain. Part of her brain already recognised it, even before she lifted it out and held it in front of her. A thin silver chain with an olive leaf pendant.

The necklace had been a present to Grace from Lloyd. Freya remembered the first time she'd seen it; the way the silver leaves captured the light, the pink glow on her sister's face as she looked at her reflection in the mirror, her eyes catching Freya's and her face breaking into a big, happy smile.

Freya remembered too, in minute and terrible detail, the last time she'd seen the pendant. It was the last time she'd seen her sister. She had been sitting on Grace's bed, watching Grace get ready to go out. At the last minute, Grace had taken off the gold chain she'd been wearing and replaced it with the silver pendant.

'An olive branch,' she said. 'Let's hope this does the trick with Joey. Wish me luck?'

She left soon after that, and Freya never saw her again.

Freya held the necklace up to the light, searching the individual silver leaves as if they contained the answer to how it had ended up here in Lloyd's bathroom. Parts of her sister would be still on it, tiny particles of skin and DNA. Grace had believed that people never truly die. Instead, she'd told Freya, their energy was transformed at death and redistributed back into the atmosphere. In this way, the world was nothing more than the combined energy of all the people who had lived before us. Freya thought of this now, trying to feel her sister's presence. But she couldn't feel anything. Wherever Grace had gone after she died, it was somewhere far away from here.

Fifty

David Verney was waiting for Dee at the same table, in the same coffee shop, as the last time they'd met. This time, however, he seemed genuinely pleased to see her, giving her a kiss on both cheeks and telling her how well she was looking before rushing off to order her a coffee.

'I got you a chocolate brownie as well,' he said, coming back a few minutes later. 'They're home-made, apparently.'

He placed the brownie and a mug of coffee on the table and sat down opposite her.

'You're not having one too?' Dee asked.

'Too early for me.' He patted his flat stomach. 'At my age, I've got to watch what I eat. You know how cruel the TV can be. Gotta look my best for the cameras.'

Dee picked up her mug and took a sip of coffee, trying not to smirk.

'Coffee okay?' he said.

'Good.'

'Yeah. This place is great. I like coming here when I'm writing. Something about the buzz of other people around me, seems to help me focus.'

He was talking too much. At first, Dee didn't understand why. Then she realised he was nervous. She almost felt guilty then. He clearly believed the story she'd fed him and was all hyped up in anticipation of his role in it.

'So,' she said, pushing the guilt aside and taking full advantage of his desire to get on her good side. 'We should probably get started.'

'Yeah, definitely. I made some notes earlier.' He opened the slim, silver laptop on the table. 'I've done a timeline of the events before and after Paul's murder.'

He turned the laptop around so Dee could look at the screen.

'You can see from this how thorough our investigation was. I know you had your doubts, but we didn't cut any corners. See these names? Every one of these people was a suspect at the beginning.'

The screen showed a detailed timeline of the murder investigation. Alongside the different dates, David had put the names of all the key people they'd interviewed.

'This is great,' Dee said.

'There's this too.' David clicked the keyboard and another screen opened. Here, he had written a brief description of each of the suspect's relationship with Paul, as well as a summary of where they'd been the night of the murder.

Dee scanned through the list until she found Joey's name.

Name: Joey Cavellini

Relationship with victim: Older brother. Employer.

'How long had Paul been working for Joey?' she asked.

'Almost two years,' David said. 'From the people we interviewed, I got the impression Paul wasn't very good at his job. Joey kept him on out loyalty, more than anything else. He had a hard time after his parents died, and Joey took him under his wing. Gave him a job and looked out for him.'

Dee returned to the notes on the screen, her eyes locking onto something she hadn't expected.

'Is this true?' she asked.

'Joey and Lizzie? Course it's true. Why?'

Dee read the notes again, trying to make sense of what David had written.

Name: Joey Cavellini

Relationship with victim: Older brother. Employer.

Alibi: Lizzie Collier.

She looked down the list until she found Lizzie's name.

Name: Lizzie Collier.

Relationship with victim: Cassie's friend.

Alibi: Joey Cavellini.

'What were those two doing together that night?' Dee asked.

'Having sex, I assume.' David grinned. 'No need to look so shocked, Dee. Joey and Lizzie were an item for a bit. Didn't last, needless to say. A girl like that with someone like Joey? It was never going to be anything serious.'

'Why not?'

'He was a successful businessman, even back then. She was a working-class girl with a part-time job in the local chippie. Pretty enough, but lacking any sort of sophistication.'

Dee thought of the elegant woman she'd met on Sunday. David Verney couldn't be more wrong about Liz Havers nee Collier. When she'd asked Joey about Lizzie, he'd implied he barely knew her. Another lie in what was turning out to be a long list of lies.

Rachel had called Dee yesterday to tell her Joey couldn't have taken those photos of Ed and Dee at the hospital. He'd been in London, at a dinner with his agent that night. Yet even if he hadn't done that, he was up to his neck in something. And Dee intended to find out what that was.

'He would have been a good bit older than her, wouldn't he?'

'Eleven years,' David said. 'So what? Plenty of men date younger women. I can't see what the problem is.'

The problem, Dee thought viciously, was so large and obvious if he couldn't see it there was no point her trying to explain all the reasons it wasn't right.

'Do you know how they met?' she asked, forcing herself to remain calm and not let his outdated sexism get to her. 'Like you said, they would have moved in very different worlds.'

'Through Cassie, I think,' David said. 'Lizzie and Cassie were best friends. Although I think they'd had a falling out a while before Paul was killed.'

'Did the name Jennifer Trevorrow ever come up during your investigation?' she asked.

'Never heard of her,' David said. 'Who is she?'

'Cassie's boss. She gave Cassie a job when she came out of prison. She said it was because she felt sorry for Cassie, but I think there might be another reason.'

'Like what?'

'I don't know.'

'I bet she's regretting that decision now,' David said. 'Having a killer on your employee list can't be good for business, right?'

He laughed, but Dee didn't join in.

'Tell me about Grace,' she said.

'Why are you so sure I met her?' David asked.

'She was looking for information about her father's murder,' Dee said. 'You would have been one of the first people she contacted.'

'You got me bang to rights, Dee. Yeah, I met her. She was a stunner. Spitting image of her mother. But she was all over the place. Convinced Cassie was innocent without a shred of evidence to back it up. I told her the same thing I told you: Cassie killed her husband. End of story. Needless to say, she didn't like hearing that.'

'And that's it?'

'Yep. I told her not to bother contacting me again, and that was the last I heard from her. You could have knocked me over with a feather when I saw her face on the news a few months

236

later. She might have pissed me off, but she was a lovely young woman who didn't deserve to die.'

Dee didn't like David Verney, and liked his attitude to women even less, but it was clear he was being straight with her now. He hadn't had anything to do with Grace's murder, which meant there was one name – at least – that she could cross off her list.

–

Dee drove straight from Bexhill to the hospital. She hadn't heard from Ed since their row. He hadn't replied to her texts or voice messages, which indicated he was still angry with her.

She'd had enough time to think everything through and, once her anger had abated, she realised he'd been right. It wasn't fair to have one set of rules for him and another for herself. So she had come up with a compromise that she hoped would satisfy both of them. She knew she'd never forgive herself if something happened to him because of her. Which meant she couldn't allow him to move in with her when he came out of hospital. Instead, she was going to offer to move in with him. That way, she would be able to make sure he was okay and – she hoped – he would see that this was a sensible solution.

She was looking forward to seeing him and hurried from her car into the hospital. His ward was on the first floor. The lifts were busy, so Dee took the stairs, which meant she was sweaty and out of breath by the time she arrived at the ward.

Pausing at the door, she got her breathing back under control before pressing the buzzer on the intercom.

'I'm here to see Ed Mitchell,' she said, when a voice spoke to her through the intercom.

'Ed?' the voice said. 'I'm afraid you're too late. He was discharged earlier today.'

'No, that can't be right. I'm meant to be looking after him when he comes out.'

'Is that Dee? Wait there, I'll come to the door.'

Dee waited impatiently, until the nurse she'd been speaking to opened the door and smiled at her.

'I'm not sure what's happened,' the nurse said. 'He got the all-clear yesterday afternoon and left this morning. Maybe he didn't tell you because he wanted it to be a surprise?'

'Maybe.' Dee didn't believe that for a second. 'How did he get home, do you know? Did he take a taxi?'

'No. His sister came. Nessa, isn't it? He said he was going to stay with her. Oh dear, I can see by your face you had no idea. Are you okay?'

'I'm fine.' Dee tried to smile, but she couldn't get her mouth to do what she wanted it to.

Ed was gone and it was her fault. She had messed everything up, all over again.

Fifty-one

Freya was in the kitchen with Mum when the doorbell rang.

'Will you get it, love?' Mum asked. She was sitting at the table, her hands wrapped around the mug of tea that Freya had made over half an hour ago. She hadn't drunk any of the tea. It would be cold by now, but Mum continued holding onto that mug as if her life depended on it.

'It's the police,' Freya said, standing up.

She had butterflies in her tummy and a pounding pain in her head. She had barely slept, spent the night tossing and turning as she went back over the last few months.

'How do you know it's the police?' Mum said.

'Because I called them this morning and said I needed to see them.'

After finding the necklace last night, she'd put it in her pocket and told Lloyd she was feeling ill. He'd offered to drive her home, but she'd insisted on getting a taxi. He had called her twice since then and left a message asking how she was feeling. She hadn't called him back, and had no intention of doing so.

Rachel Lewis was standing on the doorstep when Freya opened the front door.

'Sorry I couldn't get here earlier,' Rachel said.

'It's fine,' Freya said. 'Thanks for coming over. Do you want to come in?'

As Rachel stepped into the house and Freya shut the front door, Mum came out of the kitchen.

'Rachel,' she said. 'Is something wrong?'

'I asked to see her,' Freya said. 'I think you should probably hear this too, Mum.'

She told Mum and Rachel to go into the kitchen, and she'd join them in a minute. Last night, when she'd got home, she'd put the necklace in a clear plastic food bag and put it in her bedside cabinet. She ran upstairs now to get it.

'I found this last night,' she said when she came back down, putting the bag on the table in front of Rachel.

'Is this what I think it is?' Rachel said, lifting the bag and examining the necklace. 'Where did you get it?'

Freya glanced at Mum, who was even paler than she'd been a few minutes ago.

'Freya?' she whispered, her eyes wide and scared looking.

'Lloyd had it,' she said. 'I was at his apartment last night. I found it there.'

'But we searched his apartment,' Rachel said. 'Plus, he gave a statement saying he didn't see Grace the night she disappeared. So how did this end up in his apartment?'

'He must have hidden it somewhere, then taken it to his apartment after you searched it,' Freya said.

'Can someone please tell me what the hell is going on?' Mum said. 'Cassie has been charged with Grace's murder, and I thought that was the end of it. Are you trying to imply that Lloyd also had something to do with what happened to Grace?'

'I don't know,' Freya said. She looked at Rachel. 'But I think Grace was scared of him. He was controlling. Too controlling. She couldn't stand it. She'd tried to finish things between them a few days before she disappeared. He wouldn't accept it was over between them. He kept calling, turning up at the house asking to speak to her.'

'Why didn't you tell us any of this?' Rachel asked.

'Because I didn't understand what was going on,' Freya said. 'I didn't want to believe the things she said about him. I thought she was exaggerating. And then, after she disappeared, Lloyd told me they'd agreed to give things another go. I thought he was telling me the truth.'

She stopped speaking, ashamed. Lloyd had known exactly how she felt about him, and he'd used that. He'd manipulated her, got her to believe him instead of her own sister. Freya knew, if it turned out that Lloyd had killed Grace, she would never be able to forgive herself.

She'd assumed, the times Grace had told her about Lloyd losing his temper, that it was Grace's fault. Because Grace was careless and messy and never stopped to think about how her actions might affect the people around her. But none of this was Grace's fault.

'I think,' Freya continued, 'that Lloyd probably found her that night and tried to talk to her. I don't know what happened, or how he ended up with her necklace, but he had to have seen her that night. There's no other way he could have got that necklace.'

'But her cardigan,' Mum said, 'that was found in Cassie's house.'

'Maybe she saw Lloyd first,' Freya said.

'There's not much point speculating,' Rachel said, standing up. 'Thanks for this, Freya.'

'Hang on,' Mum said. 'What's going to happen now?'

'This will be logged as evidence and we'll bring Lloyd in to give us another statement.'

'Does this mean Cassie didn't do it?' Freya asked.

'Until we speak to Lloyd, we won't know what any of this means,' Rachel said. 'Is there anything else you need to tell me before I go, Freya?'

'No.' Freya shook her head. 'That's everything.'

Rachel looked at her for a moment, as if she was trying to assess whether Freya was telling the truth. Then she nodded her head. 'Good.'

After Rachel left, Freya went up to her room and called Patrick.

'It's me,' she said. 'Are you free to meet up later?'

'I'm free now,' he said. 'What do you fancy doing?'

'Can we go back to Falling Sands?' she said. 'Maybe see if that heron is there again.'

'Sounds like a plan,' Patrick said. 'If I leave now, I can be there in twenty minutes.'

'Perfect,' Freya said. 'Thanks, Patrick.'

She hung up, feeling lighter now it was all done. She packed a bag for the beach and then went into Grace's bedroom and lay down on her bed. The room smelled of Grace still, jasmine body lotion and Toy 2 eau de parfum. Freya knew the smell would fade over time, but for now she breathed it in deeply and let her mind fill with memories of her dead sister.

Fifty-two

Dee had two choices: wallow in self-pity and wine, or pull herself together and accept Ed was gone and there wasn't much she could do about that. After a swim, an early night and a long walk the following morning, she decided on the second of those options.

Earlier this morning, she'd received a reply to one of her posts on a Crawley Facebook group. A woman called Sue Stapleton had sent Dee a message to say that her father used to work at Cavellini Construction. Dee had sent Sue a private message with her email and phone number and hoped she wouldn't have to wait too long to hear back from her.

An hour later, Sue Stapleton called her back.

'Is this because of what's happened to Joey's niece?' Sue said. 'Because if you're a journalist, I don't want to speak to you.'

'I'm not a journalist,' Dee said, crossing her fingers as if that made up for the lie. 'I'm actually doing a favour for my uncle. He worked for CC when the company was just beginning, and he's trying to get in touch with some of his old colleagues.'

'Oh, that's lovely of you,' Sue replied. 'I'm afraid you're too late, though. My dad died years ago.'

'I'm sorry to hear that,' Dee said. 'I don't suppose you have the names of anyone else who might have worked there?'

'No. My dad left the company around the time Paul was killed, and died shortly after that. You could try speaking to my mum, I guess. She's been following the story on the news and it's got her properly upset. Although I'm not sure why, because

243

my dad and Joey didn't exactly see eye to eye. I don't know the details, but I'm pretty sure Joey's the reason my dad quit his job.'

'If I could speak to your mum that would be fantastic.'

Dee's stomach fizzed with adrenaline. Finally, she'd found someone who didn't think Joey Cavellini was the greatest living human being.

'Let me have a word with Mum,' Sue said. 'She may not want to talk to you, but I can ask her. First, though, you need to promise me you're not going to say or do anything to upset her. She's been through a lot, my mum.'

Dee squeezed her eyes shut and forced herself to take several slow breaths before responding.

'I promise I'll be careful,' she said. 'But can you please tell her this is important? It would mean the world to my dad if I could track down some of his old mates.'

'I'll do my best,' Sue said. 'But I'm not making any promises. If Mum's willing to talk to you, I'll call you back. If you don't hear from me, that means she's not interested.'

It wasn't a great outcome, but it was all that was on offer.

Dee thanked Sue for her time and ended the call. Sue said her father had left the job around the time of Paul's murder. She hadn't implied the two events were connected, but Dee thought they might be. Although she wouldn't know for sure until she'd managed to speak to Sue's mother.

She was meeting Jennifer for a drink that evening. They'd arranged to meet at the bar in Port, a new boutique hotel on the seafront. It was Dee's first time here, and she spent longer than she normally would choosing a drink from the surprisingly good wine selection. Eventually opting for a glass of Chapel Down rosé, she took a seat by the window and waited for Jennifer.

Her wine was finished by the time Jennifer finally showed up, forty minutes later than they'd agreed.

'I'm sorry,' she said, dropping into the seat opposite Dee. 'I got caught up with something and couldn't get away.'

She looked flustered and stressed, as if she'd rather be anywhere else.

'It's okay,' Dee said. 'I was very happy sitting here people-watching. This place is lovely. I haven't been before, but I certainly plan to come back. Let me get you a drink. What would you like?'

'A glass of sparkling water,' Jennifer said. 'I don't have long, I'm afraid. I've got another appointment in twenty minutes.'

'Doing anything nice?' Dee asked, as she stood up.

'What? Oh, just a work thing. One of those women-in-business networking events. I don't really want to go, but I promised a friend I'd go with her and I can't really let her down. It's in the Cavendish. Starts at seven. I don't want to be late, because my friend is a bit nervous about going.'

Dee went to the bar and ordered two glasses of sparkling water. The wine had been lovely, but one glass was enough. She had walked here, so she could have another glass if she wanted to. But she suspected she needed a clear head for the conversation she was about to have.

'Is it the Chamber of Commerce?' she said, after she'd got the drinks and sat back down again.

'What?' Jennifer frowned, sounding confused.

'Your event at the Cavendish.'

'Oh. Yes, I think so.'

'Well, I'd better get straight to the reason I wanted to see you.' Dee smiled. 'Can't have you being late for your friend.'

She took a sip of her water, wondering why Jennifer had lied about where she was going. Dee might not know much about Eastbourne's business community, but she'd been dragged along by Louise to enough Chamber of Commerce networking events over the years to know that they never took place on a Sunday.

'I've been to see Cassie,' she said.

'How's she doing?'

'Not great,' Dee said. 'Barely holding it together, I'd say.'

'Did she tell you why she did it? Why she killed Grace?'

'She says it wasn't her.'

'She would say that, wouldn't she?'

'She also told me you'd known about Grace all along,' Dee said. 'Yet when you and I spoke about it, you told me Cassie hadn't told you that her daughter was living in Eastbourne. You said it came as a total shock when you found out about Grace.'

Jennifer took a sip of her water, but didn't say anything.

'Why did you lie about that?' Dee asked.

'Who says I lied?' Jennifer said. 'Maybe it's Cassie who's lying. Did that occur to you?'

'Why would she lie about it?' Dee said. 'It doesn't make any sense.'

'And it doesn't make any sense that I'd lie about it, either,' Jennifer said. 'Don't you think if I'd known, that I'd have gone straight to the police the moment that young woman first went missing?'

'Unless you had your own reasons for not wanting to speak to the police,' Dee said.

Jennifer pushed her chair back and stood up.

'I don't have to listen to this. I came here because you said you wanted to see me. If I'd known you were going to sit there and throw all sorts of allegations at me, I wouldn't have bothered. Thanks for the drink, Dee. I hope I never have the misfortune of seeing you again.'

As she left, Dee watched her through the window. Jennifer crossed the road and turned right, onto the promenade that ran along by the beach. Dee waited until Jennifer was safely across the road before getting up and going outside too. Dee crossed the road and, keeping her eyes fixed on Jennifer's back, started following her.

Jennifer walked straight past the Cavendish hotel, confirming Dee's suspicion that she had lied. Dee knew that people only lied when they had something to hide.

A little before Holywell, where the promenade ended and the chalky hills of the South Downs began, Jennifer turned away from the seafront and crossed back over the road.

Dee held back, watching as Jennifer pushed open a gate that led into the gardens of a tall apartment block beside the Hydro hotel. By the time Dee had navigated the traffic and reached the other side of the road, Jennifer was out of sight.

The building had two glass-panelled entrance doors that didn't budge when Dee tried to open them. Peering through one of the glass panels, Dee saw a man wearing a concierge's uniform sitting behind a curved reception desk.

When she knocked on the glass, the man looked up and pointed at something to the left of Dee. Stepping back, she saw there was an intercom system with rows of buttons for the individual apartments. But there were no names beside any of the buttons, so that didn't help.

She knocked on the glass again and, with a heavy sigh that was visible from where Dee was standing, the man heaved himself out of his chair and came over to the entrance.

'You shouldn't be knocking like that,' he said, as he opened the door. 'If you want to speak to someone, you need to buzz their apartment.'

'Sorry.' She gave him what she hoped was her best apologetic smile. 'I'm here to visit a friend. I know she lives in this building, but I can't remember which apartment.'

'If you give me your name, and your friend's name,' he said, 'I can call her apartment and let her know you're here. But you'll need to wait outside while I do that.'

'Of course. Her name's Jennifer Trevorrow.'

'There's no one with that name living here in South Cliff Tower.'

'What about the woman who went inside a few minutes ago?' Dee said. 'Who was she coming to visit?'

'I can't give out that information,' the man said. 'I think you should go.'

Dee tried to get him to change his mind, but he shut the door in her face and retreated back to his desk. As she walked back towards the road, she tried to work out why Jennifer had lied about where she was going. Fifty minutes later, Dee was back home and she still hadn't thought of an answer that made any sense.

Fifty-three

The following day, Dee drove to Reading, where she had arranged to meet Liz Havers. As she navigated the busy town centre in her car, Dee deeply regretted not taking the train. The coffee shop Liz had suggested for this meeting was in the middle of a shopping centre, possibly the last place on earth Dee wanted to be. By the time she'd found a parking space in the packed car park, travelled up and down numerous escalators, and acclimatised her body to the glaring lights and pounding music, she was feeling exceptionally out of sorts.

To cheer herself up, she ordered a slice of millionaire's short-bread with her cappuccino. There was no sign of Liz yet, so Dee sat at a table near the back of the coffee shop where it was slightly quieter, and scrolled through her phone while she waited. She had a new text message from Nessa. Dee had called her yesterday and they'd had a long chat about Ed. Nessa was convinced he would come around and had asked Dee to be patient in the meantime.

'The stroke affected him more than either of us realised,' Nessa said. 'It's knocked his confidence. I'm sorry he's avoiding you. I've tried telling him he's being childish, but he won't listen to me. Please don't give up on him just yet, Dee. You're the best thing that's happened to my brother in a long time. He knows that too, even if he's acting like an idiot at the moment.'

Nessa had promised she would keep Dee updated on Ed's progress, and that's what today's text message was about.

> He went for a walk with Javi earlier. J thought he was in good spirits but when they came back Ed went to his room and hasn't come out since. I'm trying not to worry about him, but it's hard.

Thank goodness for Nessa and her partner, Dee thought, as she typed an answer as quickly as her fingers could tap out the words. At least she knew Ed was in good hands, even if she wasn't able to take care of him herself.

> Do you want me to come up?

She watched the three dots on the screen that indicated Nessa was typing a reply.

> Not yet. Give it a few more days. I'll stay in touch. X

So that was it. She had to wait until Ed decided he was ready to see her. It was difficult not to be angry with him for shutting her out, but Dee didn't have a choice. Getting angry wasn't going to change anything.

There was still no sign of Liz. They had arranged to meet at eleven. When Dee checked the time and saw it was already twenty-five past eleven, she experienced an uncomfortable feeling of déjà vu. Just a few weeks ago, she'd been sitting alone waiting for Ed. He hadn't turned up because something bad had happened. Dee didn't want to think that might also be the reason for Liz's tardiness.

At eleven thirty, she sent a text to Liz's mobile asking if everything was okay. By eleven forty-five, she hadn't received a reply and the fluttering anxiety in her stomach was growing with every minute that passed. When midday came around, it was clear that Liz wasn't coming and Dee had to make a decision about what to do next. The sensible thing would be to drive back to Eastbourne and wait until Liz got in touch. There could be any number of reasons she hadn't been able to make today's appointment. A sick child or husband, a broken-down car, or an unexpected visitor which meant Liz hadn't been able to sneak away. Except if something had come up, wouldn't she have sent a message explaining why she couldn't make this meeting?

It took less than forty minutes for Dee to drive from the centre of Reading to Bray. Another ten to get through the village to the road that led to the house she'd visited the last time she'd been here. Except today, Dee wasn't able to make it as far as Liz's house.

The entrance to the road was blocked off by a row of traffic cones and a red sign with the words ROAD CLOSED on it. Dee pulled in to the side of the road, switched the engine off, got out and walked between the traffic cones blocking the road to Liz's house. She couldn't see the house from the top of the road, but, as she walked towards it, she saw two police cars parked on either side of the gates leading into the Havers' driveway.

'Hey!' A woman, wearing a dark navy suit and a severe expression on her face, had spotted Dee and was walking towards her. 'This road is closed to the public. You'll need to turn around and go back the other way.'

'What's happened?' Dee asked, looking past the woman.

'Campbell!' the woman shouted to a uniformed officer standing by one of the cars. 'I thought I told you to get someone at the top of the road. We can't have people wandering down here to see what's going on. Get Howard or Bateman up there right away.'

When she'd finished issuing orders, the woman turned her attention back to Dee.

'You should be walking away already, but seeing as you're still here, I'll get one of my officers to accompany you back to the top of the road.'

'Is it Liz?' Dee said. 'Please, you've got to tell me what's going on.'

She saw a flash of interest then in the other woman's face.

'You want to tell me who you are and what you're doing here?'

'I'm...' Dee paused, struggling to find the words to explain properly. 'I was meant to be meeting Liz this morning. When she didn't show up, I drove over here to check she was okay.'

'Why?'

The woman was staring at her in a way Dee didn't like. She thought of Cassie, and what it would be like for the police to look at you like this all the time. As if they'd already decided you were guilty of something.

'I'm a journalist,' Dee said. 'I'm writing a story about a murder that took place sixteen years ago. Liz was a key witness for the prosecution. We were meant to meet today because she said she had something important to tell me. But she never turned up.'

'What's your name?'

'Dee Doran.'

'Okay, Dee. My name's Detective Inspector Niamh Roache. I hope you don't have any plans for the rest of the day, because we're going to need to bring you in to answer some questions and give us a statement.'

'That's fine,' Dee said, 'I'll do whatever you want. But can't you at least tell me what's going on?'

'All in good time,' Niamh Roache said. 'For now, if you could come with me please?'

She gestured for Dee to walk with her towards one of the police cars. Dee opened her mouth to say she wasn't going anywhere until someone told her what had happened and where Liz was. But something in the detective's face made her change her mind. Meekly, she allowed herself to be led to the car, where a policeman had already opened one of the back passenger doors for her to stoop down and get inside.

Fifty-four

Freya waited for the Sunday lunchtime rush to pass before visiting Albertine's. As she walked in, the sullen girl with the blue eyes saw her and scowled. Ignoring her, Freya looked around for Lloyd. He wasn't inside, but when she walked into the garden, she saw him sitting by himself nursing a bottle of beer.

'You've got a check turning up here,' he said.

'She was scared of you,' Freya said, pulling out the chair opposite him and sitting down because her legs were shaking so badly she wasn't sure they'd hold her up for much longer. Not just her legs, her entire body was trembling. A combination of anger and nerves, combined with a giddiness that came from finally seeing him for what he was.

'That is utter bullshit.'

He wouldn't look at her. Instead, he focused on peeling the label off the beer bottle and scattering the pieces of paper on the table.

'It's the truth.'

He shook his head and continued peeling paper off the bottle.

'You know, Freya, I thought we were friends. When you found that necklace, all you had to do was ask me about it and I'd have told you the truth. But you went to the police.'

He looked up at her then, his eyes flashing with an anger she'd never seen in him before but she knew now had always been there. Rachel Lewis had told Mum and Freya that they'd interviewed Lloyd under caution before releasing him. He had admitted to seeing Grace the night she disappeared, but claimed Grace had cut the meeting short because she'd had to be somewhere else.

'You told the police you had the necklace because the clasp broke and you told Grace you'd get it fixed.'

'That's right.'

'I think that's bullshit.'

'Well I don't care what you think,' he said.

'She wasn't planning to meet you that night,' Freya said. 'She was going to meet our uncle, and after that she had arranged to meet some people at the Dew Drop Inn. How did she end up with you?'

'We bumped into each other,' Lloyd said. 'We got chatting, and we agreed to give things another go. She never wanted to end things between us. It was a bit of a misunderstanding, nothing more than that.'

'If that's the case, why did she go somewhere else? Why didn't she stay with you?'

'She said there was something she needed to do.' Lloyd sighed. 'But wouldn't tell me where she was going. She was always so secretive. It drove me mad. I thought there was someone else, but I was wrong. It was that woman – Cassie. She's the reason Grace and I grew apart.'

'No,' Freya said. 'You grew apart because of your behaviour. You always wanted to know who she was with and how she was spending her time when she wasn't with you.'

'Because I knew she was hiding something from me,' Lloyd said. 'And I was right, wasn't I? She'd been lying to me. Meeting up with her mother and not telling me about it. I was her boyfriend. She should have told me what she was up to. No one can blame me for becoming a bit paranoid.'

'I don't want to hear anything else,' Freya said. 'I came here to tell you that she didn't love you. You might try to convince yourself that she did, but it's not true. She was scared of you, and she broke it off with you because she realised the sort of person you really are. A bully and a coward. And if you give any newspaper interview, saying how in love you both were, I will contact the paper myself and tell them the truth.'

She pushed her chair back and stood up.

'You're making a big mistake, Freya.'

She looked down at his hand, wrapped around her wrist. 'Let me go.'

She must have spoken too loudly, because she felt eyes turning to watch her as she pulled her wrist free and hurried away from him. She heard him calling her name, but she didn't turn around.

Outside, Patrick was waiting for her.

'I didn't think you'd still be here,' she said, getting into his car.

'Where else would I go?' He reached over and squeezed her hand. To her surprise, she found herself returning the pressure and keeping her fingers wrapped around his. 'How did it go?'

'It was okay,' she said. 'I'm glad I did it.'

'Good for you.'

She should have felt better, but her stomach was churning and there were too many thoughts inside her head. All of them bouncing off the sides and colliding with each other, creating an endless cacophony of noise that she couldn't control. The only thing that felt steady and right was Patrick, sitting beside her like he knew she needed him to stop her spinning out of control.

Fifty-five

Liz was dead. The detectives who'd interviewed Dee wouldn't tell her any details, but she'd picked up enough from the questions they'd asked her to know she'd been murdered. They had kept her in for such a long time, Dee had worried that they might never let her out again. But after five hours, Detective Inspector Niamh Roache told her she was free to leave.

On the long drive home, she had kept the radio on. News about the murder of a young mother in Bray had started to trickle through. The woman's identity, for now, had been kept from the media, but Dee knew it was only a matter of time before Liz Havers became a household name.

Too sick to eat, Dee sat on her deck drinking cups of tea and obsessively updating the news feeds on her phone, desperate for information about how Liz had died. By nine o'clock that evening, she had learned precious little that she didn't know already. The victim was Liz Havers, a thirty-seven-year-old woman from Bray. Her body had been found earlier today, and her death was being treated as suspicious.

It was a warm evening, but Dee couldn't stop shivering. Even when she went inside and shut the doors, she was still freezing. The cold was coming from inside her, fear mixed with shock and anger all combining to mess up her body's natural rhythms. The urge to open a bottle of wine was strong, but she held off. No matter how painful these feelings were, she owed it to poor Liz to experience every one of them. Because Dee knew, with absolute certainty, that Liz Havers would still be alive if it wasn't for her. This knowledge would sit with her for the rest of her life. A woman was dead. Two young children had lost their mother. A husband had lost his wife. None of these people would be going through what they were going through now if it wasn't for Dee.

Someone hadn't wanted Liz to tell Dee what she knew about Paul Cavellini's murder. Why? There was only one answer Dee could think of that made any sense. Liz had lied during the murder trial. She had blamed Cassie, when all along she knew someone else had killed Paul. The most obvious explanation for this was that Liz had killed him and lied to cover up her own crime. But if that was the case, Liz Havers would still be alive. Which meant she'd lied to protect someone else. Who? And how had that person even known that Dee and Lizzie had arranged to meet?

Dee put her head in her hands and groaned. It was late and her brain was too tired to process this unholy mess. She should get up and go to bed, but she didn't have the energy to do anything except sit here on the sofa, going back over everything in the futile hope that she would uncover something important.

The sudden sound of her phone ringing made her jump. She checked the caller ID before answering. No name, just a number she didn't recognise, which meant whoever was calling wasn't one of her contacts.

'Hello?'

She could hear breathing, nothing else. Fear crawled up the back of her throat until she could taste it, like metal, on her tongue. It was dark on the beach, the blackness deep and impenetrable. Anyone could be out there, watching her.

'Who the hell is this?' she said.

'Dee? Is this Dee Doran?'

'Yes.'

'This is Mark Collier. I hope you don't mind me calling. Nina gave me your number.'

'Where are you?' Dee said, scanning the beach half expecting to see him walking towards her.

'I'm at home,' he said. 'Why?'

'No reason.' Some of the tension left her body. 'What do you want, Mark?'

'I need to see you,' he said. 'It's about my sister.'

Dread sat in the pit of Dee's stomach as she realised he must have seen the news. All the main sites she'd visited this evening included a photo of the dead woman. If he'd seen that, then he would know.

'When do you want to meet?' she asked.

'Is now any good? I'm happy to drive to wherever you live. Or we can meet somewhere. I don't want you coming to my house. I need to keep this separate from my family.'

'You can come here,' Dee said.

As she gave him her address, she looked out at the dark beach and thought about what Ed would say if he knew she was inviting a man she barely knew to come and see her while she was alone with no one else around. But Ed wasn't here, so whatever he thought of it didn't matter. Dee was alone, and that meant making whatever decisions she wanted without having to care what anyone else thought.

Fifty-six

Before

Cassie's face in the bathroom mirror was white and alien. Like it was a stranger's face. There was a brackish brown streak on her left cheek. The smell of metal and meat clogged the inside of her mouth and the back of her throat. A ringing sound in her ears blocked out all other sounds.

She closed her eyes, then wished she hadn't. Flashing images, like a light being switched on and off. Paul's face as he lunged for her. Blackness, followed by another image. Blood pooling on the lino floor, running in between the pattern of black and white squares. The knife in her hand, heavy and slippery. Wet with his blood. Flash, flash, flash. Image after image after image, exploding behind her eyes. She turned on the tap, splashed cold water on her face, but it didn't help. Nothing would help, because this was really happening. The thing she'd wished for, except now she didn't know how she could ever have wanted this because it was terrible. Worse than anything that she could have imagined.

A sudden noise from outside the bathroom cut through the other sounds, the ones that were playing on a constant loop inside her head. A scream rose at the back of her throat and she put her hand over her mouth to block the sound. He was still alive. Pulling himself off the wet floor that was covered in his blood, picking up the knife and coming for her.

Cassie pressed herself against the wall, whimpering as she waited for the rattle of the door handle, but it never came.

And when she heard the sound again, she realised it was Grace, snuffling and shifting in her sleep.

A sob rose at the back of her throat. Grace loved him. Had loved him. Would continue to love him and would be confused and sad because she wouldn't understand where he had gone. Poor little girl.

The house phone started to ring. The sound loud and shrill. She had to stop it, because it would wake Grace up and Cassie couldn't cope with that. First, she needed to work out what to do.

She ran out of the bathroom and down the stairs.

'Hello?' she whispered, putting the receiver to her ear.

'Cassie?'

Joey. Cassie's chest tightened.

'Yes.'

'I'm trying to get hold of Paul, but I think his phone must be switched off. Is he home, by any chance?'

The phone was broken, not switched off. Lying beside his dead body, the screen smashed. Little pieces of plastic scattered across the floor, cutting the sole of her right foot. She lifted her foot and saw it was still bleeding. A trail of blood on the stairs and the carpet.

'Cassie? Are you still there?'

'Paul's not here.'

'You sure about that? He left work ages ago. Told me he was going straight home.'

A lie. He never came straight home. Always went to the pub first, so her memories of him were tinged with the stink of beer.

'Is everything okay, Cassie?'

'Fine.'

The front door was open. She crossed the hall to close it. Another memory came to her then. Mark had been here. Standing on the road outside the house. When he'd seen her, he'd turned and walked away. She'd called his name, but he hadn't turned around. If anything, he'd walked faster. As if he needed to get away from her as quickly as possible.

When had that happened? Before or after Paul had been killed? She didn't know, because everything that had happened this evening was jumbled up in her brain, like a book that had had its pages torn out and no matter how hard she tried she couldn't put them back together in the right order.

'Do you need me to come over?' Joey said.

'No!' She knew she shouldn't shout, but he couldn't come here. Not him, of all people. 'Sorry,' she said, forcing herself to speak calmly. 'I'm very tired. I'll ask Paul to call you when he gets in.'

Joey said something, but she didn't hear him and she didn't ask him to repeat himself. She hung up, leaning on the table to stop herself from toppling over.

What had she done? Each time she tried to piece it together, her mind skipped back and forth from one memory to the next. A kaleidoscope of images that briefly came into focus, then faded away again before she could make sense of them. The harder she tried, the more confusing it became, until eventually all that was left was a single memory: Paul's eyes, open and empty as he stared up at her from the cold kitchen floor.

Fifty-seven

Dee heard Mark Collier before she saw him. The growl of his car engine as he approached the house, the crunch of footsteps and the sudden, shrill sound of the doorbell.

The first thing she thought when she opened the door and saw him was that he looked dreadful. Red-rimmed eyes and a face that had aged at least ten years since the last time she'd seen him.

'I'm so sorry,' she said.

'Nina told me you were asking about her,' he said. 'Do you have anything to do with this?'

'I was due to meet her today,' Dee said, 'but she never turned up. Someone killed her first.'

'Why?'

'I don't know for sure,' Dee said, 'but I think it has something to do with Paul's murder.'

He nodded, as if that made sense.

'There's a phone number you can call if you have any information about her. I called and told the man who answered that she was my sister. He said someone would call me back, but that was hours ago. What am I supposed to do now?'

'Do you want to come inside?' Dee asked.

He hesitated, before nodding his head and stepping into the sitting room.

'Sit down.' Dee took his arm and led him over to one of the armchairs. 'I'll get us both a cup of tea.'

'Do I need to worry about my wife and kids?' he asked, after the tea was made and Dee was sitting down opposite him.

'I don't think so,' Dee said. 'Lizzie was killed because someone didn't want her talking to me about Paul's murder.'

'She lied in court,' Mark said. 'It's why we stopped speaking. I couldn't believe she would do something like that. I know she and Cassie had a falling out, but that didn't excuse what Lizzie did. She destroyed Cassie's life.'

'How do you know she lied?'

'Because I was there that night,' Mark said. 'I don't know who killed Paul, but I know for sure it couldn't have been Cassie.'

Dee nearly spat out her tea. 'You were there?'

'Paul used to hit her,' Mark said. 'I knew it was happening, but I didn't know what to do about it.'

Dee thought of Cassie, frail and vulnerable, and knew that even if she had killed her husband she didn't deserve to spend ten years in prison because of it if her husband had been beating the crap out of her.

'Cassie begged me not to get involved, but I couldn't sit back and do nothing. I saw Paul in the pub one night and I lost it. He went outside for a cigarette and I followed him out. We had a row that turned into a fight. It was a stupid thing to do and only made things worse for Cassie, not better.

'After that, I started watching the house, thinking if things kicked off, I could stop them. It was stupid. Especially because most of the time I was drunk, so it's unlikely I would have been any use to Cassie.

'The night Paul was killed, they had a row. I could hear them screaming at each other and I was about go and bang on their door when Cassie came storming out. She had Grace with her, in the buggy. She headed down the road, pushing the buggy, and I followed her. After a bit, I caught up with her and pretended it was a coincidence we were both out at the same time. As soon as she realised I'd been drinking, she made it clear she didn't want to talk to me.'

He stopped speaking and frowned.

'It's important you know that my memories from that night aren't as clear as they should be. I don't know how much time passed between Cassie leaving the house and when I spoke to her. All I remember is that she was angry. With me, as well as Paul. So much of that night is a blur, but I remember her face so clearly. She hated me for being drunk, because she knew I was no good to her like that.

'She told me to leave her alone, so I did. I was angry myself, by then. And of course I blamed Paul. Which is why I went back to their house.'

A finger of ice-cold fear trickled down Dee's back.

'I have no idea what I was planning to do,' Mark said. His voice had grown softer, the closer he got to describing what he'd done. 'I think in that moment I probably wanted to kill him. I couldn't go through another day of wondering whether she was okay.'

Dee's shoulders ached and there was a tightness in her chest. Her whole body was tense as she waited for him to continue.

'The front door was open, so I walked straight in.' He was whispering now and Dee had to lean forward to hear what he was saying. 'There's nothing like the sight of a dead man to sober you up, I can tell you that. It was horrible. No. Worse than horrible. There are no words to describe what it was like.'

'Hang on,' Dee said. 'You've lost me. Are you saying he was already dead when you got there?'

'Of course. Oh God, you thought I was going to tell you I killed him? No, it wasn't me. He was well and truly dead by the time I got there.'

All the tension left her body in a rush. As her mind readjusted to this new narrative, she realised there was still too much she didn't understand.

'How do you know Cassie hadn't killed him before she left the house?'

'He was still alive then,' Mark said, 'I heard him shouting at her as she left.'

'You're sure of that?'

'Absolutely.'

'But if you've always known Cassie couldn't have killed him, how did she end up in prison?'

'I should have called the police there and then,' Mark said. 'But when I saw him, I freaked. Everyone knew Paul and I had rowed a few weeks earlier. I was terrified the police would think it was me, that I'd killed him. So I left. I ran away.'

'But surely later you told the police Cassie couldn't have done it?'

'I tried,' Mark said, 'but they didn't take me seriously. Several people had seen me in the pub earlier, and gave statements saying how drunk I was. The police decided my statement couldn't be put forward as evidence, because I was too drunk to give a rational account of what had happened that night. It was like they'd already decided Cassie was guilty.'

'When I spoke with Nina,' Dee said, 'she told me Cassie tried to blame you for Paul's murder.'

'She saw me leaving the house,' Mark said. 'I can hardly blame her for thinking it was me. But she was wrong. Paul was already dead when I got there.'

'You must have some idea who killed him?'

'I don't know,' Mark said, dashing the last shred of hope Dee had been clinging on to. 'Paul was a proper dickhead. No one liked him very much, which means there were probably lots of people who weren't too sad when they found out he was dead. But did I know anyone who hated him enough to kill him? No. In fact, I can't think of anyone who hated him more than I did.'

Mark left shortly after that. At the front door, he paused.

'There's something else I meant to ask you,' he said. 'That day you came to my house, you asked me if I was Grace's father. Why?'

'I think,' Dee said, choosing her words carefully, 'there's a chance that Paul wasn't Grace's real father.'

'And you think the father might be me.' Mark shook his head. 'Impossible. Cassie and I had already split up when she became pregnant. The timings don't work. Whoever Grace's father is, it's not me.'

Fifty-eight

When Freya heard her uncle's car pulling up outside the house, she grabbed a bottle of wine from the fridge and went out to the garden. She couldn't cope with Jocy's restless energy and seething anger this evening. She drank some wine straight from the bottle and lay down on the grass looking up at the night sky. It was beautiful tonight. A blanket of inky black with thousands of tiny white stars sprinkled across its surface. This time of year, here on the edge of the South Downs, you could lose count of the number of times you saw shooting stars. Endless explosions of light, bright and white across the sky, before each star burned out and disappeared.

She had her phone with her, and tried to video the shooting stars, but she was never quick enough to capture one. She gave up in the end, sent a message to Patrick asking him if he could see the shooting stars where he was.

Too much light pollution in my part of town, he replied. Then, *Did you know shooting stars aren't actually stars? They're small pieces of space dust hitting Earth's atmosphere.*

Another one burst across the sky. As she watched it disappear, Freya wondered how she could have reached the age she was without knowing this basic astronomical fact. Patrick was one of the few people she knew who was cleverer than she was. Normally, she'd find that annoying, but he wore his intelligence so modestly it was easier to like him than be jealous of him.

She took a photo of the sky and sent it to him.

Maybe we could go stargazing together some time, he replied.

Maybe, she typed, then hit send before she could change her mind.

She stayed outside for another hour, watching the pieces of space dust crash into the Earth's atmosphere and explode in a flash of bright light. The combination of wine and stars made her feel dizzy and light-headed. And reckless.

She picked up her phone to tell Patrick to come over. They could spend the night sitting out here, watching stars falling from the sky. She started typing, the wine giving her an urgency and a lack of restraint she wasn't used to. But before she had finished the message, her phone ran out of charge. As it died, so did her sudden desire to tell Patrick how she felt about him.

It was getting cold. She stood up and went inside to look for a charger. As soon as she opened the kitchen door, she heard them. Raised voices that told her something was wrong.

'Why are you trying to deny it?' Mum said. 'It's definitely her. Jesus Christ, they even have the same name.'

'Keep your voice down for Christ's sake, Trish. You don't want Freya to hear.'

'It's her,' Mum said. 'And she was murdered, just like Grace. If you try to tell me this is nothing more than a coincidence, I swear to God I will scream.'

Freya felt a tickle in her nose and knew she was about to sneeze. She tried to hold it in, but that only made it worse. After a few agonising seconds, it exploded out of her nose and mouth with a loud whooshing sound.

'Freya?' Mum called.

'Hi.' She walked down the hall and pushed open the sitting-room door.

Mum and Joey were sitting side by side on the sofa, facing the TV. It was switched on, but, as Freya came into the room, Joey grabbed the remote and switched it off.

'Is everything okay?' Mum asked.

'What were you two talking about?'

'Nothing important,' Joey said, before Mum had a chance to answer.

Freya looked at the blank TV screen, trying to remember what had been on there before he'd switched it off so quickly. A news programme maybe, although she couldn't be sure.

If she'd thought either of them would tell her the truth, she would have asked again. But it was clear from the stubborn set of her uncle's jaw that he wasn't going to tell her anything. She said goodnight to them both and went upstairs.

In her bedroom, she sat on the edge of her bed scrolling through the different news websites. Unsure what she was looking for, until suddenly there it was.

She read the story several times, zooming in on the photo that accompanied it as she tried to make sense of something that didn't make any sense at all. She opened another news site, then another, skimming all of them for as much detail as she could find.

Downstairs, she could hear Mum and Joey moving into the hallway and then the sound of the front door opening. He was leaving.

'I still think you're worrying about nothing,' he said. 'It's no wonder your mind's gone into overdrive after everything that's happened. How about this? I'll make a few phone calls tomorrow and see what I can find out.'

'I'd really appreciate that,' Mum said. 'Thanks, Joey. I don't know what I'd do without you.'

'We're family, little sister. And family stick together, through bad times as well as good.'

Freya felt a surge of something dark and bitter rising up inside her. He was a bad man. The knowledge came to her as if this was something she'd known all along but had chosen – until now – never to admit. Mum was right to be scared. But it wasn't Cassie or Freya or anyone else she should be scared of. It was him.

Fifty-nine

Dee called David Verney early the following morning.

'You never told me about the statement Mark Collier gave,' she said.

'Because it was a pack of lies,' David said. 'And good morning to you too, by the way.'

'Why do you think it was a pack of lies?' Dee asked.

'Mark was off his head drunk the night Paul was killed,' David said. 'We had several witnesses who gave statements to that effect. He was in love with Cassie and lied to protect her.'

'Was he ever a suspect?'

'Of course,' David said. 'We had it on record that he'd had a fight with Paul a few weeks before the murder. But the evidence against Cassie was much stronger than it had ever been against Mark.'

'Cassie told you she saw him at her house.'

'Cassie said a lot of things. She was desperate, don't forget. She'd have said anything if she thought it would help her case. Listen, Dee, I thought we'd agreed you were going to stop trying to prove I didn't do my job properly.'

'That was before Lizzie Collier was murdered.'

'What are you talking about?'

'Google the name Liz Havers,' Dee said. 'You'll see what I mean.'

She hung up before he could say anything else. A second later, her phone started ringing. She saw David's name on the screen and diverted the call. She'd said all she needed to.

Twenty minutes later, when her phone rang again, she thought it might be him calling back. But this call was from Sue Stapleton, the woman whose father had worked with Joey and Paul.

'Hi Sue. It's good to hear from you again.'

'I've spoken to Mum,' Sue said. 'She doesn't want to meet up, but she's happy to have a quick chat over the phone if you think that would be helpful?'

'That sounds brilliant,' Dee said. 'Do you want to give me her number?'

'I can do better than that,' Sue said. 'I've got Mum with me now. Hang on.'

A moment later, someone else came on the line and said hello.

'Mrs Stapleton,' Dee said, 'thank you so much for agreeing to speak to me.'

'Please call me Olive, dear. And your name is Dee, is that right?'

'Yes,' Dee said.

'And your uncle used to work at CC? What's his name? It's possible I knew him, although I only ever met a handful of Ralph's work colleagues. He liked to keep a separation between his work life and his home life.'

Thank God for that, Dee thought, as she reeled off a fictitious name.

'Ah, I'm afraid that name doesn't ring any bells,' Olive said.

'Did your husband stay in touch with anyone from CC after he left?' Dee asked. 'If you have any contacts from that time, it would mean the world to my uncle.'

'I'm afraid I can't help you, dear. You see, Ralph left the company under something of a cloud. Actually, your father probably remembers all that business. It caused quite a stir at the time.'

'That would be the row your husband had with Joey?' Dee said, remembering that Olive's daughter had mentioned her father and Joey hadn't got along.

'The Cavellini brothers weren't nice men,' Olive said. 'I know we're not supposed to speak ill of the dead, but I'm only saying what everyone knew. Ralph always said it was the parents' fault. "If you don't bring children up the right way, they'll grow up not knowing right from wrong." That's what happened with those boys. Neither of them had a scrap of decency. Maybe that's why they never got along, because they didn't know how to.'

'Why did Joey give Paul a job if they disliked each other so much?' Dee asked.

'I think he did it to torture him,' Olive said. 'Because of Cassie, you know?'

Dee didn't know, but she desperately wanted to.

'If you ask me, it was ridiculous,' Olive continued. 'Joey didn't give a damn about her. He was a proper ladies' man in those days, probably still is. He dated more girls than most of us have had hot dinners. But he couldn't stand it when Cassie started dating Paul so soon after he'd dumped her. And my Ralph couldn't stand the way Joey treated Paul. That's what the row was about. Joey didn't like people standing up to him, but Ralph wasn't afraid of anyone. Least of all a sham of a man like Joey Cavellini.'

Dee was still processing this new information, when Olive dropped another bombshell.

'She came to see me, you know.'

'Who?'

'Grace Parker, the young girl who's been murdered. She came to see me a few weeks ago. She'd managed to find a list of everyone who'd been working at CC at the time of her father's murder. It's possible she spoke to your uncle as well. You might want to ask him about that. She was working her way through the list, speaking to everyone she could find. She was a determined young thing, absolutely hell-bent on proving Cassie was innocent.'

'When was this?' Dee asked, when she was able to formulate words again.

'Four weeks ago,' Olive said.

'You sure about that?' Dee asked.

'Positive, dear. You see, the following day she disappeared. It's not a date I'm going to forget in a hurry.'

Sixty

Freya stood on the street looking up at her uncle's apartment on the top floor of South Cliff tower. It was late, but he was still up. Most of the lights were on, and she could see him moving around from room to room. What was he doing? It was creeping towards two in the morning, yet he was pacing around up there like it was the middle of the day.

She had tried asking Mum what she and Joey had been talking about when Freya interrupted them last night. Mum had said it wasn't anything important. Which was a lie, but Freya didn't call Mum out on it. She knew, from eighteen years of being Trish Parker's daughter, that if Mum didn't want to tell Freya what the conversation had really been about, no amount of cajoling would make her do it.

Several times, she had taken her phone out to call Joey and confront him with what she knew. Each time she had chickened out. She didn't know what to say to him. Didn't know how he'd react.

When her phone pinged with a message, the sudden sound made her jump. She checked the windows of her uncle's apartment, half expecting to see him looking down at her. But the message wasn't from him. It was from Patrick.

> Just woke up and saw ur message. Is everything ok?

Unable to sleep earlier, she had messaged him on Snapchat, asking if he was still up.

I'm on the seafront, she wrote, *fancy coming down?*

She watched the three dots at the bottom of the screen, as he typed his reply.

> Where?

Then, when she typed her answer, he replied instantly.

> C u in 5.

Eight minutes later, a car approached and parked alongside her. The driver's window rolled down and Patrick's face smiled out at her.

'What are we up to?' he asked.

'I'm not sure.' Freya opened the passenger door and climbed in beside him.

'But it's to do with your uncle.'

'How do you know that?' Freya said.

'Because you told me that's where he lives.' Patrick gestured at the building across the road. 'And I can't think of any other reason you're standing here in the middle of the night.'

Freya opened the internet on her phone and went to BBC News website. When she'd found the story she was looking for, she handed the phone to Patrick.

'Look at this.'

She watched Patrick's face, illuminated in the glare of the screen, frowning as he read what she'd asked him to.

'I'm not sure I understand,' he said eventually.

'The woman who was murdered,' Freya said, 'I saw her with Joey last Thursday morning. Right after I bumped into you.'

'Liz Havers? It says here she lives in Berkshire.'

'I know, but last Thursday she was with my uncle. They were over there, outside the apartment building. It looked like they were having some kind of row.'

She was murdered. Just like Grace.

'My mum recognised her,' Freya said, trying to fill in the missing pieces from the conversation she'd overheard last night. 'But Joey tried to persuade her the dead woman was someone else.'

'What do you mean someone else?'

'I don't know. I wish I did. All I know is my mum seemed to know Liz Havers and was convinced her murder is connected with what happened to Grace. Joey told her she was mistaken. But he was lying to her. Why would he do that if he had nothing to hide?'

'Is that why you're here,' Patrick said, 'because you want to ask him about it?'

'I guess.'

'At this time of night?'

'He's still awake,' Freya said. 'The lights are on in his apartment and I've seen him moving around up there.'

'I'm not sure confronting him is a good idea. How do you know he's not dangerous?'

'I don't,' Freya said quietly.

A car drove along the road and pulled up outside the apartment building. A moment later, her uncle appeared. He ran down the steps from South Cliff tower and got into the car.

'Follow them,' Freya said, as the car started to drive away.

She hadn't needed to tell him. Patrick had already switched the engine on and was pulling away from the kerb. Taking care to stay far enough back so they wouldn't be noticed, he followed the car as it drove along the seafront towards Sovereign Harbour on the eastern edge of town.

Sixty-one

Someone was in the house. Dee opened her eyes, going from deep sleep to wide awake in under a second. She sat up in bed, heart pounding, ears straining as she tried to identify what had woken her. But the house was silent and the only sounds were the familiar ones: the sea rolling in and out over the shingle, and the wind rustling through the wild flowers and seagrass on the beach.

She realised it had just been a bad dream and lay back down. She closed her eyes and, immediately, her mind went to the idea that had gradually been taking shape ever since her conversation with Olive Stapleton. Earlier in the day, Dee had sent an email to Cassie saying she needed to see her.

Wide awake now, she reached for her phone to see if she had a reply from Cassie. She had left her phone charging on the bedside table when she'd come to bed. But when she patted the surface of the table, her phone wasn't there. She could feel the charging cable, but not the phone itself. She leaned down, patting the ground around the table, but she still couldn't find the damn thing.

It had definitely been there earlier. She remembered lying here, sending a text to Rachel asking if she was free to meet up tomorrow. Olive had told Dee she'd spoken to the police as soon as she'd heard that Grace Parker was missing. Without Ed, Dee thought Rachel might be a good person to test her theory out on. But without her phone, Dee couldn't see if Rachel had replied.

She was about to switch on the light so she could look for her phone properly, when she heard the bifold doors in the living room sliding open. Dee's heart leapt into her throat. She had one hundred per cent locked the doors before coming to bed. Now they were being opened by whoever had taken her phone to stop her calling for help.

The noise stopped. The house felt eerily silent. And too isolated. Everything Dee loved about living here made her vulnerable. The tagline from the film *Alien* had never been more relevant. Out here, on this lonely stretch of beach, there was no one to hear her scream.

She threw back the quilt and, as quietly as she possibly could, she tiptoed across the room to the window with its newly replaced pane of glass. She pulled up the blind just enough so she could reach the lock and open the window. When she turned the lock, it made a clicking sound that penetrated the silence of the night.

Dee froze, her entire body tense as she waited for the bedroom door to burst open. When nothing happened, she started to slide the window open. She did this slowly, doing all she could to reduce the sound of grating metal as the frame moved. It had needed oiling for months, a job she kept forgetting about. The logical part of her brain told her the grating was barely audible, but to the animal part that was stuck in fight or flight mode, it sounded as loud as a jet plane taking off beside her.

When it was open enough for her head to fit through the gap, she peered out and scanned the length of the deck. There was no one there. Which meant the person who had opened the doors was inside the house.

The house had been built on one level. All the rooms on the ground floor, nothing upstairs except a huge attic that ran the entire length of the house. When she was a child, Dee had been able to scramble onto the window frame and climb out through the window. Tonight, when she tried to hoist her body up, she couldn't do it.

There was a chair on the other side of the room, a pile of Dee's clothes thrown over it. She was halfway across the room to get it, when she heard footsteps in the hallway.

She hadn't shut her bedroom door properly before going to bed. Through the gap, she could see the long shadow of a person standing just outside her room. She bit down on her lip to silence the scream that rose at the back of her throat.

A hand reached out to push the door open wider, and Dee's instincts kicked in. She threw her body against the door, slamming it shut before whoever was out there could get in. Through the buzzing sound inside her head, she heard someone screaming. It took a good three seconds to realise the screams were coming from her.

The handle rattled, but Dee didn't budge, using all her strength to make sure the door stayed closed. She felt a rush of jubilation as the door held fast. She had this. Whoever was on the other side of that door wasn't going any further.

'Get the fuck out of my house,' she shouted.

A foot broke through the lower panel of the door. Dee jumped back, realising her mistake too late as the door swung open. She ran for the window, but she wasn't fast enough. There was a burst of blinding bright light and a pain that travelled down her head into her neck and back. The floor shifted beneath her, as the painted wooden floorboards rose up to smack her in the face as she fell.

Sixty-two

Near Pevensey village, the car turned right into one of the narrow roads that led to the beach. Instead of following it, Patrick kept going and turned into the next road, not stopping until he reached the beach.

'If we park here,' he said, 'we can walk back along the beach and hopefully find them.'

Out here, away from the road, it was pitch black. The moon and stars were hidden behind a thick blanket of clouds. They had to use the torches on their phones to see where they were going, which wasn't ideal as they didn't want to be seen by Joey and whoever was with him.

'It's beautiful out here,' Patrick whispered. 'We should camp on the beach sometime.'

'Camping's pretty much the last thing on my mind right now,' Freya said. 'Who's my uncle with? And what are they doing out here in the middle of the night?'

Her world had tipped upside down. Her uncle, one of the few people in the world she trusted and had always felt she could turn to when things at home got too bad, was a liar. Maybe worse. Tears pricked her eyes, blurring everything and making it even more difficult to see where she was going. She tripped over a stone, would have fallen if Patrick hadn't grabbed her arm.

'Are you okay?' he said.

'I'm fine.' She rubbed the tears away, angry with herself for the loss of control.

'You don't think we should go back?' Patrick asked.

'I can't. My sister's dead and I need to know why she died and if Joey had anything to do with it.'

'Okay.' Patrick switched off his torch and put his hands on her shoulders. 'Let me ask you something then. How sure are you that Liz Havers is the woman you saw with Joey?'

Freya closed her eyes, put herself back in that moment last Thursday right after she'd bumped into Patrick. She'd been about to go after him when she'd seen her uncle on the other side of the road.

'I'm sure,' she said, opening her eyes.

A sudden scream cut through the still silence of the night, making them both jump.

'What was that?' Patrick hissed.

Freya didn't answer. She couldn't speak. Fear froze her to the spot and she might have stayed that way forever if it wasn't for the sudden burst of light that illuminated the beach in front of them.

'Look.' She pointed at the light, which, she could see now, was coming from a house.

'We shouldn't be here.' Patrick sounded scared, and she didn't blame him. She was scared too. Terrified of what they were going to find when they reached the house. But she couldn't turn back now. 'We need to call the police,' Patrick said.

'I don't blame you if you want to go back,' Freya said. 'But I'm not coming with you. I'm seeing this through to the end.'

She moved forward, half expecting him to turn around and head back to the car. But after a moment, she heard him coming after her. It was only when he took her hand and squeezed it that she realised how glad she was that he was still here.

'Thank you,' she whispered.

They were nearly at the house. Freya could hear voices, although she couldn't make out who was talking or how many people there were.

'What do we do?' Patrick said.

'Let's split up,' Freya said. 'You go around to the front of the house and take a look around. I'll go the other way, see if I can get onto the deck somehow.'

There were stairs leading from the beach onto the deck, but there was no way of walking up those without being seen.

'I'll climb up the side,' Freya said. 'The light doesn't quite reach the edge. I should be able to get up without anyone seeing me.'

'Let me do that,' Patrick said. 'You go around the front.'

'No. I want to do this.'

He scowled and she scowled back. Their stand-off was only broken when another scream rang out.

'Stay here and don't move,' Patrick said.

Before she could stop him, he had run forward and was racing up the steps onto the deck. He was almost on the top step when something or someone shot out across the deck, moving towards him too fast. As Freya watched, Patrick flew backwards, high into the air before landing with a sickening crunch onto the shingle beach.

'Patrick!'

She ran towards him, all sense of danger forgotten in her need to make sure he was okay. He was lying on his back. Eyes closed. Freya knelt down, screaming his name and shaking him, begging him to wake up.

A hand clamped over her mouth, blocking her screams as she was lifted off the ground. She tried to kick herself free, but the person holding her was too strong, their arm too tight across her stomach. The need to breathe made her struggle even harder, her lungs screaming for air as she kicked and bucked.

'Stop fighting.'

Joey's voice in her ear, sharp and angry.

A sudden surge of movement as he propelled them both forward, towards the wall of the house. She fought harder but not hard enough. The concrete wall sped towards her face. She tried to turn her head sideways, but his grip on her head was too tight. Pain exploded across her nose and cheeks, white lights racing towards her as he let her go and she fell.

'You shouldn't have come,' he said. 'But now you're here, I can't let you go.'

Sixty-three

There was something wrong with Dee's head. A terrible pain that intensified each time she tried to open her eyes. She couldn't remember what had happened or why she was lying face down on her bedroom floor. She knew she should get up, but when she tried to move, nothing happened.

'Is she still alive?'

A woman's voice. Dee forced her eyes to open, gritting her teeth against the pain across the back of her head.

Footsteps, then Joey Cavellini's face in front of hers as he crouched down in front of her. Dee's stomach twisted with fury.

'Yeah, she's alive.'

He stood up and walked away and now she couldn't see him.

'There are two bottles of wine in the fridge,' he said. 'Go and get them for me, would you?'

'What are you going to do?'

The woman's voice was familiar, but Dee couldn't work out where she knew her from. She tried to lift her head, so she could see them, but the slightest movement made the pain unbearable.

'I'm going to sort this mess,' Joey said. 'No, don't look at me like that. You haven't left me any choice. You fucked up, Mother, and now we need to fix this.'

Mother.

The connections Dee had been making earlier all came together. Suddenly, she knew who Joey was talking to.

They both had kids that were given up for adoption.

'Please, Joey. There must be another way.'

'There isn't. Now go and get that wine.'

There was a pause, before Dee heard Jennifer walking away. Joey's face appeared again, cold and angry.

'You killed Paul,' Dee said.

'I didn't do it on purpose. We had a fight and he went for me. It was self-defence.'

'What about Lizzie? Why did she say she was with you that night?'

He didn't answer. Jennifer was back, presumably with the wine from Dee's fridge. What were they going to do? Celebrate with a drink after they'd killed her?

Joey's face disappeared again, as he issued more instructions to Jennifer.

'There's a wheelbarrow at the side of the house. You get that while I get started here.'

As Joey's feet crossed the room, Dee knew it was now or never. She started crawling towards the en-suite bathroom. Every movement was agony. Her body was bruised and battered and when she tried to lean on her right arm, the pain was so severe she thought she might pass out. But she kept going, dragging herself forward inch by precious inch.

'Where do you think you're going?'

A foot on her back, pushing her until she was lying face down on the ground. She screamed as her right arm got twisted beneath the weight of her body.

'Please,' she gasped, 'my arm. Please let me move.'

The pressure on her back disappeared and she rolled over. The moment of sheer bliss as she took the weight off her arm was replaced by fear when she saw Joey was holding a bottle of wine in his hand and was bringing it down towards Dee's face.

She turned her face sideways, covering it with her good arm, her whole body tense as she waited for the bottle to smash into her. Instead, he grabbed Dee by her hair and twisted her head around. At first, Dee didn't understand. Then she felt the bottle hitting against her mouth and teeth. Joey tilted her head back and wine poured down Dee's throat. She tried to pull away, but he was holding her too tight. She couldn't swallow fast enough. Coughing and spluttering and choking, as the wine came too fast. She was drowning and there was nothing she could do about it.

Finally, it was over. Her head lolled forward as she retched and threw up dribbles of wine. The smell of it invaded her nostrils and the taste of it was like poison on her tongue and throat.

When he grabbed her head again, she was helpless to stop him. More wine. The crack of a tooth snapping as the bottle hit it too hard. She was throwing up, then having to swallow her sick back down because the wine kept coming and she couldn't move her head.

An interminable time passed before he let her go, leaving her alone on the cold floor. The room was spinning and her face was lying in a pool of vomit and wine. She knew she had to get up, get away, but when she tried to push herself up, nothing happened. Then he was back, and he rolled her over onto her back and it started all over again with the second bottle.

Later. The sky spinning above her. White stars dancing around a fat full moon. Her head hanging backwards over the edge of the wheelbarrow that someone was pushing over the stones towards the water.

Fasten your seat belts.

Bumpy night or bumpy ride?

Her father had loved Bette Davis.

The stars and the moon disappeared. She was in water. Cold water that sobered her up instantly. Panic flared inside her chest and she tried to turn around, get back to the beach. But someone was holding the back of her head, pushing it down into the water. The taste of salt in her mouth, a flash of sad regret for the things she hadn't done. And after that, darkness.

Sixty-four

There was a crunching sound close by. Footsteps crossing the shingle to where Freya was. She had managed to crawl a few feet away from the house, before her body gave up and she'd had to stop. The pain across her face was unbearable. She'd made the mistake of touching it earlier, felt the flattened space where her nose normally was and knew the damage was bad.

As the footsteps drew closer, rage gave her the strength to fight through the pain and stand up. She retched again, leaning over to spit out the bitter bile. When she straightened up, the world was spinning and she had to hold onto the side of the house to stop herself falling over as she cautiously moved forward, scanning the beach for Patrick.

He was still there, lying on his back. Not moving. She was about to run towards him when she saw Joey and the other woman dragging something down the steps from the deck. Not something. Someone. A woman.

The woman moaned, but didn't seem capable of much else and when her body was tipped into the wheelbarrow at the bottom of the steps, she didn't react. At first, Freya didn't understand what was happening. Why were they pushing someone down the beach in a wheelbarrow? By the time she'd worked it out, they were already at the edge of the water. As they turned the body out of the wheelbarrow, Freya pulled her phone out of her jeans pocket and dialled 999.

'Emergency, which service do you require?'

'Police. No, ambulance. I don't know. They're killing her. They're going to drown her.'

'Caller, are you in danger?'

'Yes! My uncle is going to kill me.'

'Can you give me your location?'

She looked around, desperate for something she could use to identify where she was.

'The beach near Pevensey,' she said. 'Past Sovereign Harbour, right on the beach. There's a big house. Please send someone.'

The man told her he'd stay on the phone until the police arrived. But she knew that would be too late. She ended the call, put her phone in her pocket, picked up the biggest stone she could find and raced towards the water.

Joey and the woman had their hands on the other woman's body, pushing it down into the water. Fuelled by rage and adrenaline, screaming at the top of her lungs, Freya ran for Joey first. Instinct took over as she smashed the stone down on the back of his head. He let go of the woman and stumbled forward, falling face first into the water.

'Joey!' His companion shoved Freya sideways as she reached for Joey and tried to drag him back. But he must have been too heavy, because she couldn't seem to grab hold of him.

Ignoring her, Freya concentrated on trying to pull the other woman out of the water. But her clothes, soaked with sea water, meant the woman was a dead weight.

Freya knew if she couldn't turn her around, she would drown. If she hadn't drowned already. Dredging up her last bit of strength, calling on all the years of self-discipline and excessive exercise, she grabbed the woman's top and heaved her back until she was far enough out of the water for Freya to roll her over onto her side.

'Joey!'

Her uncle's body had drifted further into the water. The woman with him was still screaming and trying to pull him back.

'Please,' she said, turning to Freya. 'Help me before he drowns. I'm begging you. He can't drown. Please.'

On the ground, the woman they'd tried to drown had started spluttering and choking, coughing up all the water that had got into her lungs.

Something hard and cold had lodged in the centre of Freya's stomach. She looked at her uncle's body, then at the woman begging for her help, and shook her head.

She thought she could hear sirens, far off in the distance, but it might have been her imagination. She couldn't stand up. The last bit of energy had left her body, and her legs weren't strong enough to hold her up. She fell to her knees.

The woman on the ground reached out and took Freya's hand. They stayed like that, holding hands at the edge of the water, while Joey's body drifted further out to sea and his companion tried to follow him, screaming his name over and over.

Sixty-five

Her beautiful boy was dead. She felt empty, hollowed out, numb. It should have been her. She had failed him when he was growing up, and she'd made it her life's mission to make up for that failure. She'd done all she could, but in the end it hadn't been enough.

'Are you ready, Jennifer?'

The two detectives were sitting opposite her. DI Lewis and DC Benjamin. Lewis finished typing something onto the digital screen in front of her and looked expectantly at Jennifer.

'Joey Cavellini was my son,' she began.

It should have been a relief, after all this time, to tell the truth. But it made no difference. There was no relief, no sense of letting go of something she'd tried so hard to contain. Nothing at all.

She thought of the day, all those years ago, when she'd opened her front door to find him standing there. She'd known immediately it was him. Her son. The boy she'd given up for adoption seventeen years earlier. The joy that had surged up in her chest, rapidly replaced by a sickness in her stomach as he told her about his life. The people who'd adopted him were cruel and abusive. He had two younger siblings who, unlike him, were his parents' biological children. His parents weren't kind to those children either, although they treated them less cruelly.

Jennifer had vowed, in that moment, that she would devote the rest of her life to making up for what she'd done to him. Because she was under no illusions. What had happened to him was her fault. If she'd been braver, if she had kept him with her instead of giving him away, he would never have turned out the way he had.

She'd seen it in him that afternoon, and all the times she'd spent with him since then. There was an emptiness in him, as if part of him was missing. It was why he acted the way he did sometimes, as if he didn't care about other people. It wasn't his fault. That part of him had been beaten out of him by the people he called his parents.

She'd left Liverpool and opened a salon in south London so she could be closer to him. But it was too little, too late. When he told her his parents had been killed in a car crash, she knew it was his doing. They'd never spoken about it. They didn't have to. By then, she knew him well enough to know what he was capable of. Besides, she was glad they were dead. They didn't deserve to be alive.

'He was a good boy,' she said, telling the story she'd worked out during the night. 'Never did a thing to harm anyone. Everything that's happened, it's all my fault. I killed them. First Paul, then Grace and Lizzie.'

'What about Dee Doran?' Lewis asked.

'That was me too,' Jennifer said. 'I forced wine down her throat and tried to drown her.'

She stopped speaking and looked at the two detectives, willing them to challenge what she'd just told them.

'So you're confessing to three murders and one attempted murder,' Lewis said. 'You realise if you give a statement to that effect, there's no going back from that?'

Of course she realised that. She wasn't stupid.

'I killed them,' she said.

'I think you're lying,' Benjamin said.

'You can think what you like,' Jennifer said. 'Besides, you know I killed Grace. You found my car.'

The silver Nissan Juke that she had just signed a lease agreement for. It had arrived the day before Grace was killed. She still had her old Mazda, and had been planning to sell it. But then the accident had happened and Jennifer had had to keep the new car hidden in her garage while she continued to drive the other one.

It was true that she'd killed Grace, although she hadn't meant to. She had been planning to take the girls out for dinner, then Cassie had dropped out. When Jennifer asked why, Cassie had told her Grace had called, said she needed to see her.

After Cassie had left, Jennifer couldn't stop thinking about it. Worrying that Grace might have discovered something she shouldn't have. So she'd driven over to Cassie's house. The road was narrow and quiet. Jennifer hadn't been paying enough attention, driving too fast while on the phone to Joey. The girl had appeared out of nowhere. Weaving into the middle of the road. Jennifer had pressed her foot on the brake, but she was too late. The girl's body had hit the car with a sickening thud that she'd never forget.

Later, Joey had said it was for the best and Jennifer had agreed he was probably right. But that didn't stop her reliving the moment repeatedly in the days and weeks that followed. It was the first thing she thought of when she woke up in the mornings, and the last thing she saw at night before falling asleep.

'Who helped you move the body?' Lewis asked.

Joey, of course. She'd called him as soon as she realised the girl was dead. He'd come straight away, there for her just as she'd always been there for him.

'No one helped me,' she said.

'Why did you kill Paul?' Benjamin asked.

'Paul was causing problems for Joey, making his life unnecessarily difficult. They were always falling out, but this time Joey was really upset about it. I went over to Paul's house to try to reason with him. He attacked me and I fought back.'

'How did you know where Paul lived?' Lewis asked.

'I can't remember. It was a long time ago.'

She'd been getting ready for bed when Joey had called her. She heard the fear in his voice, and knew she'd do anything to stop him feeling scared. He told her there'd been a fight, Paul had attacked him. He was speaking too fast, words tumbling over each other, begging her to come and help him. When she saw the body, she knew Joey hadn't told her the truth. There were too many stab wounds to explain it away as an act of self-defence. He would have killed Lizzie too then, if Jennifer hadn't come up with another plan. It had involved more money, but Joey was her son so what choice did she have?

In the weeks and months that followed Paul's murder, Joey had never once shown any sign of remorse for what he'd done that night. Yet she'd stood by him, because she was his mother and that's what mothers do.

'Liz Havers gave Joey an alibi for the night Paul was killed,' Lewis said. 'I think she was killed because she was about to tell someone Joey hadn't really been with her that night.'

DI Lewis was cleverer than Jennifer had realised. She was almost right. Except she'd missed the part about Lizzie turning up at the house to find Jennifer and Joey standing over Paul's dead body. The girl had freaked out, screaming all sorts of abuse at them. Until Jennifer had grabbed Lizzie by her skinny shoulders and told her she would pay her good money if she did three simple things: give Joey an alibi, find a way to implicate Cassie in Paul's murder, and stay quiet about what had really happened.

All these years, Lizzie had kept her part of the deal. Then she'd got a visit from that interfering journalist and she freaked out all over again. She'd turned up at Joey's apartment, asking questions about Grace, saying she didn't want another person's blood on her hands.

'She dated Joey for a bit, way back when he was just starting his business. She contacted him after Grace was killed, tried to blackmail him. Said she would go to the press and tell a load of lies about him unless he paid her not to.'

Lewis frowned. 'Her husband is loaded. Why on earth would Liz need to blackmail him?'

'I have no idea why she needed the money,' Jennifer said. 'All I know is she was trying to ruin my son's reputation. I couldn't let her do that.'

'So you killed her,' Benjamin said.

'That's right.'

'How?'

Jennifer blinked. She hadn't expected that.

'I stabbed her. Just like I stabbed Paul.'

'Except Liz wasn't killed by a knife,' DI Lewis said. 'She was strangled.'

Jennifer pictured her son's hands, wrapped around a pale neck squeezing tight, and wanted to howl. He had been a monster, and yet she had loved him so much.

'So what?' she said. 'I'm telling you I did it. What more do you want? I killed her, but it was traumatic and I can't remember how I did it. It was me. Paul and Grace and Liz. The attack at the hospital and the rock through Dee's window. I did all of that.'

It was true, she'd done some of those things. The photos she'd taken of Dee's boyfriend, pushing him over when he came outside. That had been her. And Grace, of course. The rest had all been Joey's doing.

She could see from the two detectives' faces they knew she was lying. She didn't care. Let them think what they wanted. Joey wasn't here to defend himself, so she would have to do that for him. She hadn't been able to protect him when he was alive. She could, at least, protect the only part of him that was left: his reputation.

Sixty-six

A simple wooden cross marked the grave. No headstone yet, although Cassie assumed there would be one eventually. She would like to have some say in what was chosen and what words were written on it, but she doubted Trish would be amenable to that suggestion.

It was a glorious day. Sunshine poured down, bathing Grace's grave in golden light. Birds sang in the trees that bordered the cemetery, a gentle breeze chased tiny white clouds across the endless blue sky. Grace's body was here, buried beneath the freshly turned soil, but her soul was free. It was singing from the trees and flying with the clouds and deep inside Cassie's heart, where it had always been from the moment of her birth.

She had brought flowers. Yellow sunflowers because they'd been Grace's favourite. As she laid the flowers down, she remembered that day nine months ago when she'd seen Grace walk through the doors of the cafe where Cassie was having lunch.

She'd recognised her instantly. Not just because her daughter looked exactly as she'd done at the same age. But because she'd been watching her for years. The friends she'd made in prison showed Cassie how easy it was to find out someone's address. One of the first things she'd done after getting out of prison was find the house Trish had moved to in Eastbourne. People had been right to question how she'd managed to keep away from Grace all those years. There was a simple answer to that: she hadn't.

She wasn't stupid enough to get caught. She kept her distance, watching Grace but always making sure no one noticed her. Except it turned out someone had. Grace told Cassie she'd seen her several times over the years. As she'd grown older, Grace grew curious about the woman who looked so like an older version of herself. When she'd spotted the same woman inside the cafe that day, she'd come inside to speak to her. Because Grace knew she'd been adopted and she'd started to suspect the woman she kept seeing might be her biological mother.

'Cassie?'

The voice behind her dragged Cassie back from the past and her memories of the happiest time in her life. All those precious months she'd had with Grace before she died.

'What are you doing here?'

It was Trish, holding a bunch of sunflowers and staring at Cassie.

'I needed to see where she was buried,' Cassie said.

'I've been trying to pluck up the courage to get in touch,' Trish said. 'I owe you an apology, Cassie. I thought you'd killed Paul and I was so angry with you. I should never have stopped you seeing Grace. I'm so sorry.'

The apology would never be enough for all those lost years. But anger wouldn't bring Grace back. Nothing would do that. And Cassie suspected if her daughter was out there somewhere, she would want these two women who had loved her so much to be friends, not enemies.

'You took her in when I couldn't take care of her,' Cassie said. 'If it wasn't for you, she would have spent years of her life in care. I'm grateful to you for that, Trish. Thank you for looking after her for me.'

'She was very special,' Trish said. 'Beautiful and clever and so feisty you would not believe it.'

Cassie's vision blurred as her eyes filled with tears.

'I know she wasn't Paul's child,' Trish continued. 'We found that out when she was ten. But I want you to know that never changed how I felt about her. I loved her just as much as I love Freya.'

'Joey was Grace's father.'

There. She'd said it. The secret she'd kept for so many years, the one thing she had never spoken about to anyone, was finally out in the open.

Trish's mouth opened, then closed again without any words coming out.

'I should never have married Paul,' Cassie said. 'When he found out I was pregnant, he assumed the baby was his. I went along with it, because I wasn't brave enough to do anything else.'

'None of us made great choices back then,' Trish said. 'I should never have married Conor, either. But I did, and I have a beautiful daughter because of it.'

'It's why Lizzie stopped speaking to me,' Cassie said. 'She'd had a crush on Joey for the longest time. When she found out I'd slept with him, she was gutted.'

What a mess she had made of everything, Cassie thought. Sacrificing her friendship for a one-night stand with a man who didn't have the capacity to love anyone except himself.

'Does Jennifer know?' Trish asked.

'That she killed her own grandchild?' Cassie nodded. 'Apparently when the police told her, she didn't show any reaction.'

Cassie couldn't imagine what Jennifer must be feeling. Part of her hated Jennifer. All the time they'd known each other, Cassie had thought they were friends. Turned out Jennifer had only taken Cassie under her wing so she could keep an eye on her. But there was another part of Cassie that couldn't help feeling sorry for her old boss. Jennifer's life hadn't been easy. An abusive relationship, a child she'd given up for adoption to give him a better life than she could have given him. All this followed by the shattering realisation, when it was too late to do anything about it, that her baby had been brought up by people incapable of love.

'Do you think, if she knew the truth, that Grace might still be alive?' Trish asked.

'Maybe,' Cassie said. 'I guess we'll never know, will we?'

Thanks to the police, Cassie had managed to piece together most of what had happened. Jennifer Trevorrow had confessed to all three murders, although Rachel Lewis had confided to Cassie she didn't believe Jennifer had killed Paul or Lizzie. Those deaths were down to Joey. They would never know for sure why Joey had killed Paul, although Cassie suspected it was simply that Joey hated seeing Paul raising the child he must have guessed was his.

The day before she'd been killed, Lizzie had come clean to her husband, who had later given a statement to the police. It turned out Lizzie had been there the night Paul was killed. She had heard the rumours about Cassie's marriage and, despite their falling out, she had been worried enough about her old friend to go and check she was okay.

But instead of finding Cassie, she had walked in on Joey and Jennifer as they were trying to work out what to do. Jennifer had offered her money to keep quiet about what she'd seen. Desperate to escape her life, Lizzie had taken the money and kept quiet. But when she heard about Grace, she knew she couldn't keep quiet any longer. A decision that, ultimately, had got her killed.

'I saw you at the funeral,' Trish said. 'I wanted to speak to you, but when I went looking for you, I couldn't find you.'

'I left immediately afterwards,' Cassie said. 'It was too hard, being there with all those people who'd known her better than I had.'

'What are you going to do now?' Trish asked. 'Will you stay in Eastbourne or move somewhere else?'

'I think I'll stay,' Cassie said. 'I moved here to be close to her. I know she's not here anymore, but it feels like she is, if that makes any sense.'

'Yeah.' Trish nodded. 'It makes perfect sense.'

Cassie didn't want to speak any longer. Part of her wanted Trish to go, but another part of her was glad that she was here. Because despite their differences, the two women were united. Grace was Cassie's child, but she was also Trish's child. They had both loved her, and they would both spend the rest of their lives grieving her loss.

Cassie took a tentative step forward and opened her arms, the way she used to when Grace was a little girl and she wanted to give her a hug. She wrapped her arms around Trish and held her, as tightly as she used to hold Grace, while memory after memory of her daughter played through her mind on a never-ending loop.

They stayed like that, clinging onto each other, as the birds sang in the trees and the white clouds moved across the sky and the golden sun dipped lower in the sky, preparing for the end of another day.

Epilogue

The night sky was fading to a milky pink as Freya walked down the hill towards the beach. By the time she reached Falling Sands, the sun had risen above the horizon. Streaks of orange and pink and burnished gold sliced across the sky, all of it reflected on the unbroken surface of the sea.

Today was Grace's birthday. She would have been eighteen. Freya had come here because it was where she felt closest to her sister. They used to come here on their birthdays, skinny-dipping in early mornings like this one. Down here, hidden beneath the shadow of the chalk cliffs, it had been possible on those sun-drenched mornings to believe they were the only two people in the whole world.

Freya knew she would never stop missing her sister. The pain, that had already become an inescapable part of who she was, was a constant reminder that Grace had once burned through life brighter than the sun that was rising in the east and filling the world with light.

It was up to Freya, now, to live for both of them. She was going to do all the things Grace had spoken of doing, travel to the places Grace had marked on the world map pinned to her bedroom wall, and be brave about the choices she made – doing what was best for her, not other people. Just like Grace would have done.

Yesterday afternoon, Rachel Lewis had come to the house to tell Freya the police wouldn't be pressing any charges. She had acted in self-defence and, in doing so, had probably saved Dee Doran's life. After Rachel left, Freya had sat down and sent

301

an email to Cambridge University asking if she could defer her place until next year. She had no guarantee they would allow her to do this, but if they said no, it wasn't the end of the world. There were plenty of universities that would accept a student with Freya's grades.

The tide was in, water lapping against the moss-covered rocks. Freya lifted her dress over her head and let it drop to the ground. The morning air felt cool against her bare skin. She shivered, glad she wasn't doing this by herself. Beside her, Patrick took off his glasses and folded them carefully on top of his shorts and T-shirt, lying on the ground beside Freya's dress.

'Ready?' she said.

'Ready.' He smiled and took hold of her hand.

A grey heron swooped down, its wings skimming the surface before it landed. It turned its head so that one orange eye was trained on Freya and Patrick, watching as they walked over the rocks towards the water.

In the silence, a sound. Faint and distant like the last fragments of the night sky. But Freya recognised it, nonetheless. A sound she'd heard thousands of times in her life and one she'd never thought she'd hear again. Grace's laughter.

She understood, then, that her sister hadn't really gone away. She was the heat of the sun, the icy coldness of the sea and the energy that drove the tides in and out over the smooth white stones. She would always be here; dancing on the white beach with the sunlight captured in her crazy curls and her laughter ringing in the air.

–

'I think we should get married.'

'You do?' Dee said.

Ed took her hand and smiled. 'Yes, Dee. I'd like to marry you and spend the rest of my life with you. Neither of us know what the future has in store for us. But I know that no matter what happens, I want us to be together.'

Dee stood up and walked to the edge of the deck. The tide was in, water lapping against the white shingle. She hadn't been in the sea since that night. For the first week after it had happened, she hadn't been able to come outside at all. She had needed to stay inside, doors closed and curtains drawn. The only way she'd been able to feel safe.

The memories were still raw. There were times when they became too much and it was like being back there again. The pressure on the back of her head, the rush of water into her lungs, and the terrifying certainty that she was going to die.

She had spent the rest of that night in hospital, and had woken the next morning to find Ed sitting by her bed. When she was discharged from the hospital, he'd come back to the house with her. A month later, he was still here.

Last night, he'd told her he was selling his house and finally buying that camper van. Now he was asking her to marry him.

Marrying Ed and taking off into the unknown would mean turning her back on the career she had worked so hard to build up. She would be able to write, but the TV and radio work would have to be put on hold. If she turned him down, he would go without her and that would mean accepting – once and for all – that their relationship was over. Whatever decision she made, it would be final. There would be no more second chances.

Across the shingle, the sea glistened in the afternoon sunshine. A sudden rush of joy surged through Dee as she realised she knew exactly who she was and what she wanted for the rest of her time on this earth.

'I'm going for a swim,' she said.

'Oh, Dee.' Ed touched her arm, and she could see the consternation on his face. 'Are you sure?'

'I've never been more certain of anything.'

She kissed his cheek and went inside to get changed into her swimsuit. She could feel Ed watching her, as she came back outside and ran down the steps and across the shingle.

As the cold waves lapped against her ankles, a snapshot from that night came rushing into her head. She almost turned back, but didn't.

When she was in far enough, she put her arms above her head and dived down. As she went beneath the water, she saw her future – laid out before her in glorious technicolour. Her life, the one she was going to grab with both hands and live in the fullest way possible.

She rose out of the water into the clear light of a perfect summer's day, refreshed and revitalised. Across the beach, the house shimmered behind waves of heat rising up from the shingle beach. She was too far away to see Ed, but she knew he was there. Sitting on the deck, watching out for her and making sure she was okay.

Acknowledgements

Thanks as always to my parents, for your ongoing support and for your tireless work promoting my books at every opportunity.

Thank you to the wonderful people at Canelo, who I just love – Louise Cullen, Francesca Riccardi, Nicola Piggott, Siân Heap, Jade Craddock and Abigail Headon. Thanks also to my lovely agent, Laura Longrigg for all you do for me. Thank you, too, to the dedicated community of book bloggers who do so much to support and promote authors.

A big shout out to my fellow crime writers Lorraine Mace, Marion Todd and Chris Curran. We keep each other going and I value your friendship enormously.

A very special thank you to Jennifer Price (née Trevorrow) who won the opportunity to have a character named after her. Jennifer, your character changed so much in the writing of this book – thank you for going along with all the changes with such humour and good grace.

Thanks too to Chris Simmons for all the years of friendship and books. I hope your brilliant blog, crimesquad.com, continues to thrive for many years to come. You're a wonderful person and I'm so happy we know each other.

Thank you to the brilliant group of people who run the UK Crime Book Club, particularly my pal Samantha Brownley. Sam, I don't know if I've told you this, but I was close to giving up at the end of last year. Your support and kind words got me through a very difficult time. Thank you.

Finally, I couldn't do any of this without the fam-a-lam (sorry guys, I couldn't resist!): Sean, Luke and Ruby – you are my everything.